To: -

Congrats!!

Hope you enjoy

Thanks for the Support.

11/16

To: Tracey

Congrats!!

Hope you enjoy

Thanks for the support.

Jim

NECESSARY DEATH

R. Michael Markley

BALBOA.
PRESS
A DIVISION OF HAY HOUSE

Necessary Death is a work of fiction. Names, characters, places, and incidents are the product of the author's imagination or are used fictitiously. Any resemblance to actual events, locales, or persons, living or dead, is coincidental.

Balboa Press books may be ordered through booksellers or by contacting:

Balboa Press
A Division of Hay House
1663 Liberty Drive
Bloomington, IN 47403
www.balboapress.com
1 (877) 407-4847

Because of the dynamic nature of the Internet, any web addresses or links contained in this book may have changed since publication and may no longer be valid. The views expressed in this work are solely those of the author and do not necessarily reflect the views of the publisher, and the publisher hereby disclaims any responsibility for them.

The author of this book does not dispense medical advice or prescribe the use of any technique as a form of treatment for physical, emotional, or medical problems without the advice of a physician, either directly or indirectly. The intent of the author is only to offer information of a general nature to help you in your quest for emotional and spiritual well-being. In the event you use any of the information in this book for yourself, which is your constitutional right, the author and the publisher assume no responsibility for your actions.

Print information available on the last page.

ISBN: 978-1-5043-2760-2 (sc)
ISBN: 978-1-5043-2762-6 (hc)
ISBN: 978-1-5043-2761-9 (e)

Library of Congress Control Number: 2015902002

Balboa Press rev. date: 07/27/2015

I would like to thank S.E. Hinton, whose book, *The Outsiders,* was the first book I got lost in. After finishing it, I knew I wanted to write a story. Forty-three years later, it's finally here.

To Jeri… your initial edits and insights were a huge help in the development of this story. Thank you so much.

My designer Chad… your artwork on the cover is just what I wanted.

Nadine Brandes… author, editor. First, congratulations on the release of your first novel, *A Time to Die.* Your editing skills have made *Necessary Death* so much stronger. Thank you for working with a novice and helping me grow through this journey.

Sara… the time you took to read, and the suggestions you made, has helped the story to be smoother and gripping. At times I would want to pull my hair out because of your thoroughness, but the finished product was well worth the wait. Thank you.

Most of all, to the love of my life, Kristine… Your constant support and encouragement while writing has been so gratifying. The time it has taken from start to finish has been tedious, and at times frustrating. Your endless reads, suggestions, and direction have been the best. To have you come along on this ride has been the best time spent together. Thank you for being my best friend, and my wife. If not for you, this would have never come to be. Your sweet spirit and tender heart makes it very easy to love you. Hold on because the ride is just getting started. Oh, thank you for the walk on the trail.

To the One who gave me the gift of writing, the One who has allowed me to write for Him with the opportunity to reach thousands. I am humbled and grateful to my Lord and Savior Jesus Christ. May Your name be lifted up. Use this gift You have given me to advance Your Kingdom.

PROLOGUE

STEVE PRESSED THE barrel of the gun to the back of Rhino's head. His arm twitched. He had never killed before. This would be his first. The fact that Rhino had been his mentor and had been like a father to him didn't make it any easier. It seemed impossible to pull the trigger. Did he really want to taint his life with murder?

The thick muscles of Rhino's neck and wide shoulders tensed. Would a single bullet truly collapse such a stocky man? Yes. Yes it would. No matter how big Rhino was, it wouldn't stop the bullet from sending him face first onto the chilled concrete floor.

Steve sniffed. The stale air carried a musty odor. Dampness hung around him. Oil and bloodstains splattered the floor. Cobwebs filled the corners and rafters, while dust collected everywhere. Spiders lay their traps to catch their next victim. The irony flirted with Steve's thoughts, but there was nothing humorous in the old garage tonight.

"You are responsible for the horror and the brutality that is legendary for this old garage," Steve said. "What has happened here is all in the past, but unfortunately for you, the past has returned. Don't take it personally, it's just business."

He pulled the trigger.

The shot resounded, and the vibration shook the dust from its resting place. Rhino fell forward and landed with a thud. The shot was louder than Steve had expected. Maybe it was the empty garage or maybe he was more scared and nervous than he had thought. The bullet's impact splattered skull fragments and brain matter. Something slid down Steve's cheek, and he wiped it off with his left hand.

Rhino's big, bad lifeless body looked like a pile of—

Shouting came from outside. Steve raised his .45 semi-automatic. Kevin opened the door. "You did it?"

Kevin stood an even five feet, and his small stature made him seem incapable of doing the job he was recommend to help do. His jet-black hair and brown eyes made him look even younger than the twenty-five years his driver license said he was. He could never stand still and was always rocking back and forth. It drove Steve crazy.

"What do you think? Didn't you hear the shot?" Steve responded abruptly. "You need to shut up and relax!"

"I thought maybe you would scare him a little, make him beg for his life. You know, like in the movies." Kevin circled around the body on the floor, checking out the legend they used to call Rhino. This wasn't the movies, and it wasn't Hollywood either. This was real.

As Steve cleaned the gun and Kevin wrapped the body in plastic, Steve's mind went back to his last words to Rhino. Couldn't he have thought of something more creative? He tried to shake the thought from his mind. This was not the mafia or the mob. This was not the way things were done anymore, but Rhino changed all that.

Again, Steve thought, *maybe the past has returned.* Titan wanted Rhino dead, but Michael, Rhino's brother, ran Titan like the mob. There was the *omerta*—the code of silence, the old saying, *once in, you're in for life—no turning back*, and of course the idea of family first. You never turn your back on your family. Well, when word of this got out, the game would change. What had Steve just gotten himself into? They killed only to protect. In the early days, they used intimidation and threats, physical threats. That's why they kept the garage, but Rhino took care of that side and only Rhino.

"Hurry up," Steve commanded.

In the middle of their clean up, feet crushed gravel outside and someone made a shushing sound from the other side of the wall. Steve and Kevin darted to the secret crawlspace. Once inside, Kevin hissed, "Don't forget to pull the drawstring."

"Shut up will you? I'm not a fool." Steve pulled the rope, and a load of dirt dropped from the floor rafters and filled the crawlspace. Now, if someone found the trap door and opened it, they would see only a bunch of dirt.

They followed the dark and chilly underground tunnel. Steve crawled behind Kevin, spitting out the kicked up dirt. The tunnel was filled with cobwebs. "Where is this leading us to?" Kevin wiped cobwebs off his face.

"It will take us to an old junkyard that has a shanty disguised as a boiler. It gives the impression that it's uninhabitable. The rule is we need to stay there for twenty four hours."

"I hate that rule." Kevin sounded like a child.

"Tough, that's what we're going to do. Now shut up and move!" They made it to the shanty and settled in.

With time on his hands, all Steve could think about was what just transpired. He had seen Rhino's brother twenty-four hours ago. Did he really just take another man's life? Then, it hit him; they had left the body behind. What would happen now? Who was outside the garage? What would they do when they found the body? When they found out who the victim was, they would wonder who had the power to take the life of such a high profile member of Titan. The more he contemplated about it, the more powerful he felt. *I will make a name for myself, he thought. I will be known as the one who took down the great Rhino.*

His smile grew the more he reflected on it. He was now a killer. No one would touch him. He would have the group on his side, well, everyone but Rhino's brother, Michael. Steve started working on his next move.

1

Five days earlier…

THEY MET WHERE they always did—in the clubhouse of the Wooded Hills Country Club, which was owned by Titan. Four men sat at the big oak table where they would do their business. Steve stood attentively at the foot of the table in the haze of cigar smoke and cheap aftershave. He looked around at the men who had called him there today, anxious to prove himself to the leaders of Titan. They needed to discuss what to do about Michael's brother, Rhino.

Moe Giovan, also known as the Mole, sat at the table. Steve kept getting distracted by the mole the size of a dime on his right temple. William Cozzoni—Willy—sat to the left of Moe, his trademark cigar sticking out of his mouth. Next to Willy, sat Sammy Salluci, and next to Sammy, was Paul Delemonni. Paul was the cool-headed one of the four and looked to Steve as if this meeting should not be taking place. He squirmed in his seat and tugged at the collar of his shirt. Judging by the perspiration on his forehead, he didn't seem to have much control right at that moment.

They all sat there, smoking and not saying a word. Willy finally broke the silence, "Probably wondering what you're doing here, huh kid?"

Knowing better than to answer, Steve waited them out.

Sammy spoke up, "We have a problem we think you can handle."

There was a pause. "Are you willing to do this for us?" That question came from Moe. Steve waited for Paul to speak, but Paul remained silent. Steve answered, "I'm in. I'll do whatever you ask. Just tell me what you want."

The tension grew in the room. "Are you sure you want this responsibility?" Sammy pressed. "You have no idea what we are going to ask."

"I can handle whatever needs to be done." This was Steve's chance. "I have been ready to step up and prove myself for so long. I'm ready to take charge and show you guys what I'm worth," Steve spoke boldly, even forcefully, hoping the men would see he could be trusted with the responsibility.

"We want you to take care of someone." Sometimes when Moe spoke, the words came out faster than his mouth could move, which made him hard to understand. "This individual is very close to the group and very close to you."

Each member looked at each other, then at Steve.

"Once we tell you what we want from you, there will be no turning back," Moe continued in the fast talking manner he was known for. "If you refuse, do it now. Once we tell you, for the protection of the group, we cannot let you leave this room alive should you refuse," Moe repeated.

Steve straightened his shoulders and stuck his chest out so the men of Titan could see he meant what he was about to say, "I have been a foot soldier too long. It's time I stepped out and made a name for myself. Mr. Giovan, I know of all the connections you have in the city, and because of those connections, you have the right people in the right places. Ask around. You'll find out I'm not one to back down. I'm in. Tell me what you want."

A smile came across Moe's face, "See, boys? I told you Steve was our man and that he could handle it." Moe sat directly across from Steve and stared him down. He took a long drag on his cigar and then blew the smoke right in Steve's face. "We want you to kill..."

At the word *kill*, Steve's mind started racing. He could hear everything and nothing at all. Moe's mouth moved, but he didn't hear any words come out. He closed his eyes to focus on what was being said to him. They didn't do that anymore. He could not remember the last time they offed someone, took someone out, or eliminated somebody. All nice ways of saying *kill.*

When he cleared his thoughts, he heard Moe ask, "Did you hear me, kid?"

"I'm sorry," said Steve. "What is it you want me to do?"

"We want you to kill Rhino." This came from Sammy.

Steve's skin turned cold, yet he started sweating.

Willy asked, "You gonna be alright? Want some water?"

Why would they want to get rid of Rhino? He could not believe they were asking him to do it. His stomach started churning. He was in it now. If he refused, they would kill him. He'd have to act like it would be no problem. "If that's what needs to be done, I'm your man. Do you mind if I ask why, though?" He desperately tried to keep the quiver out of his voice.

They were asking him to kill the man who saved his life—the man who was like a father to him. Rhino had taught him everything, the ins and outs, the scams, and the ways to survive an attack, to get out of a ticket, and to be a ladies' man. He owed all that to Rhino. And now, they want him killed?

"So, can you tell me why?" Steve repeated.

"It won't change how we feel about it," Sammy said.

"He has been squealing like a pig," Willy interrupted. "For years, we've been doing things a certain way, and it worked. Now, we got someone telling others about our business dealings. Nobody else needs to know anything!" By this time, Willy was out of breath and turning red.

Sammy put his hand on Willy's shoulder, "Slow down, big guy. Take it easy. We all want to see this come to an end, but don't get so riled up about it. That's not healthy." That concern from Sammy struck Steve as out of the ordinary. Sammy had the reputation of being a cold-blooded and heartless individual.

Paul took control of the meeting, "It began about a week ago. Rhino started going around to some of the businesses we've dealt with in the past apologizing for what he'd done or what we'd done. He was even going to family members of the guys we'd taken out."

Paul took out his handkerchief and wiped his brow, "Rhino was seen several times during the week coming and going from the police station downtown. Rhino's turned on Titan, turned into a snitch."

What? No. Steve must have heard wrong. Not Rhino. Not a snitch. Paul showed him photos taken of Rhino meeting with different people who had been dealt with in a bad way by the group. There were several photos taken of him going in and out of the police station, never in handcuffs. Steve could see why Michael gave Paul the power that he had. Paul was very deliberate and precise in his presentation of the evidence and yet very calm. Steve also thought that to be unsettling. Paul was so calm while the rest of the men around the table where adamant of Rhino's wrong doing.

Steve looked at all the pictures, talked to the men, and tried to justify to himself what he saw. But in the end, he knew what had to be done to protect Titan, and he'd volunteered to do it. What a fool! How was he going to pull this off? How was he going to live with himself after killing the only person who had ever been a like father to him? Then it hit him. How was he going to explain this to Michael?

"Doesn't the vote need to be unanimous?" he asked.

"We know the rules, Steven," Paul said, "and there are some—"

"We are all in agreement here," Moe looked right at Paul. "All we need to do is to get Michael to come on board. That will be your job, too." Moe worked a toothpick around in his mouth while he spoke.

"And how do you think I could do that?" Steve replied.

"Explain the situation to Michael," Sammy chimed in. "Tell him the rest of the board is for it and that Rhino broke a major rule. He'll have to go for it."

"We feel you are the only one who could make Michael believe that his brother broke a major rule, Steven," Moe continued, "and that he needs to die." That was twice now they called him Steven. He liked that. It made him feel important.

"Rhino will trust you," Willy encouraged him. "It will be a total surprise. You will be the one in control. You will be known as the one who brought down the Rhino."

Steve liked the sound of that, but how would Michael take the news? Well, Steve could worry about that later. First, he needed to figure out how and where. The how was pretty simple—one bullet in the back of the skull. The more he thought about the group's confidence in him to take care of this and the reputation he knew he would earn, the smaller the problem of dealing with Michael seemed. After this, he'd have the whole group on his side.

"Can I have help?" Steve asked.

"Steven," Willy's eyes gleamed, "you can have one person help you. But, you better be sure he can be trusted. It all falls back on you if he squeals. If this was to get out, we wouldn't back you to the police. We would back Michael and whatever he felt was the best way to punish you however he wishes."

"So, choose your partner wisely," Sammy advised. "Make sure you can trust whomever you pick."

With the instructions and deadline set, they left one by one. Each man stopped by Steve to shake his hand and tell him he was a good man, everyone but Paul.

Steve sat there for a moment by himself thinking. He had until the end of the week. If he couldn't get it done by then, the group would find someone else to take care of Rhino and Steve. Steve still could not believe they wanted Rhino killed.

That was not his only worry now. He had to protect himself, too. But, he'd get the job done. Steve left as the first golfers walked into the clubhouse.

SITTING IN HIS car and listening to the ball game while earning time and a half was not a bad deal to Mark Capwell. He needed the extra money. The bad part—and what he really grew tired of—was being a cop on the take, a loner. Mark's best friend was his own reflection.

While sitting outside the coffee shop, Mark swore under his breath as he burnt his finger trying to smash one more cigarette in an already over-stuffed ashtray. Smoke filled the car even though he'd rolled down the window.

He cleaned the dirt from under his fingernails with a matchbook as Joy approached the car. "Hey baby what's the good word?" She stood outside the car in heels that were too high and a skirt that was too short. Her blonde hair pulled back into a ponytail exposed a face adorned with way too much makeup.

Mark snapped back, "Not tonight, I'm busy."

"What's the matter big man?" she purred. "Can't handle the job, home, and another woman? Thought you were the man?"

"Shut up!" Mark yelled. "I told you, not tonight." He'd been with Joy the last six months, but tonight he was in no mood for games.

"You're feeling guilty. Having second thoughts about us or about leaving your wife, sweetheart?" Joy leaned in the window and caressed Mark's cheek with the back of her hand.

Mark grabbed Joy's wrist and pulled her halfway into the car. He whispered fiercely, "Look, you no good tramp. I said to get out of here and leave me alone, and I meant just that." He pushed her back out through the window.

She stumbled backward on her high heels and landed on her backside, "You no good son of a—"

"Shut up!" Mark yelled. "Or I'll arrest you for loitering, prostitution, and for being a pain in the—"

"Fine!" Joy stood up and brushed herself off. "But just you wait and see if I'm ever around when you need something!"

Mark got out of his car, grabbed her, and pushed her forward, "Get out of here, tramp!" He gave her a kick and started to chase after her just when his cell phone rang. "It's a good thing for you I have to answer this! Now get out of here." He flipped open his phone, "What?"

The voice on the other end was the same one it always was, "Excuse me, but I feel I need a more proper greeting than *what*."

"Sorry," he mumbled. "Just dealing with some low-lifes. What do you need?"

"Where are you?"

"Outside the coffee shop," he replied.

"Is the mark in your sight?"

Mark's gaze drifted to where Rhino sat at the counter talking to some guy Mark didn't know, "Yes, he is."

"Does he know he's being followed?"

"No."

"Are you sure?"

Mark rolled his eyes, "Yes, I'm sure. I've been doing this long enough to know when I've been made."

"I want you to lose Rhino," the voice ordered. "Stop tailing him."

"I can't do that. What will I tell my boss?"

"I don't care what you tell your boss. I'm telling you to lose the tail and lose it now." The line went dead.

Great, Mark thought. *The rumor is true, and they're going to take Rhino out.* This was Mark's shift, and he had the responsibility of trying to keep Rhino safe. He didn't like Rhino, but he liked the thought of being in trouble with his boss even less, even though he hated him also. Mark closed his cell phone and put it in his pocket, swearing under his breath.

He never worried about a call being traced because they always called his cell phone and the call was always made from a pay phone. Now, Mark would have to figure out how to tell Ryan he lost the tail. Mark swore under his breath again as he lit another cigarette. He got back in his car, glad to see that Joy had left, and dumped the ash tray contents on top of the pile of cigarette butts and ashes he'd left on the street from last time.

He reached under the front seat and pulled out a flask filled with vodka. Vodka never left a smell of alcohol on his breath, but it sure left a lasting effect on his mind. As he sat there nursing his drink, a car pulled up. Steve looked way too big for the car he got out of. Close to six feet tall with a crew-cut style haircut, his brown hair matched his brown eyes. He wasn't what you would call muscular, but with his broad shoulders and small waist, he looked very trim and fit. He walked into the coffee shop.

So, this was going to be the patsy they would use to wipe out Rhino. Mark started up his car, and a big cloud of blue smoke coughed out of the tail pipe. He revved the engine a couple of times and dropped it into drive. The car lurched forward, and the tires squealed. He tossed his cigarette at the car Steve had come out of making a miniature explosion on impact.

He drove off, wondering what he would tell his boss. When he got to the intersection, he picked up his radio. "My car just died," he told Ryan. "What should I do now?"

Mark could tell by the silence at the other end of the radio that Ryan did not like the sound of this. "Get a squad car to your location now. As soon as they pick you up, head straight to the abandoned garage. Got that?"

"Yes, sir," he mocked, "will get right on that." As soon as he got off the radio, he pulled into the parking lot across the street from The Hidden Agenda. It was his favorite watering hole. He laughed at the irony as he walked across the street and in the door.

He found a spot at the bar and lit another cigarette. The place was filled with smoke, and the jukebox blared out the southern rock song called, "I'm Not Gonna Let It Bother Me Tonight."

"Vodka," Mark told Big Jack, the bartender. When Big Jack returned with the shot, he said, "What a fitting song."

"What do you mean by that?" Big Jack asked.

"Well, after tonight there is going to be a small war. A blood bath really, but I'm not gonna let it bother me tonight," He downed the shot of vodka.

Big Jack smiled his famous toothless grin. He slapped Mark on the shoulder, "Want another?"

"Yep," he replied and waited for Big Jack to return as the song continued to play.

THERE HAD NOT been an execution in over five years. The details of who the target was would definitely rattle things. Steve still could not believe he was going to kill Rhino. The more he thought about it, the more personal it became. He shook those thoughts out of his head and put the security of Titan first. If he could keep that in mind, he could get through this job.

He would pick up Rhino as if all was fine, drive him to the garage, and take care of business there. They'd remove the body just like Rhino had instructed him many times before. Then, they would report back to the group.

Steve and Kevin drove up to the coffee shop. Sammy had recommended Kevin to help with the hit. Steve thought it best to take the advice of Sammy, even though he knew nothing about Kevin. He was too afraid to pick someone who might have loose lips.

Steve saw Rhino through the front window, sitting at the counter talking to a stranger. He got out of his 1972 Monte Carlo. It was a deep midnight blue, and even in the dim light of dusk, it had a deep shine.

“Wait here,” he said to Kevin.

For a moment, he allowed himself to think back to five years ago when he first met Rhino. His father owed Titan money, and Rhino went to collect. What happened after that he hated to recall. *Focus.* He once again tried to concentrate on the job at hand.

Steve completely respected Rhino, that is, until he heard Rhino was spilling his guts to all the people who’d been on the wrong side of Titan. Rhino broke a sacred rule of the group. They both knew it was punishable by death.

Steve had to forget about his loyalty to Rhino and the respect he had for him. He wanted to be the big guy now. When the group called him in last night, he had no idea that they would be asking for Rhino’s head.

The bell on the coffee shop door jingled. Rhino turned toward the sound, “Hey Steve! Come here.” The guy Rhino was talking to shoved his hands deeper in his pockets, staring hard at Steve.

“Steve, meet Charles,” Rhino said in his hoarse voice.

Steve tipped his head to Charles then ignored him as he turned back to Rhino, “Where you been, man?”

“Here and there,” Rhino answered. “Been talking to some people, tying up loose ends. You know, like Mikey does.”

Steve looked at Rhino strangely for he never referred to his younger brother’s nickname in public, “We need to talk.”

“In a minute. I got something very important to share with Charles first,” Rhino turned back to Charles.

Rhino knew how to control situations. He would manipulate this and work that, and things would come out just the way he wanted. The clock was ticking, and the longer Steve allowed Rhino to have control, the harder it would be to get the job done.

Grabbing Rhino's coat, Steve took hold of both his shoulders. He looked Rhino right in the eyes, "We have to go, now!"

He thought for sure Rhino would take a swing at him, but instead Rhino just looked at him and quietly said, "Okay."

That's when Steve knew something was wrong. Rhino was different. Any other time, Rhino would have dealt a knife or bullet wound before his opponent could blink, but not this time. Rhino didn't even put up a fight, "Okay, let's go."

Rhino looked at Charles, "Remember what we talked about. Don't wait much longer to make a decision."

That sounded kind of funny. As they walked out, Steve asked, "Who's Charles, and what did you mean by that parting shot?"

"He's just a homeless guy who needed a friend, so I told him about a friend who could help."

"Who?" Rhino stopped walking and turned to face Steve. *Here it comes*, Steve thought. *Here's when he resists and tries to run.*

"Let's go to the garage and talk about it." It wasn't a command, but more like a request. Rhino wanted to go to the garage? If Steve would have suggested it, Rhino would no doubt have known something was up and been on edge, looking for a trap. "No one will know we're there, and I could share with you a lot more than here on the street. So much has happened this past week. I need to let someone know who I can trust."

It was too late for that. The trust game was over. Then it hit him. Rhino trusted Steve to keep him safe. Steve pushed that thought out of his mind and reminded himself of Rhino's betrayal.

As they walked up to the car, Rhino pointed to Kevin in the front seat, "Who's your friend?"

If Steve ignored the question, Rhino would know something was up. But, he wanted to be sure that Rhino didn't get a chance to take over the conversation, thus taking control of the situation.

"His name is Kevin," Steve offered, "someone I'm taking under my wing, like you did for me." Steve tapped on the window and motioned for Kevin to move to the back seat.

"Stay there," Rhino told him as Steve opened the door. "I'll sit in the back."

Rhino settled in the back seat, closed his eyes, and laid his head back. Steve got in and started the car. As he drove to the outskirts of the city, the thought of actually killing Rhino started to eat at him. He focused on his driving instead.

Rhino's voice broke into his thoughts, "The city sure has changed since I was a kid. At the time it happened, I felt some of those changes were good. But now, looking back with a different perspective, I wonder how many people suffered in order for us to gain."

The very idea, let alone voicing it, was out of character for Rhino. He was definitely different tonight.

"I wish I could go back and change things, but since I can't, I just want to make sure people know I'm sorry for what I've done."

"What are you mumbling about back there?" Kevin asked. "Can't you just shut up?"

Steve looked in the rearview mirror and saw Rhino shake himself out of whatever this mood was. "What did you say to me?" he asked darkly.

Steve struck Kevin's cheek, "You fool! You don't talk to Rhino like that. He could have you killed!"

Kevin sat dumbfounded. Steve stared hard at him. He hoped Kevin would remember to treat Rhino like he's a friend and not the enemy that he was. Any disrespect, and he'd know something was up.

Kevin muttered an apology, and that seemed to put Rhino right back in his earlier mood. "No problem, Kevin. I forgive you;

and there is no way I would take your life, not anymore that is, since I accepted—"

"You sure are lucky Rhino's in a good mood," Steve grumbled at Kevin. "Otherwise, he would have your head."

The three men grew silent. Every time Steve glanced in the rearview mirror, Rhino had his eyes closed. It kind of looked like he was talking to himself.

The city was quiet and looked beautiful in the darkness.

"Steve," Rhino broke the silence, "do you ever wonder what will become of all this once you're gone?"

Steve hesitated. Was Rhino trying to feel him out? "What do you mean, Rhino?" He had learned early to respond back with a question when unsure.

"You know, after you die and the city still goes on, what do you think will happen to it?"

Steve shot a look into the rear view mirror to assess the expression on Rhino's face. Was this Rhino's way of telling him he knew what was coming and was letting Steve know he'd fight for his life? In the back, Rhino stared out the window looking at the disappearing skyline.

Steve relaxed, "I don't worry about dying. It's gonna happen someday, and I can't stop that. I just hope that whenever it happens, I'll end up in a better place than what I left. If not, then I'll probably be with the same bunch I'm with now, and I guess that won't be too bad either."

Kevin looked in the back seat, "So, what do you think about that, Rhino?"

Steve slapped Kevin upside the head, "Shut up! No one's talking to you!"

As he turned onto the gravel drive leading up to the garage, Steve saw in the rearview mirror that Rhino was still just staring out the window. Something wasn't right. Kevin was getting edgy. In a way, Steve wanted to find out what was different about Rhino, but he knew if the conversation got personal, he wouldn't be able to do the job Titan required him to do.

The small garage just east of the city sitting off old Route 6 was barely noticeable to the occasional passerby. A high ridge surrounded it for privacy. That made the property a great place to do the things that needed to be done privately. It also made it a perfect place to just sit and do nothing.

They parked the car at the back of the garage. Rhino quickly got out of the car and headed to the west side of the property. Was he going to run for it? No, Steve hadn't played his hand yet. Rhino should still feel safe.

A distant train whistle broke the still of the night air as it crossed through the city. The sound of a train being switched in a nearby yard and empty boxcars banging against each other reminded Steve of rolling thunder. Steve slowly followed Rhino to the top of the rise, and they both stood in the cool night air looking west to the city in the distance.

Rhino examined him. "So, what's next?"

The question took Steve aback. Again, he answered with a question of his own, "What do you mean, what's next?" He got the feeling that Rhino knew what was coming and why they were there.

"Come on, Steve. I've been in this business too long to not know why we're here."

"We're here because you wanted to come here," Steve crossed his arms. "You said, 'Let's go to the garage.' So, here we are."

Rhino turned back to look at the city. He knew, "Do you think I'm that dumb? I know what I've been doing is against the rules. I knew sooner or later I would be a marked man."

Rhino paused for just a second, "We wrote the rules to protect each other and made sure if they were ever broken, it would mean death to the one who broke them. I knew as soon as I spoke with the first family that it would bring the group together for a vote. I thought that with Mikey on the board, I'd be safe for a little longer. I thought he'd at least ask the group for a couple of days to think about it and find out what was going on."

He took a deep breath, "But, I guess my time is up. I am surprised that you're the one… Let me rephrase that. I am not surprised you're the one they chose, but I am surprised that you accepted the hit. I taught you well. I just thought that if they asked, you would have said, 'no'".

Steve couldn't look at Rhino, "They told me I'd move up in the ranks if I did this one job. I said 'yes' before they told me what I had to do. They also said that after I heard what the job was they'd kill me if I refused to carry it out. I can't believe you put me in this position!" He was yelling now. "After all you taught me about loyalty and respect and about how we always come second and the business comes first, now you turn around and do this. Was that a bunch of—"

He hesitated. He'd said too much without guarding himself. "I'm doing this to save my own life. I hate this, but you messed up man. You should've known that what you were doing was going to make you a target."

"So, what are you waiting for?" Rhino pushed. "What has to be has to be. I accept that."

"Why did you have to turn into a snitch? You were going around town telling people about Titan and talking to the cops. Why, Rhino? Please tell me why." His feelings were taking control. He had to focus on what had to be done and why it had to be done. "Look, it really doesn't matter to me why you did what you did. I have a job to do, and I will see it through to the end."

Rhino held up his hand, "I believe that still, but I found out my loyalty and respect need to go to someone else."

"Someone else? Who?" Steve's anger helped him concentrate on the job. That was good. Kevin made his way up the ridge before Rhino could give the name of who now had his loyalty.

"Look!" Steve shouted at Kevin. "You're being a big pain tonight. Did I call you up here? Go sit in the car until I tell you to get out!" Kevin stared at Steve, then slumped his shoulders and headed toward the car.

"How do you know Kevin?" Rhino asked.

"That really doesn't matter right now. I told you earlier that he's someone I'm taking under my wing to teach the business."

"Why is he here?" Rhino pressed.

"I was told I could choose one person to help. I chose Kevin."

"So, you trust him?" Rhino's tone sounded earnest.

"Yes, I trust him."

"Where'd you meet him?" Rhino eyed Kevin, who stood rocking back and forth at the car smoking a cigarette.

"Sammy introduced me to him. Said he'd make a good protégé."

Rhino put his hand on Steve's shoulder, "I'm going to tell you why I did what I did, and then you'll do what you have to do. But, watch your back after this."

Steve abruptly turned away from Rhino, "Let's go inside."

Steve let Rhino go first and followed close behind. They reached the front door, and Steve took the keys out of his pocket. His hands shook, making it more difficult to grab the rusty lock that secured the door. Once he unlocked it, he shoved it open. The deafening creak scared him. Maybe he wasn't ready for this like he thought.

Once inside, Rhino sat down on a stained office chair. It had been years since the garage had been used. It still looked and smelled the same way. Rhino started reaching into his breast pocket. Steve jumped forward and grabbed his arm, "Whoa! cowboy, what are you doing?"

Rhino looked at Steve. "It's okay. I'm not up to anything. If I wanted to get away from here or from you, you wouldn't be able to stop me. Trust me."

Truth was behind those words. The small book Rhino pulled out looked like a Bible, not that Steve had seen a lot of Bibles, let alone read one. Rhino thumbed through some pages and then looked at him with a crooked smile, "If you were to die tonight, where do you think you'd end up?"

Steve went rigid. The little book really *was* a Bible. Was Rhino really talking about death?

"Remember when I asked you earlier what you thought would happen to the city—to all this—once we're gone?" Rhino began. "You said you aren't worried about dying. Do you remember that?"

"Yeah," Steve snapped, "what does this have to do with you turning into a snitch?"

"I'll get to that, but first I have something you need to hear. I told you I still believe in loyalty and respect, but now I give it all to Jesus Christ. I became a Christian. I don't really understand it all yet, but now I live for Him because He forgave my sins. All my sins. Even the sin of murder. I know, I know, I still find that hard to believe, but I know in my heart He forgave me of all of them. I know you don't believe the Bible, Steve. It was hard for me to understand, but when I read it, it was like someone punched me in the gut. It says that 'It is appointed unto man once to die.' After death, then there is judgment."

Steve had never wanted anything to do with religion, and he didn't want to stand here now and listen to any more of this. Rhino had turned his back on Titan, on his brother, and on his friends—all for a myth? Steve was almost glad he took this hit.

"Did you get that?" Rhino asked.

"Are you kidding me?" Steve asked incredulously. "I want nothing to do with this, with you. I couldn't care less!"

"You should care," Rhino whispered. "At one time, I didn't care either until I read the words, 'For God so loved the world that he gave His only begotten Son, that whosoever believeth on Him should not perish, but have everlasting life.' These words made me think."

Steve wanted to plug his ears, but Rhino kept on talking, "I was living only for myself and for what I could accomplish for Titan. Now, I want to do the right thing and live my life for Jesus Christ and—"

"Shut up!" Steve broke in. "Are you telling me that you gave up everything you have and all that you've done, not to mention putting Titan and even your own brother in danger of going to jail, all because of religion? You have totally lost it." Steve's voice rose with every accusation.

"Steve, settle down and listen to me," Rhino leaned forward and reached for Steve's arm. "I am not trying to put anyone in jail. I haven't given any names to anybody. This is something I have to do for me, for Christ, because Jesus died on that cross for me. He died for you, too, and He took away the sins of the world when He died on that cross."

"Don't try to bring me into your little fantasy," Steve jerked his arm away. "I got all I need right here. I have friends who watch out for me, and I got endless resources. I don't need help from no one."

"Steve," Rhino started very softly, "the Bible says…I can't remember word for word, but something to the effect that we can have everything we want and still be lost. I was lost; you need to realize you're lost. Steve, I love you, and I want to see you understand your need for a Savior. That Savior is Jesus Christ. You need to ask Jesus to forgive your sins."

That was enough. He went to the door, "Kevin! Get over here and help me bind and gag him!"

When Kevin arrived, Steve hissed, "Stay here and watch him. I'll be right back."

As he jumped in the car and peeled down the drive, he could not get what Rhino had been telling him out of his mind. What was all this "getting forgiveness" stuff? It reminded him of the television preachers he would see as he flipped through the stations. They always yelled and pounded on the pulpit. He wanted no part of that. He tried to keep his mind clear as he turned the car in the direction of Michael's estate.

4

MICHAEL MARELLO SAT at his desk looking at the computer screen, a smile spreading across his face. Computers made it so much easier to move money from one place to another and so much easier to conceal it. No more having to worry about so-called bagmen who risked getting caught and putting a snag in the money trail. Then again, Michael's bagmen hardly ever got caught, not in this city.

He was in his late forties, and as he stretched his six-foot frame, he stared at the reflection in the computer screen. The amount of gray seemed to be increasing every day. His brown eyes were strong, and he still had no need for glasses. Michael was an attractive man according to the latest newspaper interview. The reporter wrote a scathing story on Titan. But, she must have been intrigued by his appearance, for she wrote that he looked nothing like a person who was involved in the business of running a ruthless organization—an organization that had control of the city.

The city was changing. No longer was it an industrial city, but for economic reasons that Michael had no control over, it was emerging as an entertainment venue, of which Michael did have a measure of control. It would never be Vegas, but the changes taking place would bring Michael and his group a lot of money.

He leaned back in his chair and thought of the sight he would have if his office sat in a high rise. Surrounded by windows, everywhere he looked he would see the city he was making better—better for him, better for Titan. But right now, all he had were four walls, a desk sitting in a corner, and a couch pushed against a wall. That was best though. No reason to bring attention to himself or the group. It kept his enterprise strong, with no cracks. He had solid contacts in all the right places, loyalty from the underlings, and unity in the leadership.

Michael's thoughts wandered as he sat in that small office, his one lamp lighting up the computer. What an organization Titan was, and he had pulled it all together. His favorite movie had always been *The Godfather*. This was his mafia, and he was like Don Corleone. But, he kept that part to himself. No need to make any of the guys feel they had to answer to him alone. Still, he enjoyed the fantasy.

Was it corrupt? Sure. Was it illegal? Yes. Did they take care of people with violence or hush money? You bet they did. Most important of all, though, they kept a very low profile.

His favorite symphony, "The Titan" by Gustav Mahler, played in the background; it was the inspiration behind the name for his business. The mere word conjured up visions of strength and power. It was enormous in size and grandeur. Mahler had increased both the brass and the timpani of the orchestra to accommodate the need to execute the finale, and Michael loved the excess needed to accomplish that. He also loved the sound of a full orchestra playing with a ferocious vindictiveness. It mirrored the way he ran Titan, and he was determined to orchestrate his environment.

The phone rang at the same time someone knocked on his door, bringing his thoughts back to the present. His caller ID flashed his sister's cell phone number.

"Hello," he said into the receiver and then yelled, "Come in!" at the door.

Steve pushed open the door and walked straight to the desk, "Michael, we have a problem." He leaned into the desk.

"Mike, we have an emergency," Michael's sister cried into the receiver. Sue was one of the very few who could get away with calling him Mike. Everyone else called him Michael, which sounded more important, more authoritative, and more respectful.

Michael held up his hand, telling Steve to wait. Steve stepped away, "Michael, I need to talk to you now. We have a big problem."

Michael leveled a practiced glare at Steve. Steve shut up and sank down on the couch.

"Go ahead, Sue," Michael told his sister gently.

"Michael, Dad just had a heart attack. They're taking him into surgery, and you need to be here."

"See you in a couple of minutes," He hung up. They'd have taken his dad to Silver Cross Hospital near his home.

His mind raced with all the things he had to do before heading to the hospital. He had to take care of the information on the computer screen and call the rest of the group to inform them of what was going on. He needed to call Rhino whom he had not seen in a week, but was nothing to worry about. He glanced at Steve, but didn't say anything yet. Even though Rhino wasn't as close to their dad, he would want to know what happened.

Michael began shutting down the computer, filing all his notes away, and shredding the notations that he had been working on. Even in a crisis, he knew better than to leave any information lying around; he always tied up all loose ends. Anyone could pick up unfiled information, and before you know it, they know all about you and your business.

Even in his hurry, Michael encrypted his computer files and destroyed his computer history before turning it off. He made several calls to people who needed to know where he could be reached. Where could Rhino be? A half hour had passed by the time he finished all these tasks. As he stood up from his desk, he remembered Steve, but only because he still sat on the couch.

"What is it?" Michael asked roughly.

"We have a problem," Steve told him. "Something needs to be done about it, and it needs to be done now."

Michael had no time for this. The phone rang again.

"You haven't left yet?" Sue whispered.

"I am leaving now," he told her and slammed the phone down. "Look," he said to Steve. "Whatever the problem is, just fix it. I do not have time to deal with anything right now."

"The rest of the group feels this needs immediate attention and should be taken care of now," Steve pushed.

"Fine," Michael put on his coat and walked toward the door, "you have been with this business long enough to know that if the group felt that something had to be done, you have permission to just do it."

"But…" Steve grabbed Michael by the coat.

Michael turned and snapped, "Get your hand off me. Do you even know what you are doing? Do you know who you are messing with? Get your hand off my coat, now!"

Steve cowered like a puppy, "I'm sorry. I just need you to know what needs to be done."

"What are you doing here, telling me about a problem? Where is Rhino anyway?" Michael demanded.

Steve looked at Michael's feet and mumbled.

Michael didn't hear his answer, "Why are you looking at the floor? I cannot hear you."

Steve raised his head and cleared his throat, "I haven't seen him all week."

It bothered Michael that Steve still could not look him in the eye. He did not like dealing with Rhino's little lap dog, but he was in a hurry and wanted to get to the hospital.

"Find him and tell him to call me. I've been trying to get in touch with him and have failed to do so. Anyway, you need to find him. In the meantime, you have worked with Rhino long enough to know I hate this type of decision making. Rhino knows that if the rest of the group is for something that is all I need to know. 'Just take care of it,' is what I would tell him. And since I cannot find him, I am telling you to take care of it. Fix it. I do not care how. I do not want to know why. I just want it done. Period."

He left Steve standing there and headed out to his car. He did not need this to deal with right now, not when his dad might be dying.

Driving to the hospital, Michael's hands tightened around the wheel. Steve had *grabbed* him. Michael could have him killed, or even do it himself. But, he would not hurt Rhino that way.

He opened the glove box, pulled out his cell phone, and turned it on. As much as he liked the electronic world in which he lived, he hated cell phones. He barely used his and always left it in the car.

He glanced at the phone. It had a voicemail from Rhino. He dialed in for voicemail, keyed in his password, and listened.

"Mikey? Rhino." The nickname always made Michael smile. Rhino never used it in public. He sounded nervous, which Michael thought was odd. "Mikey, look. There are some things I need to do. I uh… I uh… have to see some people, and then, I'll come to see you." Michael did not like the sound of that. "I made a decision that is going to change a lot of things. It changed me, and I want you to hear what I heard, and maybe it'll do the same to you. I'll call you tomorrow. I love you and am praying for you."

Michael passed the hospital. His thoughts started racing. Did his big brother just say, "I love you?" What happened there? Did he go soft all of a sudden?

* * *

Steve headed back to the garage. He'd gotten the green light from Michael without Michael even knowing it. Steve thought for sure there'd be questions, at least who and why. Never did he think he would get the okay so quickly. Now with the whole group in agreement, Steve had a free pass to kill.

He found Rhino right where he'd left him.

"Kevin, untie Rhino and go back to the car."

Kevin made short work of it. Once he left, Rhino and Steve just stared at each other and didn't say a word. Finally, Steve asked, "What are you doing Rhino? What made you change?"

Rhino tilted his head, "I told you Steve. Jesus Christ changed me, and He can change you, too. I finally saw how what I was doing separated me from God. I read about it in the Bible. I also read that even despite all that I've done, God still loves me and wants me to be in heaven with Him."

Steve held up his hand as if to say enough, but Rhino pushed on.

"You are going to listen, Steve," his voice sounded commanding. "My sins and your sins put Jesus on the cross. He never did nothing wrong. He was perfect; He had to be. God gave us His Son as a perfect sacrifice. Jesus willingly died so that we can have eternal life."

Rhino leaned forward in his chair, his eyes boring into Steve's, "That's what changed me, Steve. It was nothing I did on my own. Jesus gave me eternal life, and now I want to tell everyone close to me, everyone I love, about this gift that God has given to us."

"So, you turn into a snitch, you turn your back on all the things you've believed in for all these years, and you change all of that because someone told you a story about what Jesus did for you? I thought you believed that what we're doing was better for us than anything. What about your friends and family? Where's your love for me, that love that once made you kill a man to save my life?"

Steve's emotions were taking over again. He had to stop before he failed at this job.

"It's all still there, Steve," Rhino reached for him. "Like I told you earlier, I have different priorities now."

Steve shook his head. Here he was sitting across from the man who killed his father, the man who was now saying that he has different priorities.

"I'm sorry."

"Sorry for what?"

"Sorry I killed your father. Sorry I gave you this kind of a life. Sorry you..."

Steve got up, walked to the door, and called out to Kevin.

Rhino stood, too, "Can I pray with you, Steve?"

Steve exploded. "Just shut up, will you? I've had about enough of this stupid talk about Jesus, about dying, about forgiveness. I don't want to hear about it anymore. In fact, you want to pray? Then, you get on your knees right now, and you pray. Go on. Get on your knees now."

Rhino got on his knees and closed his eyes. The shot rang out into the night as the train whistle blew in the distance.

5

THE ELEVATOR DOORS opened to the fourth floor, and the smell of disinfectant rushed up Michael's nose, bringing back memories of the last time he was in a hospital. He walked aimlessly, searching for his sister as the memory flirted with his mind.

"Michael. Michael!" Sue's call brought him back to the present.

How had the smell of the hospital brought back such a rush of recollection? He'd walked right pass the waiting room. He turned and took the few steps back. Sue ran to him and gave him a hug.

"How is he doing?" was Michael's first question.

"He is in surgery right now," she began to cry.

"It is all right, Sue. I am here now."

Sue backed out of his embrace, "Sorry, big brother, but you can't buy Daddy's health no matter how much money you've got now." She turned back to her chair.

"Obviously, sis, what I meant was I am here for you now. Just relax and take a seat. I am here to comfort you."

"I don't need or want your comfort!" She sat down. "You and your lifestyle don't mix with mine. I pray one day you will see that if you dance with the devil, sooner or later, you are going to pay."

"Please, I do not want to have this conversation again. You know I considered not coming here because of how you condemn me all the time." He hated how she cornered him at family gatherings to talk about "what he really needed in his life."

"I'm sorry. I just want you to know that you can spend eternity with God after you're done here on earth. I pray God will one day show you and Rhino how much He loves you, and that you'll understand the gift He gave you," She blinked fast and sniffed.

"Someday," Michael tried to sound convincing, "just not today. Speaking of Rhino, have you seen or heard from him lately?"

Sue allowed him to change the subject. "No, I haven't. Have you tried his cell?"

"Not yet, but I will."

Other family members started to arrive, crowding the waiting room with noise and tears. They greeted Michael and offered Sue comfort. Michael watched from the corner, sharing only the occasional nod as someone new entered the room. Of course, Michael considered anyone who did not agree with or condone his business practices or his associates to be an enemy. Often times, he considered even his own sister to be an enemy

That left plenty of enemies in the room. He judged each person as he always did, wondering who might be an enemy or a friend. He wished he could get a hold of Rhino. Had Steve found out anything about his brothers whereabouts? Steve must know where Rhino was.

* * *

Steve had been stuck in that tiny shanty for only a couple of hours, but it felt like an eternity. The powerful feeling Steve had felt after taking a human life—and not just any human—was beginning to wear off. Claustrophobic and more than a bit bored, a sick feeling began to overwhelm him, making him want to throw up. Steve started to shake. The more he thought about what he did, the more nauseous he felt and the more he shook. Not only did he feel guilty, but he also regretted his action. Rhino had been the only man who had ever been like a father to him, and out of his own selfish desire to make a name for himself, Steve killed him.

Kevin spoke up with juvenile-like glee, making Steve wish he were there alone, "I still can't believe you took down the great Rhino. How cool is that?"

"I don't want to talk about it," Steve responded sharply.

"Oh, come on, that had to be—"

"Shut up, will you?" Steve shouted. "Just keep your mouth shut. I don't want to hear you again." Kevin glared, but he kept his mouth shut.

In the silence, Steve rummaged through the duffle bag they'd stuffed with Rhino's things before escaping through the tunnel. A small box against the wall held a flashlight, some matches, and a couple bottles of water. There was also some chewing gum and a granola bar. A rat or some other animal had chewed on the granola bar, and there was no water in the bottle, as it appeared that whatever attacked the bar also chewed on the bottle. Steve checked the flashlight. It still worked. He kept it close to the bag so the light would not fill the shanty.

Rhino's keys, license, wallet, a little spiral notepad, and surprisingly, that Bible he'd been waving were in the bag. Steve shoved the Bible back in. The last thing he needed right now was a reminder of what made Rhino turn his back on Titan and all he'd taught Steve to believe. But, what was in the notebook? He flipped through the pages.

The notebook was a detailed work of information from every little job Rhino did, to everyone who was involved, to the reasons why he did it. If the police ever got a hold of this, it would bring the group to a close and completely halt Titan's operations. The first entry was dated over twelve months ago.

So, there must be more notepads. By the looks of this one, Rhino kept track of everything. The notes showed Rhino's proficiency and dedication to Michael.

Then, it hit Steve like a runaway train. If Rhino had turned into a snitch, then why did he still have this notebook? If he'd gone to the police, wouldn't he have turned in the notebook? Rhino said he wasn't trying to put anyone in jail and that he had not given up names to anyone either. His voice echoed in Steve's head, "This is something I have to do for me, for Christ." Maybe Rhino had not snitched.

Steve flipped to the back of the notebook to see if there was anything that would tell him what was going on in Rhino's life—anything that would answer his questions. Kevin had fallen asleep. The quietness of the shanty helped Steve concentrate on what he read. He saw the dates Rhino had marked with a detective but there was no name identified. They met twice this week. He also noticed on the bottom right hand corner of a few pages Rhino had written some sort of code with abbreviations and numbers. A couple of the entries had the name John. The way it was written looked vaguely familiar to Steve, but he couldn't pin point where he'd seen it before.

Steve turned back several more pages. Written in red ink and with large letters, the note "NEED TO TALK TO MIKEY" filled the page. A couple pages before that Rhino had written a notation about a meeting with Ryan and again the name John and the numbers 3:16. Then, it hit him; the numbers and abbreviations were Bible verses.

Steve decided to check out these bible verses to see if he could get the answers there. He dug out the bible he had thrown back in the duffle bag. The first one was John 3:16.

"For God so loved the world that He gave His one and only Son, that whoever believes in Him shall not perish but have eternal life."

Rhino mentioned that verse. Another one written down was Rom. 6:23. He used the table of contents to figure out it was the book of Romans. Steve read the words. It was as if Rhino himself was saying them. *"For the wages of sin is death, but the gift of God is eternal life in Christ Jesus our Lord."* This still made no sense to Steve. The answer of who or why was nowhere in this book.

As he continued to search, Rhino's words just before his death rang in Steve's mind. He could not turn them off. The more he replayed them, the more he was convicted.

Last night, Rhino had made those same references, "You need to realize you're lost, just like I did. I love you, and I want to see you understand you need a Savior." Now sitting in the quietness of the shanty while Kevin slept, it all came rushing back to Steve with each new verse he continued to look up. A reference to Rom. 5:8 read, *"But God demonstrates His own love for us in this: while we were still sinners Christ died for us."*

Steve could hear Rhino's voice in the shanty, "I became a Christian, and now I live for Him because He forgave me my sins." *This* was the reason why Rhino did the things he did. It wasn't that he'd turned into a snitch, but he'd become a Christian. Being a Christian had changed him. The last conversation Steve had with Rhino played back so clearly. Steve could hear Rhino telling him how he still believed in loyalty and respect, but it was Jesus Christ who Rhino would give his loyalty to now. Maybe Rhino had not turned into the snitch the group claimed he was.

Steve closed the notebook and tried to digest what he had just read. All he could picture was Rhino's lifeless body lying in a pool of blood on the cold concrete floor of the garage. Steve had taken the life of the only person who ever loved him. Rhino's love was unconditional, and he would have given his own life to protect Steve.

Hot tears ran down Steve's dusty cheeks. He sat there sure of it now. Rhino had not snitched; he'd become a Christian. Now, Steve could not stop the tears even if he wanted to. He should have thought things through. Rhino had always told him to stop and think and to check every angle before making a choice.

He sat there for another half hour looking through the Bible. He knew what he had to do next. Steve needed to get back into town, get in touch with Michael, and explain to him what had happened. If Michael did not kill him, he would then take Michael to the group and let them tell their side of the story.

He threw Rhino's things back in the duffle bag, but tucked the notebook in his back pocket, "Kevin, wake up."

"What's up?" he responded a bit groggily.

"We have to go," Steve ordered.

Kevin was still not fully awake, "It hasn't been twenty-four hours yet, and we need to stay put."

"We'll go north through the woods until we reach Old Barn Road. That's over a mile away. The cops won't be looking that far. We'll take that west back into the city."

Kevin still in a daze, sat up, "And we're doing this why?"

"I need to get back into town to talk to Michael," Steve's voice came out terse.

Kevin leaped to his feet, "What did you just say?"

"I said I need to get back into town to talk to Michael," Steve threw the duffle bag over his shoulder. "While you were sleeping, I realized some things that Michael needs to know."

"You're kidding, right?" Kevin sounded agitated. "You just shot Rhino, and now you want to go talk to his brother?"

"That's right," Steve said. "You got a problem with that?"

"Sammy told…" Kevin stopped talking.

"Sammy told you what?" Steve asked.

"Nothing, never mind."

"Well, he must've said something; otherwise, you wouldn't have brought his name up. So, what did Sammy tell you?" Steve folded his arms.

"Nothing really. If we're going, let's go, though I still don't think it is a good idea unless the twenty-four hours have passed."

"Get your stuff together, and let's go now," Steve pulled up on the rusty lock to swing the boiler's door open. Rhino's warning about Kevin rang in his mind.

6

MICHAEL GLANCED AT his watch. He had been at the hospital six hours. He still had not heard from Rhino or Steve. He was starting to get mad and worried. Something was not right. His dad had made it through surgery, but now they had to wait and see how he did in post-op. People continued to show up, and others would leave because of the late hour as word of his dad's heart attack got around. Sue had calmed down and kept busy answering everyone's questions and relaying what was happening. Michael once again glanced around the room. Who were his friends, and who were his enemies?

He had never been close to certain family members because of distance. Now, seeing everyone show up during this crisis when Sue needed the family support made him think he ought to try this family thing again. Family, in the form of Rhino, had always been important to Michael. He had always been closer to Rhino than to Sue, Dad, or even Mom. It really bothered him that he could not get in touch with Rhino.

Sue approached Michael cautiously, "What are you thinking about Mike?"

"Childhood memories. My time with Rhino always included fun and danger in equal doses. Rhino would put me in the swing in the backyard, twisting it around until the chains knotted up. He would let go of the swing, and I would laugh so wildly as I was spinning."

Michael shared how Rhino would place him in a wheelbarrow and run up and down the sidewalk, "I use to feel bad I could never return the favor because Rhino was too big for me to push. Rhino would tell me not to worry. He had fun just watching the look on my face as I wondered if he would stop too fast and leave me flying out of the wheelbarrow."

"Of course, Rhino had a mean streak, too," Michael told her. "There was the time he got a hold of a book of matches and we went down to the house on the corner of our block where old man Taylor lived. We were just playing around when a lit match fell into a pile of dried twigs. It immediately caught fire, and we both ran off. Before we knew it, the hedges that surrounded the house had caught fire. We both ran into our house and woke up Mom, telling her there was a fire down the street. We all ran to the front yard and looked down the street. We could see the fire trucks and firemen spraying water on the hedges. Mom looked down the street and said, 'I wonder how that happened?' Rhino and I responded at the same time, 'Don't know.' That's when Rhino mumbled under his breath, '*That'll teach old man Taylor.*'"

Susan sat there with her mouth open. Michael placed his hand under her chin and pushed it closed.

"What did he mean by that?" she asked.

"Are you sure you want to know?"

"Well, you can't leave me hanging with just half the story," she pleaded.

"It may make you understand Rhino a little bit better, but it is up to you."

"Well, as much as I dislike the way you both live your lives, maybe, just maybe, it will make me understand why."

"That night, as I lay in the bunk beneath Rhino, I asked him what he meant about old man Taylor. He leaned over the edge and looked down at me and said, 'That old man needed to be taught a lesson.' I'll never forget the chill in his voice."

Sue just sat there with a look of amazement as he continued, "Rhino confided that he dropped the match on purpose because old man Taylor yelled at him and called him fat. He'd taken a bag of candy Rhino earned and smashed it into the concrete. You know how Rhino always says no one would take what belonged to him without a fight. Well, he made old man Taylor his fight. You know as well as I do, sis, that Rhino lived up to that throughout our childhood and his adult life."

Susan was at a loss for words and shook her head. "It's a wonder you are both still alive." She stood and walked away.

Where could Rhino be? He never had a reason to be before, but now for some reason, Michael was worried. Before he had left for the hospital, he called the other guys from Titan to tell them what had happened to his father. No one had returned his call. No one had come by the hospital either, which Michael thought was strange. He remembered the brief conversation he had with Steve in his office. It was strange that Steve came to talk to him about a problem instead of Rhino. *Where are you, Rhino?* Michael almost said out loud. He jumped at a tap on his shoulder.

"Relax, big guy. It's just me," Sue said. "I'm sorry for judging you and Rhino. I just don't understand…" Michael put his hand up, which silenced her. Then, he reached out to hold her. Susan accepted, "Where's Rhino?"

"I was just wondering the same thing," Michael told her. "Last time I heard from him was a voicemail he left at the beginning of the week. I have not heard from him since."

"If you don't mind me asking," she paused for a second, "what did the message say?"

"He said some pretty strange things that I am still trying to understand."

"Like what?" Sue pushed.

"He said something about a decision he made, that he needed to talk to me, and that he loved me. But, here is the real strange thing," Michael paused for a moment. "He said he was praying for me or something like that."

"That *is* strange," She rubbed her tired eyes. "I've never heard Rhino talk like that."

Michael reached out to pull her closer, "Neither have I. That is why I am worried."

"With the type of life you both live, I'm always praying for both of you," she reminded him. "Who knows what could happen—"

"Please." Michael again raised his hand. "Not now. I do not need to be preached to right now."

"I'm sorry," she returned the embrace. "You still haven't called his cell phone?"

Michael stood up. He intended to use the pay phone in the waiting room to dial Rhino's number but remembered he had taken his cell phone out of the car and put it in his pocket. He flipped it open and began dialing Rhino's number just as his cousin Tom came up. Tom embraced Michael, "Let me know whatever you need."

"I will," Michael lied. "I am fine right now."

It seemed Tom's embrace opened the door to everyone else to approach Michael. He was surprised at how good it felt to be surrounded by family. He talked to old family members he had not seen for a very long time. There was laughter and tears and hugs and handshakes. Michael again realized how much he missed this.

After a while, he wished for the quietness of being left alone. It was getting late, and eventually, just he, Sue, and a few others were left to wait out the doctors. As things started to quiet down, Michael replayed the meeting he had with Steve in his office before he left for the hospital. Steve had told him that there was a problem that needed to be taken care of right away. Michael did not like dealing with those issues, and if it was that important, why didn't any one from Titan call Michael about their meeting?

And why had none of the men called to see how things were with his dad? That, along with not being able to get in touch with Rhino and the strange voicemail that he had left and his meeting with Steve, made Michael wish he had Steve's cell number. He sat there and closed his eyes. Michael was tired from all the emotion and being at the hospital. Sleep softly crept upon him so quickly that he forgot to get in touch with Rhino.

* * *

Steve and Kevin made it to Old Barn Road without being seen, and they headed west back into town. Steve knew this part of town even in the dark. Small, one-story cookie cutter houses lines the streets. Most of the houses had not aged well, and several of the yards were victims of neglect. Once in a while, there was one that stood out because of a well-manicured lawn, and it always made Steve smile. It reminded him of the perfect home he missed out on.

"I don't think we should have left before the twenty-four hours were up," Kevin kept repeating. "I can't believe you're going back to talk to Michael."

"I have to," Steve finally told Kevin a little apprehensively. "I found something out while you slept, and I think I have to let Michael know about it."

"What did you find out?"

"Rhino hadn't turned into a snitch. He became a Christian," Steve murmured. The word felt foreign on his lips. "He got saved. That's why he was acting different this last week."

"I have no idea what you're talking about," Kevin replied. "Saved from what? How does that prove that Rhino didn't turn into a snitch?"

"Well, I was going through Rhino's things while you were sleeping and found a little notebook," Steve held a branch back so that they could pass between two tight trees. "Rhino kept notes on everything. If he'd turned into a snitch, he would have given the notebook up. The information he'd compiled in that little book would bring the whole operation down."

Steve's pace picked up at the same rate as his speech, "So, I need to get back into town to tell Michael what happened. Then, we need to go back to Titan to tell them that there was no reason to kill Rhino."

"You're crazy," Kevin told Steve flat out. "You're telling me that you're going to tell Michael you killed his brother and then you and him will go to the group and tell them they were wrong for ordering Rhino's execution?"

"That's right," Steve gave a quick nod of his head.

"If Michael doesn't kill you," Kevin's voice rose with each word, "the group will definitely have your head when they find out you went to him."

They walked closer and closer, arguing about returning to Michael. "Before you get a chance to talk to the group, Michael will kill you himself when he finds out you killed his brother," Kevin warned Steve.

"I don't think so," Steve tried to sound confident. "When I met with Michael to tell him what the rest of the group wanted, he gave the order to 'just get it done.' He made it a unanimous vote." They started over the bridge that crossed the railroad yard. "He ordered his own brother's death without even knowing it. According to the code, he can't hold me accountable for that."

Steve turned to face Kevin and said, "Rhino's life changed because Jesus came into the picture. I figured that out after going through Rhino's stuff. He spelled it all out in the notebook. He even wrote how he needed to talk to Michael about it."

Steve took the notebook out of his pocket as he continued, "As I sat there reading Rhino's Bible, a strong feeling came over me. I can't explain it, but it felt like a guilty or convicting feeling. I saw it in the book of Romans—Jesus died for me even though I'm a sinner. I realized He would forgive my sins if I told Him about them. Jeez, if anyone needs a Savior, I do. I just killed Rhino! So, sitting in the shanty, I prayed and asked Jesus to save me."

Looking directly at Kevin, Steve pleaded, "Kevin, you need to be saved, too."

In the distance, a train whistle blew, cutting the silence of the crisp early morning air.

"Do you mean to tell me," Kevin started slowly, "that because of a *prayer,* God forgave you and now *you* think that Michael will forgive you, too?"

"I'm not worried about Michael right now," Steve told Kevin. "I'm worried about you and your soul. You need a Savior just like I needed one." Steve dug into the duffle bag looking for Rhino's Bible. He got his hands on it and feverishly turned the pages, looking for John 3:16. Even though it was just starting to get light out, to Steve, it was as if the sun shone full force on the page. The words were so fresh to him, for he'd just read them, absorbed them really not long ago back in the shanty.

"You've heard of John 3:16, right? You know, it's behind the goal post at every football game. '*For God so loved the world He gave His only begotten Son, that whosoever believeth in Him shall not perish but have everlasting life.*'"

Kevin replied, "So what?"

"So, we're all sinners, Kevin," Steve tried to explain. "Because we sin, we're separated from God. It's only when you accept Jesus Christ as your Savior that you can get back to God."

"And you say that's what you and Rhino did? You both became Christians? Let me see the notebook," Kevin held out his hand.

As Steve reached with the notebook, Kevin grabbed his wrist and kneed him in the gut. Steve doubled over as he dropped the notebook and the Bible. Kevin swung an upper cut with his left fist that caught Steve squarely in the jaw, smashing it. He let go of Steve's wrist and grabbed the hair at the back of his head. Holding him tight, Kevin's right fist came straight at Steve, breaking his nose. Steve tried to catch his breath. He had blood all over his face and his jaw hung loose.

Kevin grasped the back of Steve's head. "Sorry, buddy," he whispered directly into Steve's ear, "but you're not going to say anything to anybody. Not to Michael. Not to the group. Sammy told me to make sure you didn't make it back alive, and I'm going to see to it that you don't."

"You know what?" he continued. "I don't want anything to do with your Jesus or your God either. You're a fool, and well, you're going to die because of it."

Kevin grabbed the duffle bag off Steve's shoulder and shoved him over the railing of the bridge. As Steve fell backwards, it was as if he was falling in slow motion. He could still see Kevin standing on the bridge with a look of satisfaction on his face. Just before he landed, Steve saw a truck come over the bridge and strike Kevin. Then, Steve landed on the tracks with a thud. The train passed over him, cutting him in two.

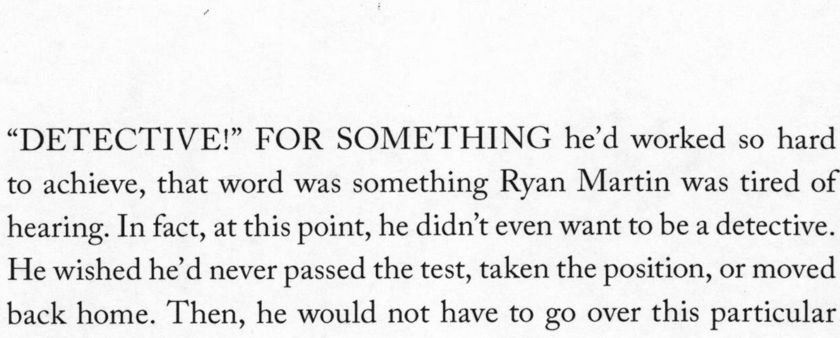

7

"DETECTIVE!" FOR SOMETHING he'd worked so hard to achieve, that word was something Ryan Martin was tired of hearing. In fact, at this point, he didn't even want to be a detective. He wished he'd never passed the test, taken the position, or moved back home. Then, he would not have to go over this particular crime scene.

For the first time in his career, he personally knew the victim.

"Detective!" Mark Capwell's insistent voice brought him back to the present. When Ryan looked up, Mark continued, "The press is showing up, and we need more manpower to keep them at a distance. What a worthless life."

Ryan didn't like Mark's style of being a cop. How could he be so cold-blooded and uncaring?

"Well, it looks like he got what he deserved," Mark said callously, standing in the dim light of the garage.

Ryan pushed Mark against the wall with just one finger and got right up in his face, "No one deserves to die like that." He would love to take Mark outside and make him eat those words.

Mark shoved Ryan away, "What's your problem, man?"

"Hey, you two knock it off!" Captain Altman pointed to Mark. "We have a crime scene here, and I don't want either one of your DNA to contaminate it. Capwell, go outside and see if they found a weapon yet."

After Mark stalked out the garage door, Ryan turned to his boss, "Sorry, Captain, I've never really liked Detective Capwell. In a way, I sometimes don't trust him."

"I'm not worried about him right now. What I am worried about is how this happened. You told me to give you some room with this and you would give me something in return. Well, all I got is a dead body," Captain Altman surveyed the crime scene.

"Are the reporters out there already?" Ryan asked.

"They're out there, but we're keeping them at a distance," Altman responded testily.

"I know this looks bad, Captain. I mean we have a body shot gangland style, and the victim is the brother of one of the most powerful men in the city. Just tell the press that we started an investigation into the murder of a single victim. Leave it at that for now. When word gets out about the property involved, that will clue in the people likely involved. I have to make a phone call. Give me a little more time before we release the victim's name."

"We're not going to release any name until you're sure who it is. Are you sure it is who you say it is?" Altman asked. "There's no ID."

"Nick Marello, known as Rhino."

The captain's voice rose again, "I thought you had a tail on him. How did this happen?"

"Look, Captain, I don't want to imply anything or accuse anyone, but I've got a strong suspicion. I've come to the conclusion that Capwell's a loner and his best friend is his own reflection. In my investigating, I found—"

"Wait a minute. You're investigating a fellow detective?"

"Sir, just listen to this before you condemn. This, sir, needs to stay off the record. He's been on the force for fifteen years and a regular at the gambling boats. I did some checking, and found out that's when Capwell first met Rhino. While I was investigating Capwell, I learned that Rhino hired all the security for the boats, and since Capwell needed extra cash, he got himself hired. After starting security, Mark was soon addicted to gambling.

Here's how it works—whatever cops win, they can keep. Titan covers whatever they lose, and they always lose more than they win. Always. That's how they had so many cops on the take. As long as Titan covered a loss, the cop owed a favor or two in return. By covering the losses, Titan earned the cops' loyalty and their compulsory service. Mark has a wife and four kids to provide for. He needed Titan to cover his gambling losses. In return, Titan owned Capwell.

"I can keep this off the record for now, but I can't keep quiet for long," Captain Altman reminded Ryan.

"I understand, sir, but I've got serious cause to believe Mark Capwell's involved," Ryan began as he looked at the bagged body of the late Rhino. "When Mark radioed that he had car trouble and lost the tail, I sent a car to pick him up, but Mark wasn't there. In fact, he didn't show up for an hour. I made my way to the garage with a couple of patrolmen, not the quietest of the bunch. Whoever killed Rhino was gone by the time we entered. We found the victim lying there just as you see him now. The initial search hasn't turned up anything yet."

"With Rhino's cooperation, we were poised to take down the Marello Empire. He gave me all the ins and outs of the business, no names though. Rhino was just about to go to his brother to let him know he was ready to quit."

"Really," Altman rolled his eyes, "and why was he going to do that?"

"Because he was changing his life," Ryan shrugged.

"You know this how? "Altman asked stepping closer to the body.

"Well, sir...he...well…he became a Christian," Ryan answered.

"I've told you how I hate it when you bring in your personal beliefs to the job, Detective!"

"Yes, sir, this was on my own time, and Rhino was ready."

"You're always talking about how it can change a life. Well, you really changed Nick Marello's life. He's dead, and I don't like that at all."

"Sir, I can explain if—"

Altman cut Ryan off in mid-sentence, "I don't care. I've heard it before, and I don't agree. If it works for you, fine. Me, I'll be good to my fellow man, keep the law of the land, and take my chances. Now, what you can do is find out who did this before the media blows it out of proportion."

Altman walked out the door with Ryan trailing him. As they stepped out of the garage, they met Mark Capwell, who slid his cell phone into his pocket.

"Who was that?" Ryan asked narrowing his eyes.

"Forensics," Mark replied with a quirky smile. "Said they'd be here in a couple."

"Find anything?" Altman asked Mark.

Mark pointed north, "Over there's a junkyard that has an old shanty with a boiler in it. We'll have to wait for a little more daylight to search for a weapon." Mark lit a cigarette.

"We're not going to find a weapon," Ryan told him.

"Why not?"

"This was a hit, a professional hit," Ryan explained. "We came upon the body before they could get rid of it. So, I know we won't find a weapon. We need to be looking for a suspect or suspects. We need to canvas the area and do it now. Wait too long and we'll lose them for sure."

"How do you know it was a professional hit?" Mark was playing dumb Ryan could tell.

"Are you serious?" Ryan pointed back at the garage, "Do you know whose body is lying on the floor of that garage with a bullet through his head? —Nick Marello, brother of Michael Marello, the person who has the town wrapped around his finger."

"Nick Marello," Ryan emphasized the name again, "does not wind up on a garage floor with a bullet through his head unless it was done for a reason and by someone who knew what they were doing. Like I said earlier, the only reason we found the body is because we almost caught the killers in the act. If you hadn't lost the tail because of your supposed car trouble, Marello might still be alive," Ryan finished on a softer note.

"What? You can't be blaming this on me. I can't help it that my car died."

"Yeah, how convenient is that?" Ryan said under his breath as he turned to leave.

"What'd you just say, Martin? You think I let this guy get killed? Look, I've been a cop a lot longer than you. What right have you got to judge me or assume anything about how I do my job?"

"All right, cool off," commanded Altman.

"Detective!" An officer called as he walked up to Ryan. "Sir, I've been trying to get your attention, sir. They want you on the radio."

Ryan took the officer's portable radio and spoke into the mic, "Detective Martin here."

The radio crackled back, "Detective, we're at the bridge that runs over the railroad yard. You need to get over here."

"Officer," Ryan tried to sound patient, "can this wait?"

The officer's voice came back, "I don't think so, sir. I have two more bodies here that may be linked to your crime, sir."

"I'll be right there," Ryan gave the radio back and walked briskly toward his vehicle.

8

SAMMY SALLUCI SAT in his den with a beer in one hand and the remote in the other. Watching the late local news kept Sammy up on any local events and how they might either favor or hurt Titan. Tonight's report made him mad and worried at the same time.

"We have breaking news," said the anchor on the TV while holding onto his earpiece. "Police have found a body in an abandoned garage along old Route 6. The garage is believed to be owned by Titan Incorporated, which has also been suspected to be a part of the Marello Empire managed by the very powerful Michael Marello. The body may or may not be connected to the Titan enterprise. We are waiting for an official confirmation. That's all the information we have at this time. Stay tuned to learn more as this story develops."

Feeling furious, Sammy stood up and shut off the TV. He paced back and forth seized with an anger that made him pace even faster and kept him tight lipped. He would stay tight lipped until he heard whom the body belonged to. Right now, it could be one of three people he knew would be at that garage—Steve, Kevin, or Rhino. Common sense and calm reasoning told him it had to be the body of Rhino. If it were Steve, then what happened to Kevin or vice versa? Or, maybe if it was Kevin's body, then Rhino flipped Steve and got him to talk. That meant that Rhino would be on his way to see him. Sammy's pacing grew faster as the anger started to control his thoughts.

His cell phone rang, "Mr. Salluci?"

"Yeah, what is it?"

"Capwell here. We have a problem. They found the body."

Sammy was silent for a moment, "I was watching the news, something about a garage and a body. Is that what you are calling about?"

"Yes. There was no one around, and no weapon has been found," Mark tried to assure him.

"Your job was to make sure there would be no police interference," Sammy charged.

Capwell replied, "Detective Martin interfered. Got there before I did. There was nothing I could do to stop it. What would you like me to do now?"

"Right now, nothing. I'll get back to you. Wait, they never gave a name of the victim. Is there a need to worry?" Sammy asked still pacing.

"No sir, no need," Capwell assured him.

The pacing stopped, but now Sammy's mind raced. There was still a small need to worry. He had to call the rest of the group to let them know that somehow things didn't go as planned. Yes, Rhino was dead, but the body was found. That was not supposed to happen. Now, Willy and Paul might turn on Moe and him. Those two argued the most against the hit on Rhino and had to be coaxed into it. Sammy would have to cover his tracks. He didn't have to worry about a paper trail. Decisions like this were never documented. All the meetings they had were at the country club, so no recordings either.

Sammy was anxious to get to Willy and Paul to make sure they would still be on his side. He picked up the phone and started dialing. He stopped and hung the phone up when he thought of Kevin and Steve. Had Kevin done his job? Was Steve dead, or were they on the run? Sammy swore under his breath. What should he do next?

9

"I HAVE BODIES everywhere," Ryan Martin yelled to the dispatcher. "Send a squad to keep the press away, and get a forensic team down to the south end of the train yard." Ryan snapped his cell phone shut and started to put it in his pocket when it rang again. It was Detective Capwell. Ryan sighed, "What do you need, Mark?"

"Forensics just arrived at the garage, and the Captain's here. So, I was just wondering if you need help where you are."

"Yeah, sure. I'm at the train yard, and I have several people who need to be interviewed." Ryan closed his cell phone again and crossed the remaining distance to the old switchman. "Okay, tell me...um, what's your name?"

"Homer." The switchman said as he turned and spit tobacco juice onto one of the steel rails, missing an ancient coffee can by at least five feet, "Shoot, missed again." He wiped the spittle off his chin with his worn denim shirtsleeve.

"Right," Ryan huffed, "tell me, Homer. What did you see?"

"Well, I was standing right here by the north seven switch. I always stand at the north seven switch because it is the best place to see the sunrise. You ever watch a sunrise, Detective?" Ryan nodded, motioning with his hand for Homer to continue.

"Right," Homer got the hint, "anyway, as I stood by switch seven, I looks up at the bridge and see these two guys, and they looks like they're wraslin' So's, I yells up at them to get off the bridge. Don't think they heard me though, what with the train whistlin'." Homer spit again. This time, it landed with a ping right in the coffee can. He turned and smiled real wide, baring his yellow stained teeth and the remaining tobacco in his mouth. "Good hit, don't you think, Detective?"

"Look, Homer," Ryan jotting down notes in his pad. "It's been a long night, and it's going to be an even longer day, so don't get offended if I tell you I really don't care for your target practice or your tobacco chewing."

"Different folks," Homer shrugged and wiped at the spit on his chin again. "Anyways, these two guys were wraslin,' and all of a sudden, I see one of them falls off the bridge. At least, I'm pretty sure he fell. I don't think he jumped. Course, he might have been pushed. Anyway, I start to run over to him, but the train got there before I did. It messed him up, somethin' awful. Then, I look back up at the bridge, and I heard the truck horn and the brakes screeching. I thought maybe the trucker was stopping because he saw the guy fall from the bridge, not because he hit the other guy."

The radio Ryan had borrowed from the officer at the garage went off. It was Officer Lansing on the bridge, "Sir, you better get up here. We found something you need to see."

"I'll be right up," Ryan turned back to Homer. "Anything else?"

"Nope," Homer replied.

"Well, here's my card. If you do remember anything else, give me a call."

"Yep, I sure will, Detective. Now, you go and have yourself a good day," Homer turned to spit another perfect arc of tobacco juice into the coffee can, causing him to once again flash his yellow stained teeth. Ryan's stomach churned.

By the time Ryan got to the bridge, Mark Capwell had arrived and was pacing next to the semi talking on his cell phone and holding his hand up to his open ear to hear better. Ryan walked past him and stopped in front of Officer Lansing. Kyle Lansing was a rookie cop who wanted to impress the detectives by getting everything right. This was his first murder scene investigation, and he was going by the book.

"What did you find?"

"Well, sir, we found this duffle bag, and inside, we found some personal effects of one Nicholas Marello," Lansing handed Ryan Nick Marello's driver's license. He proceeded to inventory the contents of the bag, "Nick Marello's wallet, a cell phone, and this." The officer pulled out a .45 automatic and what looked to be a note pad or some sort of journal or log. He also found a Bible lying on the ground.

Ryan took a pair of rubber gloves from his pocket and pulled them over his hands. He took the gun and sniffed the barrel. It had recently been fired. "Tag everything and make sure to keep an eye on it. I guess I was wrong about the murder weapon. More than likely we just found it and the two guys who used it. Now, we just need to know what happened here and at the garage."

Mark walked up to Ryan, stuffing his cell phone into his pocket, "I'll tell you what happened. These two botched a hit, and they were both taken out so they couldn't talk. They either put the Marello family in jeopardy by taking out one of their biggest defenses; or they planned a hit on their own, and the Marello's retaliated."

"And just how do you know this?" Ryan asked derisively.

"Just a guess," Mark shrugged.

"Have we identified either of these bodies yet?" Ryan asked Officer Lansing.

"The I.D. on the victim hit by the truck is one Kevin Marino, and the one sliced in two is Steven Silinger," Officer Lansing told him.

"Run the names through BCI and find out what we can. Let's make sure we get this investigation right! I want whoever is responsible for this arrested, and I want them convicted. Don't screw it up!" Ryan nodded briskly at Lansing.

"Yes, sir," Officer Lansing headed toward his squad car.

Ryan turned to Mark, "Do you have any idea who either one of them could be working for or why they'd go after Nick Marello of all people?"

Mark turned away from Ryan and looked over the railing of the bridge, "They look familiar, at least what I can make out from what's left of them, but nothing definite yet."

Ryan shared with Capwell what information he got from the interview with the switchman as he rummaged through the duffle bag. He found Rhino's note pad and a quick turn of the pages brought a tear to his eye. In the short time since he'd been able to introduce Rhino to his Savior, Rhino had been much disciplined in his daily devotions. He flipped a couple more pages and saw the page that Rhino had written in red ink the words, "Need to talk to Mikey." Ryan could not find an entry that indicated if Rhino ever had a chance to talk to his younger brother, so Ryan grabbed Rhino's cell phone to check the call records.

"What are you looking for?" Mark sounded a bit frustrated.

Ryan ignored him as he searched Nick's phone book on his cell. He looked up Michael's name and made note of the number. He then went to Nick's outgoing calls and looked for the last time either Michael called or Nick called Michael. Nick had called Michael a week ago, Sunday. The incoming call log also showed that Michael had tried to get in touch with Rhino late last night. Although it was completely against protocol to do what Ryan was about to do, for some reason he was drawn to do just that. Even though he was hesitant to call with Capwell standing right in front of him, Ryan didn't care. He highlighted Michael's name in the contact list and pressed talk. The phone began to ring as Ryan looked at the sun rising in the eastern sky, which was turning the sky more blue than black.

* * *

Sammy's cell rang. He flipped it open when he recognized Detective Capwell's number, "What do you want?"

"Relax, Sammy. I think we're safe," Mark said calmly.

"What do you mean *we*?" Sammy replied.

"Got some good news for you," Mark began. "We found two bodies. The names are Steve Silinger and Kevin Marino."

"How?"

"Not really sure yet. One was sliced in half by a freight train; the other was killed when he stepped in front of a semi," Mark paused as he cleared his throat, "according to a switchman by the name of Homer. I'm serious, Homer is his name. Is that classic or what?"

Sammy gave no response.

"Anyway," Mark continued, "he saw two men on the bridge who appeared to be fighting. One of them either was pushed or fell, and the other was struck by a semi."

"Are you sure it's Steve and Kevin?" Could Sammy believe his luck?

"Yes, I'm sure. Now are you going to tell me what's going on?" Mark asked impatiently. "You need to let me know so I can deflect any tie to you or Titan that may come up. I've got to steer the investigation the way it needs to go. Otherwise, it could turn back toward you, if you know what I mean."

"You little punk! Are you trying to blackmail me? I don't owe you anything, let alone an explanation, and for you to ask for more than you deserve is a very bold attempt on your part," Sammy warmed to his outrage. "You are in no position to ask for anything. You work for us, remember? If you want to keep your job and your health just keep your mouth shut and do as I say. It's not the other way around. Don't be a fool. You know whom you are dealing with and what happens when deals go wrong. Be smart, be safe, and you'll stay alive. If not, we will mail you back to your family in a cardboard box. Got that?"

"You're right, Sammy, but the captain and the lead detective think this is a sign of a power struggle and there's going to be an all-out bloodbath. You need to tell me what's going on so that I'll be able to take the heat off you."

Sammy didn't bite, "For right now you just keep the focus off Titan and make it look like an inner struggle between foot soldiers wanting to move up the ranks. Maybe, Steve got tired of working for Rhino or taking orders. He wanted to be out from under his wing. Maybe, if the police fear a bloodbath, it could be a good thing for us. You just do as I say, and you'll stay alive. Got it? Call me when you have more."

Sammy snapped his phone shut but let a small smile loosen the lines of his face.

10

THE WAITING ROOM windows allowed the morning sun to shine right on Michael as he stirred in his chair, turning his face away from the light. In the course of one blink, he noticed Sue's friend, Elizabeth, watching him.

Elizabeth sat across from Sue. Michael sheepishly kept his eyes closed to listen to the conversation. It was something he became very cunning at—eavesdropping on others. It was a craft and an art that Michael prided himself on mastering.

"Just look at Michael," Sue commented. "He's the spitting image of my father, and yet he is nothing like him. Our dad is a strict man, even harsh at times when we were growing up. He has a hard time saying how much he loves us, but he's nothing like Michael or Rhino. Our father is a loving man who loves his kids, and even though he divorced our mom, he was never a dead beat. He provided like he should and was always there when we needed him. That is until Michael and Rhino got involved in the things they do now. Now, they think only of themselves."

Michael wanted to jump up and assault Sue with a defense of his lifestyle. Had she forgotten how it had benefitted her? Didn't he and Rhino take better care of her than her abusive husband? Did he not make sure that she and her two daughters were always taken care of, never to want for anything?

"I know they do their best to take care of me and the girls," Sue brought these thoughts into her conversation. "But, I have never agreed with how my brothers lived their lives. I really do try my best to be a testimony to them. I always tell Michael and Rhino they need a Savior, but they don't seem to want anything to do with religion. I tell them to look at the way they live their lives and how wrong it is. They need to turn from their sin and repent." Michael could hear disappointment.

"I know how that frustrates you. I feel for you each time you share the concern of your heart," Elizabeth said.

"They just blow me off, and they never hear my words," Sue continued. "They would come to Grace of Christ Christmas programs that my daughters were in. They came a couple of times when our church had a guest speaker mainly because I begged them to come until they agreed. But, they have never been convicted to turn their lives over to Jesus."

She paused. Michael didn't dare peek. "Rhino has defended me to Michael before. Michael is just so arrogant. He'll say things like, 'I do not need your religion' or 'I do not want to hear it again.'"

He wanted to wake up from his pretend sleep and tell his sister how much her nagging turned him away from what she believed. Her persistence was making it undesirable.

"But, Rhino always gets Michael to show some respect toward my beliefs. Actually, I need to talk to Rhino about some things Michael was just telling me about last night. Michael told me that

Rhino left a message on his phone that ended with him saying, "I love you and that he was praying for Michael also". That's unusual for Rhino."

"They really do care about you and your two girls," Elizabeth said.

Yes, Michael thought, *bring Sue's attention back to the positive side.*

"Michael and Rhino are so different, and they have completely different styles in defending me." Sue had always acted a little embarrassed about her childhood, but Michael rarely heard her talk about it with her "church friends." Michael could tell it was good for Susan to talk with Elizabeth about her brothers. It was also a benefit for him to learn how his sister really felt about her brothers.

"Rhino always used his muscle, while Michael would use words. One time in high school, a boy took me under the bleachers at a football game and took advantage of me. I have never told anybody else this story Elizabeth, so you need to promise me that this stays between the two of us. I hate reliving this part of my life, and it sickens me to tell it. But, I just feel I can be completely open with you."

Michael continued to sit there and was amazed and impressed by Elizabeth's response and dedication to his sister, "Sue, you can trust me with whatever you want to share. I'm here for you now and always."

Sue smiled and continued, "I didn't want to go to the police, but Rhino found out about it and said he would take care of it. Rumor had it that at the next home game Rhino found the guy, took him under the bleachers, and proceeded to beat him silly. He stretched out the guy's arms and tied them to the bleacher supports. Rhino kicked him in his groin, busted his nose and his jaw, ripped the guy's shirt off his back, and spray painted 'I am a pig' on the guy's bare chest. I was never mistreated or messed with again in high school."

Michael couldn't help it. He peeked. Elizabeth's jaw hung open in surprise and possibly horror, but she shut it quickly.

"You said that Michael used words instead of muscle? I'm hoping you've got a story about him as well."

Michael barely caught Sue's smile before his eyes closed again. "Oh, yeah, I've got a story to tell you, and it is definitely different from how Rhino dealt with any threats."

What would she say?

"When I was in college, a classmate in my freshman English class would whisper all these dirty things he would like to do to me. I told Michael about it, and the next day he came to visit me on campus right after class got out. I introduced Michael to the guy. Michael shook his hand and pulled him in close to whisper something in his ear. The expression on this guy's face changed immediately. He looked Michael right in the eyes and nodded, and then he tried to look at me, but he couldn't bring himself to do it. He called out that he would see me later as he walked quickly away from us. I never saw the guy again. I asked Michael what he'd said to him, and Michael told me not to worry."

"Did you ever find out what he said?" asked Elizabeth, sounding like a school girl.

"Well, he told me that Rhino once said that if people feared you, you would be safe. 'This guy now fears you,' he said."

"Are you going to tell me what he said or just make me sit here and beg?" Elizabeth started to laugh.

Sue laughed, too, "One day in the cafeteria I overheard some students talking about this guy and Michael, and I asked them what they knew. One of them told me that he heard Michael had told the guy that if he ever touched me he would chop off his hands and cut out his tongue so that he would not be able to tell anyone who beat him to a bloody pulp."

Elizabeth didn't laugh after that. Finally, after what seemed like a minute had passed, all she said was, "Wow!"

"Yeah, wow," Sue mocked. "Those are my big brothers, and now look at them. They live their lives with such lawlessness and don't care. They need a Savior, but whenever I try to share with them, they tell me not to worry. Well, maybe, I should stop worrying. Don't get me wrong, even though I despise their approach to dealing with problems, they have always made me feel safe and secure. I also realize how much they love me."

A long silence passed, and Sue spoke up again, "What's wrong? Did I scare you?"

"No. It's nothing really," Elizabeth assured her. "It's just that as I sit here and you talk about how much you love your brothers, I don't see that love when you talk to them about their need for Christ in their lives."

"What do you mean?" Sue responded.

"You always tell me that you tell your brothers how wrong they are, how their lives are full of sin, and that they need to change the way they live. Granted, all this is true, and they do need to change. But, this is the only life they know, and to them, it has been a good one. Michael and Rhino need to have Christ in their hearts and have Him cleanse them. I agree with all of that, Sue, but don't you think you should share this with them with a heart of love and compassion? Let them see Christ's love in you and in your love for them."

Michael took a quick peek and saw Elizabeth lean forward in her chair and grasp both of Sue's hands, "If all you ever do is condemn them, you will do nothing but continue to push them away and turn them off to the saving grace of Jesus Christ. Jesus never did that. He met people where they were, and He used stories to teach them and convict them of their sin. He did it all with a compassionate and loving heart. He desired for them to come to that saving knowledge. If you want to see Michael and Rhino come to know Jesus, let the Holy Spirit do the convicting, not you. You need to love the sinner even though you hate the sin."

He squinted, just barely enough to catch sight of Sue crying. Did she truly feel badly about how she treated him? It would be a relief if she stopped slamming her Jesus down his throat. Maybe she really did care about him. Sue and Elizabeth hugged, "Thank you, Elizabeth, for your honesty. I guess I didn't realize how I might have been pushing my brothers away instead of drawing them to Jesus. You know that my biggest desire and most urgent prayer is that not only Michael and Rhino come to know Christ, but my dad also."

Michael was getting a little uncomfortable feigning sleep and was glad when Sue shook his shoulder to wake him up as Dr. Thompson walked into the waiting room.

Dr. Thompson stopped in front of Sue, "He had a rough time, and for the next twenty-four hours, he'll be in intensive care and monitored closely. We almost lost him twice on the table, but we were able to get his heart going again. His heart has taken a beating. He had a quadruple bypass and was under anesthesia for a long time. He's not out of the woods yet. In a couple of hours, he should be out of recovery. I'll come back then to let you know when you can see him."

Sue cried again and turned into Michael's open arms. "Thanks, we will be waiting here for word from you," Michael nodded at Dr. Thompson. To his sister, he said, "It is going to be okay. He is alive and hopefully will get better." He did not have much experience in consoling, but he tried.

"I know," Sue said. "Just the thought that he died twice on the table is scary. I just hope I have another chance to talk to him." She stepped back and patted Michael's heart.

"Just let him be for now," Michael said to Sue. "Do not go preaching religion at him now; his heart cannot take that."

"You want me to leave my…our father alone and not preach religion to him? Is that what you are telling me?" Each word came slowly out of her mouth, "Our father is near death, without Christ, and you just want me to shut up and say nothing?"

"I just do not want you to go in there with all that foolishness and get him upset," Michael tried to explain. That is not going to happen. He knew Sue was not only getting frustrated at his pretensions but also his non-use of contractions. It made conversations with people sometimes long and laborious. Michael would always blame his grandmother for this. Growing up she would always correct him if he ever used the word ain't. She would scold him and tell him "Michael, ain't is not a word. If you are going to grow up to be someone, you need to converse in a proper way; otherwise, no one will take you seriously if your language is sloppy." Michael took those words to heart and always did his best to use proper English when talking to others. It was a habit he had developed, and it drove him as crazy as those who had to listen to him.

Sue grabbed Michael's arm and raised her hand as if to slap him. Then, she stopped. "Foolishness? This is not foolishness! Foolishness is what you and Rhino do. What I want for our father is security in knowing that there is a heaven and a hell and to let him know he needs to make a choice between the two. What you and Rhino do I just don't care anymore. I give up."

Her gaze shifted to look over his shoulder where she knew Elizabeth was standing, watching the whole thing. Sue's demeanor changed, and her face visibly softened. She pulled Michael close to her again, "You're right, and I'm sorry. I need to let dad rest and pray that he will get strong and that I will be able to talk to him a little later. Thank you, Michael, for being here."

"I am glad to be here, Sue," Michael responded, a little confused at his sister's mood swings.

Michael caught Sue looking back at Elizabeth as she mouthed the words, "I'm sorry." He then glance toward Elizabeth and saw her smile and nod in acknowledgment. As Sue stepped away, Michael told her that he needed something cold to drink and asked if either of them wanted anything. In unison, they both said, "no."

11

WHEN MICHAEL RETURNED from the cafeteria, he stepped back into the waiting room but stopped himself when he saw that Sue and Elizabeth were together on the couch. He wanted not only to hear what they were talking about but also wanted to see what more he could learn about Elizabeth. She was an outsider. He needed to figure out the motives behind why this outsider would spend so much time with someone who was not family. And it didn't hurt that he was drawn to this Elizabeth. He didn't know why. He'd never been romantically involved before.

He stayed right outside the room and again eavesdropped on their conversation.

Elizabeth said, "I've been wondering how long before you would finally open up and share with me about your past. I want to know what I can do to be there for you in any way you may need."

Again, Michael was taken aback by such compassion for someone who was not family.

Elizabeth continued, "You told me earlier that Michael was the spitting image of your father, but nothing like him. Tell me about your dad. Why are your brothers so different?"

Sue's voice lost its softness, "They are completely different. Michael may look like our dad, but that's where it ends. Dad was totally devoted to our mother right until the divorce. Even then, he was always there whenever we needed him. My father works hard every day, and he always told us to never be embarrassed about how we looked at the end of a day of work. He taught us good moral values, respect for those in authority, and right from wrong. Before the divorce, Michael and Dad never seemed close. Rhino and Dad seemed like best buds. Hunting, fishing, and camping—they would do it all. But, after the divorce, the whole thing shifted. Michael stayed close to our father, and Rhino resented him so much he never really forgave him for leaving our mother."

"One thing about Dad was that he was not what you would call compassionate. Michael grew up with a lot of insecurities. Dad knew it, and it bothered him. He would always point out Michael's flaws and failures and make Michael feel worse than he already did. Actually, I think that's why Michael got involved in what he did, just to prove to his family that he was somebody who could take care of a huge operation without failing. Michael is a very proud person. He likes having power more than having money. Having the ability to get the things he wants or get things done his way gives him a big high. Dad never thought much of Michael's abilities, so this is Michael's way of throwing it back at him."

"So, what about Rhino?" Elizabeth asked. Why was she changing gears? Michael wondered.

"Rhino is like a big soft teddy bear. On the outside, he may look rough, but on the inside, he has a heart of gold, not harsh or cold like Michael."

Michael could not wait to see how Sue was going to describe his older and bigger brother as a teddy bear, but all of a sudden, his cell phone rang. Since he was sure that Sue and Elizabeth heard it, he walked into the room as if just retuning from retrieving his cold drink and grabbed for his phone in his pocket.

Michael recognized the incoming number, "Rhino, where have you been? Dad is in the hospital; he had a heart attack last night and just got out of surgery after six hours."

The voice at the other end was not Rhino's. "Michael Marello?"

"Who is this?" Michael asked.

"This is Detective Ryan Martin with the Pine Bridge Police Department."

"Obviously, you know who you called, Detective. As you have heard, I am in the middle of a family crisis. What can I do for you, and why are you calling me on my brother's phone?"

"I would like you to come down to the station. It's important," Ryan told him.

"I just told you, Detective, I am in the middle of a family crisis. You have my brother's phone, so that tells me this has something to do with him. He is a big boy. He can take care of himself," Michael tried to let him know how annoyed he was by this phone call.

"You need to come down to the station," Ryan insisted. "I'll send a car for you."

"Look, call my lawyer. He will take care of whatever needs to be taken care of," Michael responded.

"Your lawyer cannot take care of this, and it's something that I don't want to do over the phone."

"Well," Michael said, "it looks like you are going to have to, Detective, because I am not leaving the hospital."

"Mr. Marello, your brother's been shot. He's dead."

The color left Michael's face, and judging by Sue and Elizabeth's expressions, they could tell something was not right. "What is it?" Sue asked.

Michael just stood there staring out the window, "I will be there as soon as I can." He slowly closed his cell phone.

"What is it Michael? Please, tell me," Sue pleaded.

"Nick is dead," he responded in a barely audible voice.

"What?" Sue leaned in to hear him better.

Michael turned and took his little sister in his arms. "Our brother is dead," Michael barely got the words out before the tears started. He had not cried since he was a child.

Sue held Michael as his sobs shook his entire body. She, too, wept for Nick. After a few minutes, Elizabeth came up next to Sue to offer what little comfort she could. When Sue took one arm off Michael and wrapped it around Elizabeth, he took the opportunity to remove himself from Sue's embrace.

"I have to get down to the station," He wiped his eyes.

"I'm so sorry about your brother," Elizabeth told him. Even in the midst of this tragedy, her beauty caught Michael's eye.

"I better go," He nodded toward Elizabeth.

"Could I go with you?" Sue asked.

"You should stay with Dad," Michael suggested. "If Dad wakes up, whatever you do, do not tell him about Nick. I will tell him when I feel he can handle it." Michael's tears had stopped by now, and the thoughts of who, when, and why started to fill his mind, along with anger and a desire for revenge. He was determined to find out who killed his brother and planned to exact the same payment from them.

Michael had always put his business before his family, which was one reason he never married. Already, he was pushing aside the need to mourn his brother in favor of working to avenge his murder. By the time he reached his car in the parking lot, Michael was in full business mode. Now, he was glad to have a cell phone, and he wasted no time in calling the other members of the group.

He called Moe first, "Rhino's dead. I want answers, and I want them fast. You got the informants you need to do what you can to find out." He ended the call before Moe had a chance to respond.

Michael then called Willy. The conversation—if you could call it that—started the same way, but he gave him a different job to do. "Freeze all our assets and clear the special accounts. You know where to deposit the money. I want it all there in the next hour. Got it?"

"Yes," Willy responded. Michael hung up.

When the phone rang at Sammy's, the answering machine picked it up. Odd. Sammy usually answered. "Rhino has been shot. He's dead. You need to take extra care. I will call back with a time and a place to meet. If there is anything in the warehouses that someone might kill for, I need to know." The conversation ended there.

Next, Michael would call Paul. If Michael had what could be called a friend, Paul was it. Paul answered with the sound of a shower in the background.

"Paul, Rhino is dead," Michael started bluntly.

"What?" Paul shouted.

Michael didn't repeat himself, but gave Paul his instructions, "We are going to need more protection. Get your guys together and do what is necessary to protect my family. Sue and my dad are at the hospital. Get someone there first and do it now! Also, add protection for Moe, Willy, Sammy, and you. Also, get a couple of guys to guard my house and to wait outside the police station.

They can follow me home. I will call back to let you know when we are going to meet." Michael snapped his phone shut.

Michael opened his cell phone one more time and pressed the voicemail button. His brother's voice spoke to him again, "Mikey, look there are some things I need to do. I uh… I uh… I have to see some people, and then I will come see you. I made a decision that is going to change a lot of things. It changed me, and I want you to hear what I heard. Maybe it'll do the same to you. I'll call you tomorrow. I love you…" As he sat there in the silence of his car, Michael wept.

Nick did not have any more tomorrows.

Michael sat in his car, wiped the tears from his face, and tried to compose himself. He had no idea how long he had been sitting there. He did not even remember the drive from the hospital to the precinct. He opened the door and placed one foot on the asphalt parking lot. A sudden fear entered his thoughts, and he immediately brought his foot back into the car and closed the door.

"Dominic," he said aloud, "what will I say to him?" With everything that was happening, Michael had completely forgotten about Rhino's son. Rhino had been in a pretty bad place in his life when Dominic came along.

Now, sitting in his car, Michael wondered how to tell Dominic his father had been killed. Dominic would want revenge for any attack against Michael or Titan and would want it fast. Even though he was never close to Rhino, he had respected him and would want to avenge his murder. It was a personality trait he'd inherited from his father and learned from his uncle.

He did not have time for this now, but he was here. Anyway, he had no idea where Dominic was and even if he could meet. Michael pulled out his cell phone and called Dominic, but got his voicemail, "Dominic, I have some bad news. Whatever you hear on the streets do not react right away or do anything stupid. Please call me first. Please!"

Michael pressed the end button and opened his door to get out of the car. He walked briskly into Precinct Seven right up to the desk sergeant, "I am here to see a Detective Martin."

12

SO MANY DIFFERENT scenarios ran through Sammy's mind as he finished his beer. What would Michael's next move be? He had settled down, and the pacing had stopped. The anger was still there, but he had it under control. Now, instead of pacing, his anger followed the normal path to drinking. Even after several cold ones, his mind remained clear, working at devising a plan. He always worked better with a little liquid courage.

Michael knew nothing as far as who, what, where, or why. He would be closing ranks though and protecting his associates, which was normal. Good thing Michael was acting normal. That meant he believed this was an attack from the outside and not a hit from within. With both Steve and Kevin dead, no one could turn snitch. Moe would not be a problem, and Willy could be scared into silence. Paul, on the other hand, may just have to be silenced. He was the most reluctant. That was everyone…except Mark Capwell.

* * *

Dominic spent the morning doing his usual routine of checking to see that things were running well. Michael had accelerated Dominic's rise through the ranks as a personal runner. That way Dominic could be taught by Michael without Rhino finding out who he really was. Michael had a place for Dominic in the family business once Dominic graduated from high school.

Dominic pulled out his cell phone to call Luther and ignored the voicemail indicator. Dominic and Luther had become friends the day Dominic's car stalled in an unfamiliar neighborhood and he ran into some gang members ready to protect their turf from outsiders. Luther, because of his size, had a reputation in the neighborhood. When he stepped in to defend Dominic, whom he recognized from shop class, the punks just took off running.

Dominic had learned from Michael to never forget a favor. He told Luther that if he ever needed anything to give him a call.

Dominic dialed Luther's number. Luther started the conversation almost before he answered the phone, "—Dominic, is it true?"

"Is what true?" Dominic asked.

"Man, word is out on the street that the Rhino is dead." Silence. "Hey, man, you there?"

"Yeah, I'm here," Dominic heard himself respond when he could talk again. "Where'd you hear that?"

"Everybody's talking about it. I thought you were calling to tell me, too," Luther continued. "So is it true?"

"I have no idea what you are talking about, Luther. I haven't heard anything," Dominic remembered his voicemail. A cold shiver ran down his spine. Less than a handful of people had this number.

"Luther, did you leave me a voicemail?" he asked suddenly.

"No, man, I just got the news, and I called you first," Luther replied.

"Listen, I have a voicemail; I'll call you back as soon as I have anything to tell you."

Dominic ended the call and immediately checked his voicemail. It was Michael, but his message really told him nothing and made him even more confused. He called Michael.

"Hello," Michael answered hoarsely.

"Michael, its Dominic. What's going on? I just heard through a good source that Rhino's dead. So, I check my messages, and you tell me to call you before I do anything and not to react to what I may hear on the streets. So, what's going on?" Dominic's words ran into each other.

"Before you go anywhere else or talk to anyone else I need to meet with you at the Wooded Hills Country Club. Wait for me in the clubhouse. Right now, I am a little busy, but I will be there as soon as I am free. Go there now. Do not go anywhere else; just go there and wait, please," Michael sounded comforting and persuasive at the same time.

"Michael, what's going on?" Dominic demanded.

"Dominic, go to the club house now. Do not go anywhere else. Wait for me there, and I will be there as soon as I can. Got that?"

"Yes, sir," Dominic answered back almost by habit. The line went dead.

Dominic started up his car and called Luther as he pulled onto the road heading south, "I got no confirmation from Michael, but his voice sounded guarded. I'm going to meet with him as soon as he can get away from what he is doing. Put your ear to the streets. Find out from your sources anything you can. I don't care how insignificant the info you get is. Whatever is out there, I want to know about it. If Michael doesn't want me out on the streets right now, then you're going to bring the streets to me. Can you do that?"

"You don't even have to ask, man," Luther responded quickly. "I'll find out what the word is, and when I get anything, I'll give it to you. Is there anything else you want or need?"

Dominic could hear the concern in Luther's voice. "I don't even know what to think, let alone what I need."

"What I have heard so far is from a very reliable source," Luther reassured. "He usually doesn't wake up till the wild dogs roam, so to get something from him this early isn't good. But, he is a night crawler, and you know how they suck up any information they can get a hold of in order to sell it to get a quick fix or make a quick dollar. I'll grab him to see what he knows. Talk to you soon."

Dominic set his phone down on the passenger seat and headed for the country club.

* * *

Michael waited as patiently as he could for the detective to arrive. Everything that had happened in the last twenty-four hours ran through his mind. Who would want Rhino dead and why? Why was it that Steve came to talk to him instead of Rhino? His father almost died during his heart surgery. Why hadn't anyone from the group called him? He had left messages, and even when he called to tell them about Rhino, no one asked about his father. Sometimes Michael hated how his mind worked, always analyzing and looking for holes in a person's story. Something was just not right, and he could not quite figure out what. It drove him crazy. The door swung open. Ryan Martin came up the stairs and immediately headed in Michael's direction. With his hand extended, he said, "Michael Marello?"

Michael just nodded and did not offer his hand. Ryan brought his own hand back down to his side, "Okay, I'm Detective Ryan Martin. Let's step into my office."

Ryan led Michael down the hall and stopped at a door with his name on it. He stepped aside and allowed Michael to walk past. After he closed the door, he began to speak, "Sorry we have to meet like this—"

"Where is my brother?" Michael interrupted before he could continue with his pretty speech.

"Mr. Marello, your brother is at the county morgue. I will be happy to take you there, but I need to ask you a couple of questions first."

"Detective, I am not going to sit here and play twenty questions. I will save you some time and tell you I have no idea who would want to kill my brother. Let me take that back. You know as well as I do that because of my reputation and the people I associate with there are plenty who would want my brother dead. Do I know who did this? No. All I know right now is that I need to start making arrangements for my brother's funeral," Michael needed to get out of there and start his own investigation.

"There are a few things that we need to finish up. Remember, this is a murder investigation, and there are some things we just can't hurry through. Please, Mr. Marello, have a seat," Ryan Martin pointed at the open chair as he walked behind his desk to sit in his own.

"I am not likely to forget this is a murder investigation, Detective. Can I see the body to make sure it is my brother?"

"We've had a reliable ID, Mr. Marello. I can take you to the morgue later, but I do have some questions to clear up. First, let me tell you what we have got so far, and maybe you can shed some light and clear a few things up. Do you know who either Steve

Silinger or Kevin Marino is? We found their bodies about six miles west of where we found your brother."

Michael had trouble keeping his poker face. He sat there in silence for so long Ryan asked the question again, "Do you know either of them, Mr. Marello?"

Michael slowly and deliberately answered him, "Steve Silinger was adopted by my brother a few years back. He raised him from the age of fifteen until he was able to take care of himself. I have no idea who this Marino is."

This *must* have been an attack from an enemy. Not only was Rhino killed, but they took out Steve as well. Michael had no idea who Kevin Marino was, but he would definitely find out.

"We found your brother in an old garage on Route Six just east of town. Do you know where I'm talking about?" Ryan Martin's voice invaded Michael's thoughts. "Your brother died from a single shot through his head. We found him in the old garage on Route 6. Do you know that place?"

Rhino shot dead at the garage? Shot one time with a bullet in his head? Shot in a place that the group used for that specific reason? It made no sense at all. "Yes, I know where you are talking about."

"Well, that's why I need to ask you some questions. Not only because it's your brother, but also because he was found on a property that you own. Do you know anything about this?"

"No." The last time he talked to anyone who seemed to be involved with this was when Steve came to his office. He had been interrupted with the call from Sue about his dad. Steve told him something had to be taken care of and the rest of the group had unanimously agreed with it.

He had barked at Steve to take care of it, no matter what is was. Did that have anything to do with why both Rhino and

Steve were now dead? Is that why no one at Titan had called him? Nothing seemed out of place when he called them with the news about Rhino except he did not talk to Sammy but only left him a message. Now, Michael's thought process was in full gear deleting, analyzing, and filtering. He scrutinized everything and anything he could remember about the last forty-eight hours.

Martin cleared his throat, "So, you can't give me anything as far as a who or a why?"

"No, sir, I cannot," Michael would not share the thoughts racing through his brain at that moment.

Detective Martin leaned on the desk and spoke quietly, "The following is completely off the record. Your brother and I became friends over the past couple of weeks. I think I know who killed him and why. Take a closer look at your associates. Do you trust them completely?"

"What?" Michael responded. "You have no idea what you are talking about. We do not operate that way. I run a distribution enterprise, not a criminal enterprise that takes people out—"

"Mr. Marello, not only does the department have a file cabinet full of records on your operation, but I, myself, have been studying it for the past six months. There have been several people 'taken out'—to use your words—over the last fifteen years. There have been people on the take even longer. I know that some of the cops who work security on the gambling boats are in your pocket, also. Don't play me for a fool or think I don't know who you are and what you can do. I am very aware of the power of Titan."

Michael did not respond, so Ryan continued, "I used to live in Pine Bridge. In fact, Rhino and I knew each other as kids. One day, I almost got my butt kicked playing football. Your brother stuck up for me. I never forgot that. When I moved back, I looked him up. We sat for hours at Margie's Coffee House just catching up. We talked about growing up in a tough neighborhood and how I got out. That's when Rhino opened up and shared how he always saw I was different than most guys he talked to or met up with. What is that difference he asked me? I told him I was no different or better than anyone else, but maybe it was because I had Jesus Christ in my life and because I live for Him."

"Nice story," Michael said. "Let us get to a more important issue here. You implied that my associates had my brother killed? Next, are you going to tell me Steve did it? Rhino was like a father to Steve. Maybe it was this Marino character. If you know so much about my business affairs, you should know of the loyalty I have and the respect I am given. There is no way my brother was killed by either my associates or anyone in my organization. What kind of evidence, if any, do you have? How can you even make such a statement?"

"We found some private items belonging to your brother in a duffle bag on the bridge that goes over the railroad yard. Kevin Marino, who was struck by a semi-truck, was also on that bridge. On the tracks below the bridge, the other victim, Steve Silinger, was cut in half by a passing train. According to a car switchman working in the yard at that time, it appeared that Marino and Silinger were fighting and Marino either pushed Silinger off the bridge or he fell. Looking at Silinger's facial injuries, it appears he was beat up pretty good. Marino's hands looked like they had been in a fight. We don't have the test results, but more than likely, the blood on his hands will match that of Silinger's."

Martin set a box on his desk and opened it, "These were the contents of Rhino's duffle bag."

Michael stared in eerie silence at each item as Martin laid it on the desk. There was a small spiral notepad along with a three-ring notebook, a Bible, a wallet, car keys, a watch, a money clip, some loose change, and a cell phone. The money clip appeared to have about two hundred dollars, and the keys were to Rhino's Bronco.

Michael wanted to take the three-ring notebook immediately, for he knew that it contained all of Rhino's personal notations of what happened with Titan in the past what was currently taking place, and what was to come. Hopefully, Detective Martin had not looked through it. Martin picked up the little spiral notepad and flipped through its pages. He stopped and turned one page around so Michael could read it. In big red letters it said "NEED TO TALK TO MIKEY!!!!" The date on that entry was Monday. Today was Friday.

"When was the last time you talked to your brother?"

Michael eyed the cell phone, "He left voicemail on my cell phone on Monday that I just picked up yesterday. That was the last I heard from him."

"Monday? Don't you check your voicemail?"

Michael did not answer. He was staring at one particular item besides the change, the watch, and the money clip that he thought was completely out of place but yet was not talked about.

"What are you thinking?" Ryan asked.

"What is that?" Michael pointed at the small Bible on the desk.

"That's Rhino's Bible. I gave it to him two weeks ago when we talked," Martin got up from his chair to sit at the edge of his desk.

"Why would Rhino have a Bible? My sister would maybe have one, but not Rhino. It makes no sense."

"Because I told him about the need in his life that could only be met by Jesus Christ." This detective was starting to sound like his sister.

"What? You told him what? He 'had a need,' and it could only be met by whom?" Did Rhino finally fall for this nonsense? After all this time had Sue's words infected Rhino to the point that he believed all this Jesus talk? "Let me tell you something, Detective. Any needs my brother may have had and would have had, *I* always met them. You told him someone else could meet his needs? You are unaware. *I* take care of my brother and my family. *I* meet all the needs they have."

Ryan Martin held up his hands and shrugged, "Look, I never talked about meeting material needs. I am talking about spiritual needs. Rhino told me that even though he had everything, he felt cold and empty like a lost soul out of place. I just shared with him that those feelings could be replaced by asking Jesus into his life."

"You told my brother about religion? He gets enough of that from our sister!" Michael stood, "Look, I am not here to argue what my brother does or did with his life. I came down to answer questions, and you still have not told me anything to make me believe that Silinger or Marino killed my brother. So, unless you have got anything else, can I see his body now?"

"Well, we do have something. Also, in the duffle bag was a forty-five; it had recently been shot. We found gunpowder on Silinger's hands. Your brother was shot once in the head. Something tells me that if we find the bullet, the ballistics test will match. That is why I feel that Steve Silinger is your brother's killer."

Michael's mind was at work with these new facts. His cell phone rang. It was Sue. He flipped it open, "Yes, Sue?"

"Michael have you seen Rhino yet?'

"No, I am still at the police station."

"Well, what are they waiting for? You need to get everything taken care of. Then, you need to get back here. Dad just woke up."

"I am trying, but they will not let me see him."

"Don't hesitate to call that lawyer of yours. Will you do that please?"

"Yes, I am going to call my lawyer if they do not let me see him. What did you say?" Michael walked to the hall to try and get some privacy for the conversation.

"Dad's awake," she said. "He's groggy and doesn't really know anybody yet, but he's awake."

"That is great. I will be back at the hospital as soon as I can, but right now, I have a lot of business to take care of. I have to make arrangements for Nick's funeral. I need to find out who is responsible for taking his life."

"You're not going to do anything that will cause trouble are you?" Sue asked.

"Look, Little Sis. You do not need to worry about that. I will take care of what needs to be taken care of the best way I feel it has to be done."

"How are you doing, Michael?" Sue's voice softened.

"I am fine right now. I have a lot on my mind, and that is making me numb. Business first. I always deal with things better when I deal with it that way."

"Rhino is not business, Michael. He's family, and maybe if you didn't have your business—"

"Susan! Let me deal with it the best way I know how." He never called his sister Susan unless he was either mad at her or very concerned. It was hard to tell which one it was now. "I will call you with all the details and preparations for Nick's funeral." Without waiting for a reply, he ended the call and walked back through Detective Martin's open office door.

"Mike," Martin began. "Do you mind if I call you Mike?"

"Yes, I do as a matter of fact," Michael replied coldly.

"Okay then, Mr. Marello, I couldn't help but overhear part of your conversation. I need to warn you right now that if there is any retaliation on your part I will haul you in and lock you up so fast that even you won't know what to do."

That was enough. "Is that a threat, Detective? Are you honestly threatening me? Let me tell you something. Obviously, your six months of studying Titan has not taught you enough. You do not and cannot threaten me. I will do what has to be done to find out who is responsible for my brother's death!"

Michael stood in the office doorway, "I run this city. My connections are so high up that you will be writing traffic tickets after a single phone call from me. You say you grew up in this town, that you left, and then came back? Well, things have changed, Detective. This is my city now! Welcome home. Now, I am going to see my brother." Michael turned and walked down the hall, leaving Martin to gather his coat and hurry after him.

13

SUE TURNED TO Elizabeth after ending the conversation with Michael, "I'm worried. I think Michael is going to do something that will get some, if not a lot of people hurt. We need to pray." They bowed their heads.

"May I pray?" Elizabeth asked.

Sue smiled, "Please."

"Our Heavenly Father, we come to You now. First, we want to thank You for bringing Sue's dad safely through the surgery. Thank You for being a God who answers prayer. Father, we ask now that You will be with Sue's family in a comforting way through the turmoil, uncertainty, death, and fear. We ask that You be with Michael at this time. May cool heads prevail, and may he not do things that will cause harm to himself, his family, or others. May You use these tragedies to draw Michael to Yourself. We ask these things in Jesus' name, Amen."

Elizabeth lifted her eyes, "What was it that Michael said that's got you worried?"

"He told me he would do whatever needs to be done to find the answers he is looking for. You know, as much as I disagree with the way Michael lives his life, his dedication and love for family is so strong."

"I've never seen a man so committed to his family," Elizabeth replied. "My dad and I weren't close; he was uncommitted and distant when it came to family. His ministry came first and his personal stuff a distant second. It was always about what was best for him and his church. He felt that his ministry was to meet the needs of his congregation even if it meant his family suffered. It would often make me rebel against some of my father's strict rules. It was not the best childhood. That was the extent of my father's involvement in my life. He was always ready to point out my faults, but the compliments were scarce. It's neat—almost endearing—to see Michael take the lead in dealing with these family matters."

Sue looked at Elizabeth, "Did you just use the word *endearing* when talking about my brother? You *like* the way he's threatening to deal with this situation?"

"No!" Elizabeth assured as she threw her coffee cup away.

"What I'm trying to say is that you don't often see someone care so much about his family. That's all."

"I know what you mean, and it's one of the things I love the most about Michael. Nick and Michael were always close. It must be tearing Michael up inside knowing that his brother is dead and he couldn't do anything to save him. I know he will get through this, but I want to show him Christ cares about what he's going through right now. Christ can help him get through the pain."

"Michael is not the only one suffering. You lost your brother, too. I know you're a strong woman dealing with that and the reality of your father's open-heart surgery. Remember, Christ is there for you, too."

* * *

Dominic sat in the country club's conference room waiting for Michael to arrive. His mind desperately searched for answers, going over antidotes and clues about what happened and why Michael wanted him off the streets. Did Luther have it right? Was Rhino really dead? He took his cell phone out and called Luther.

"What do you need, man?" Luther answered.

"It's driving me crazy sitting here and not knowing anything. Michael told me to wait on him, and that's what I am going to do. I thought I told you to get yourself out there and start asking questions. I need to know if the rumors are true, if they are who is responsible, and how we are going to take revenge. Did you forget that or what?

"Aren't you going to wait to see what Michael wants to do? He has his ways of dealing with things, and if this is true, he's gonna want to take care of this himself. Don't you think?"

Dominic knew that acting outside Michael's orders could bring Michael's wrath down on him no matter that he was his nephew. But, he was not doing anything he shouldn't be doing. Michael said to get to the country club, and Dominic was here waiting. He had his own contacts, and Michael didn't say anything about not getting in touch with them.

"If this rumor is true, I want to be able to either take care of it or have it taken care of, so that Michael doesn't have to. This is going to kill him," Dominic told Luther.

"Right," Luther agreed.

Dominic swore as he got off the phone with Luther, "I am who I am, and I like it." Dominic was conceited, and he knew it. Michael had warned him that it could one day get him in trouble.

Dominic brushed aside the advice just as he did any of Michael's lessons that he thought to be unimportant. He was Michael's greatest student, but he did have after all the family arrogance. Most times, Dominic's looks got him out of any trouble his conceit got him into. His charm and handsome features won over more ladies and more favors than anyone else. He thrummed his fingers on the table and waited for Michael.

* * *

Sammy finally got on the phone to call the group. He called Moe first and told him everything, "There were no eyewitnesses because Rhino, Steve, and Kevin are all dead. Capwell is going to steer the investigation to make it look like it was a power struggle from within."

Sammy's confidence rose, "All's we have to do is play along with what Michael wants to do. If we do that, Michael won't suspect a thing, and we will have accomplished what we wanted without Michael ever knowing. You couldn't ask for a better scenario."

"Have you talked to Willy and Paul? Are they still on board?" Moe asked.

"When I tell Willy about the story, he's going to love it. Paul's a little different. If there is a crack in the plan, it's with him. We need to make sure he's with us before Michael talks to him. I'll call you if and when I hear from Michael."

* * *

Michael could not shake the image of Rhino lying on that cold steel table. He could not bear to see Rhino like that—so helpless, so quiet, so cold, so still, so…dead. Michael stood there with Detective Martin and the coroner beside him controlling his emotions when all he wanted to do was scream.

Now, out of the building, he promised Detective Martin that he would keep in contact and help with the investigation in any way that he could. Michael stopped by the funeral home and made arrangements for the funeral director to meet them at the hospital in an hour. He would honor Nick's life and give him a very humble and quiet funeral.

Finally, driving to meet Dominic at the country club, Michael got hit by a wave of emotion so strong he pulled off the road. He did not like this feeling. He had shut down emotions a long time ago, and he did not need them returning at this moment.

But, everything had happened at once and so quickly in the past twenty-four hours. He could not control those emotions he had shut out so long ago. For the second time in a day, he sat in his car and sobbed like a child. So many thoughts competed in his head for prominence—memories of his childhood with Nick, his father lying in the hospital, Sue pleading with him to change his ways, and family members consoling and supporting him. Nothing seemed to add up. He could not stop the tears. He would miss the closeness that he and Rhino shared. Then, he remembered the last voicemail he received and how his brother had told him he loved him. When was the last time he told Nick that he loved him? Now, facing the hard reality of his death brought on more tears and sorrow. He would never be able to completely get over what had happened.

Michael tried his best to stop the tears and bring himself back to business. He needed to find the culprit. He needed to pull himself together so that Dominic would not see the weakness.

After ignoring and repressing the emotions for so long, they poured out in a magnitude that Michael could not control. He felt an overwhelming need for comfort and closeness to someone. He'd been such a recluse that he had never wanted or needed others in his life. Now, with his father in the hospital and his brother dead, the need was there, and he did not know how to meet it.

He sat in his car…

…empty and alone.

14

AS MICHAEL ENTERED the conference room of the country club, Dominic stood. They embraced and Dominic asked, "So, what's going on Michael?"

He sat down and motioned to Dominic to sit, but he respectfully said, "I will stand if you don't mind."

"Nick is dead."

The color drained from Dominic's face, and he swayed, "So, who is responsible? Who needs to pay for this? When do we make them pay?"

Again, Michael held up his hand, "Sit, please. There are several things I need to tell you like what has happened in the past twenty-four hours, what should have happened, and my theory on what needs to happen." Dominic sat and gave Michael his full attention.

Michael began, "You need to mourn your father's death. Do not rush to take revenge until you are confident that the person you suspect is in fact the person at fault. Before that though, we will mourn our loss and make sure Nick is given the proper burial."

Dominic sat there, "Why are you calling Rhino, Nick?"

"When my brother was alive, he earned and deserved the name Rhino. Now that he is gone, out of respect to him and our family, I want to remember him as Nick." Dominic's bottom lip quivered. "Go ahead and cry. You are no less of a man if you cry."

"But, I never see you cry," Dominic replied.

"I know. I have always thought that it was a sign of weakness, but have come to realize that you become stronger when you allow the emotions to fill you but not control you," Michael stood and opened his arms.

They embraced and both cried, mourning Nick. "We'll make sure whoever is responsible for this will pay, right?" Dominic asked.

"Absolutely. But first, we need to examine what has brought us to this place before we can make our next move. It's time I tell you how I started Titan. You need to know these things to protect yourself. One of the most important things I have learned is this: *when people owe you, you own them.* That is how I started Titan. Let me start from the beginning."

Michael folded his hands, "The business in which I worked for was called Trait Bindery. It was a small but prosperous business controlled by Bruce Trait. It was not a direct supplier to the funeral home industry but was a subcontractor in the same field. Although Trait was never in direct competition with Beverly Funeral Supply, Trait did service their opponents. That made Bruce Trait a difficult man to trust, at least in the business he was in. At one time, Bruce worked for Beverly Funeral Supply. That is how he got his start. But, he was smart and decided to compete for the business that was controlled by Beverly.

"When I started at Trait, business was booming. I would never miss a day of work. I quickly became the Production Supervisor and a part of the management team. That allowed me to find out things others did not know about. The position I had meant I was always the last to leave and lock up. Business was good, and the company was growing. The need for a second shift came, and the boss asked me to manage it. I saw it as another opportunity to move up the corporate ladder, and I eagerly took on the challenge."

He sat straighter in his chair, "Bruce's son, Jerry, came up with the ideas for cutting benefits and increasing workload. Jerry was a carbon copy of his father. I remember times at the plant when he would adopt hastily developed procedures even before I had a chance to trouble shoot it and expect me to run those procedures flawlessly. When I found a flaw in the process, he would tell me, 'That's why we put you in this position. If you can't handle it, we'll find someone who can.'"

He shrugged, "I went along with it until I started running the second shift and saw what a little empathy could do in terms of productivity. I treated my workers much different than Bruce did. Not long after, I started managing the second shift and found an opportunity to speed up my rise in the corporate world. They kept the office open in case I needed to access a file or a work order. There was never a secretary working because the business was running production and was closed to the public."

Dominic nodded and leaned closer.

"It is not that I started out doing anything too terribly wrong. I had to be in the office because of my position. But, one night when I went into Bruce's office and saw that the computer was left on, I snooped a little. I learned that night that when you finish with business, you do not leave anything out for others to find. You must always shut off the computer."

He leaned back in the chair and rested his voice.

"Wait a minute. You can't stop now," Dominic said.

"I will tell you everything, but right now, there are other things we need to figure out," Michael promised.

"Well, what are you feeling right now?" Dominic asked.

"Right now, I feel betrayed, but I have no real facts to back that up. For some reason, I do not think this was a hit. According to the police, two of our guys were involved. I'm sure you know who Steve Silinger is right? What was he doing, and who is this Kevin Marino? Do you know anything about him? I know that this is the first time I ever heard his name. Those questions need answers. The street gangs all respect us, and they especially respect Nick. So, I feel that rules them out. Nick was not involved romantically with anyone, at least not that I was aware of. Do you know of anyone in his life?"

"You know as well as I do that once he straightened up, he was a loner. As far as I knew, he kept it that way. He lived for you and your interests, which was his main concern and I have never heard of this Kevin guy either." Dominic stood from the table.

Michael shared what he had learned from the police and his own assumptions.

Dominic's eyes widened, and he plopped back down in his seat, placing his hands on Michael's shoulders, "Where did they find Rhino's body?"

"That is the one thing I do not understand," Michael answered. "According to Detective Martin, Nick's body was at the garage out on Route 6. That is our place where we take care of our business, so why would Nick be killed there?" Michael looked at Dominic and they both came to the same conclusion.

Someone inside wanted Nick dead.

"Why would someone want Nick dead?" Dominic asked.

"And, if Steve was the one who shot Nick, why did he do it? Nick was like a father to him. Nick even saved his life."

Dominic frowned, "What makes you think Steve killed Rhino?"

"When I was down at the police station, the detective told me that tests showed traces of gun powder on Steve's hand. They had reason to believe that the gun they recovered was the murder weapon."

"Sounds to me like whoever did this was pretty sloppy," Dominic rose again.

Michael motioned for Dominic to sit back down, "I think we need to sit here until we find a scenario that fits."

"I agree, but where do we start?"

"First, and the most obvious is the fact that Nick was found dead on our property and supposedly killed by one of our own. But, the question is who did it and why?"

For the next hour, they discussed different scenarios that may have happened. Still, with no clear-cut answer, Michael finally suggested that they meet again sometime after the funeral. He didn't want anyone to get suspicious if they were to act out of the ordinary.

Before they left, Dominic said, "I've asked Luther to find out what he can about Nick's death."

"Be careful." Even as he said it, Michael knew Dominic would handle this the way he wanted to and would probably find something.

As they were leaving, Michael noticed the little red light flashing on the motion-activated video camera. He had learned early on to watch everyone and trust no one. Dominic probably set off the tape when he entered the room. Michael locked up and left.

Out in the parking lot, he embraced Dominic, "Nick was a good man and will be missed."

As expected, Dominic responded, "And, we will make sure that whoever killed him will pay."

Michael pulled back, "Just like your old man, you are ready to protect, defend, and react without first thinking things through. We will do this my way. We will look at this from every angle and make sure we do what is best to avenge his death. In the meantime, you need to mourn. Remember, we will not make a move until we are sure that we have all the information. Then, and only then, will we make our play. The house always wins, and right now since we do not know what has happened, we are betting against the house. If you play your hand too early and the house calls your hand, you could be caught bluffing."

"I don't think you need to worry about that," Dominic assured Michael.

Michael opened his car door and got in. As he started his car, his cell phone rang. He ignored it and looked back at Dominic, "I know you Dominic. I am warning you. Do not get caught bluffing."

"I got it. I understand."

Michael pulled away.

* * *

As soon as the car was out of sight, Dominic pulled his phone from his pocket and called Luther. After Luther's typical greeting, Dominic filled him in on what Michael told him.

"We can't figure out why Rhino was killed at the garage or why Steve may have been the one to pull the trigger. As soon as the sun starts to set, I want you to head out and see what you can learn. Michael wants to wait 'til after the funeral, but I can't wait. I want to know now! Also, find out what you can about a Kevin

Marino. Get back to me with anything you find out," Dominic closed his phone without waiting for a response.

* * *

Michael hoped the warning he gave Dominic would be enough to keep him from doing anything rash. He did not want anything to interfere with Nick's funeral. He was about to call Dominic when he looked at his phone and it told him he had a missed call from Sue. He called her back, but it was not Sue who answered.

"Hello, who is this?" Michael asked.

"Michael, this is Elizabeth, Sue's friend."

Michael remembered her—the attractive woman in the waiting room. "Yes, I remember. Where is Sue?"

"You need to get back to the hospital. Your dad had a stroke and now is in a coma."

Michael did not know what to say.

"I'm sorry I had to tell you like this, but Sue said that if you called, I should tell you what happened. She is in with your father now."

Michael was in an instant daze. His father was now in a coma, and his brother had been murdered, possibly by someone within Titan. It was too much for Michael to handle. These were the types of things he paid people to take care of.

At that moment, he was alone with nowhere to turn, "I am on my way."

As he drove back to the hospital, he mulled over the fact that Nick was killed at a place where it should only have happened if it were ordered. Even though Michael tried to exclude himself from this part of the business, he was no fool. He knew people had been eliminated in order for Titan to become what it was. He just made sure he never had a hand in or personal knowledge of the grisly part of the business.

He couldn't rid himself of the nagging feeling that he had been betrayed. The more he contemplated it, the angrier he became. Who did it, why it happened, and how it happened played in a continuous loop in his head. Dominic, his dad, Sue, and even Sue's friend, Elizabeth, raced around in his thoughts.

What could he do?

* * *

Paul Delemonni sat at his desk, feeling like Benedict Arnold. He'd betrayed Michael—*betrayed* him. He'd been against Sammy's plan from the beginning. Why had he let himself get coaxed into agreeing? He hated himself for always being easily persuaded into making certain decisions. Michael would never make him feel uneasy about the decisions that he made, but he did feel so unsure of himself with the idea of killing Michael's older brother.

Sammy was so convincing and so adamant about getting it taken care of quickly. Paul didn't have the confidence that he usually had when *Michael* wanted something taken care of. He so badly wanted to talk to him, but until he understood what he was thinking, it would be like suicide to even contact Michael.

Paul had been the first one Michael invited to join the group. They had worked closely together with Paul's business when Michael was the foreman and ran the second shift. When Michael took control of the business, he first contacted Paul with the idea of buying his company. With the ten million dollar buy out, Paul, just like the other three, couldn't pass it up. Michael made them all rich and powerful. The more Paul remembered, the sicker it made him feel. He ran to the bathroom and emptied his stomach of the breakfast he recently finished.

The telephone rang as Paul wiped his face. He walked into the kitchen and reached for the phone, "Hello?"

"Paul, it's Sammy. Has Michael called you?"

Paul cleared his throat, "Yes, he has called."

"Are you okay, Paul? You sound funny."

"Actually, to tell you the truth, I'm not all right. You went ahead and had Rhino killed. I think you're crazy for ordering the hit."

Sammy's tone turned calm and direct, "We all agreed with this. You are just as guilty as the rest of us. If you think you are going to back away from this and try and hang the rest of us, let me warn you ahead of time. I've been working on this for a long time, and I have backing that Michael doesn't even know about. I will take you out. If need be, I can take Michael out, too."

"I can't believe you talked me into this. Michael has been nothing but good to me. In fact, he has been good to all of us, you included. Now that we have killed his brother, you seem ready to take him out. Are you nuts? Bite the hand that feeds us? The one that's been buttering your bread and making you fat? Now, you want to take that and ruin it? Sammy, you had better catch your breath and step back."

"Settle down Paul. I'm not even thinking of taking Michael out," Sammy tried to sound convincing, but Paul knew better. "I just want you to remember that we all agreed on this and we need to stay strong and convince Michael we had good reason to go through with it. What did Michael say to you when he called?"

"He just told me to be sure to get protection for everyone and to be careful. He also said he would call with a time and place to meet."

"It seems that's the message he gave everyone. What do you make of it?" Sammy said.

"Well, it sounds like Michael is going into defense mode and wants to be sure everyone is protected. I don't think he suspects anything. The way he's acting is normal. Considering what has happened, what do you think?" Paul stared at himself in the mirror, disgusted with his own image.

"Well, my contact on the police force told me both Steven and Kevin are dead and that the police believe it was a power struggle between foot soldiers. So, I told him to steer the investigation that way. With both Kevin and Steven dead, we don't have to worry about them. All we have to do is wait and see which way Michael wants to play this, and we can come out of this in good shape," Sammy finished.

"How reliable is your source?" Paul asked.

"He's good, but sometimes a little arrogant. He's deep in debt with the boats, so he's in tight with us."

Paul was silent for a moment, "Do you really feel it was a good thing to kill Rhino? Did you think it completely through? I just wonder if we should have discussed it more before we blindly went at Rhino."

"Are you forgetting something, Paul? You are in this just as deep as the rest of us. Don't you begin to consider for a moment that you're clean! You voted the same as we did. It was unanimous. Otherwise, we would have waited. Michael loves power more than money. I want the money, and Michael seems to be moving toward the influence and power side of it. *I want my money.* I could care less about the power."

Paul squeezed the phone so hard it made a cracking sound, "So, this has to do more with Michael than it ever did with Rhino. You have been planning to overtake Titan, and if necessary, take

Michael out too, aren't you? You used me and the rest of us to accomplish your agenda and get Rhino out of the way. You knew you would not be able to get near Michael if Rhino was still alive! If I had known that, I would have never given the go ahead to have Rhino killed. I would have warned both Michael and Rhino. I just might tell him anyway."

"Don't be a fool!" Sammy yelled. "I've warned you. You don't want to turn on me or have me turn on you. You will keep your mouth shut if you know what's good for you. Just do as you are told by Michael, and we'll take care of the rest. If you say one word to him, I'll have your head! Are we clear?"

Paul was silent.

Sammy growled through gritted teeth, "Don't be stupid. Keep your mouth shut, and you'll stay alive. You understand that? You will regret it if you don't." He hung up.

Sammy called Moe, "We got a problem with Paul. He's talking about having regrets, feeling sorry for Michael, and said that he might tell Michael. We can't do anything yet, maybe after the funeral. Maybe then, we can make Michael believe Paul was the one who wanted to turn against him. We'll have to wait and see."

15

AFTER A LONG day, Ryan Martin was just finishing up his paper work when a knock sounded on his door, "Come in."

Mark Capwell opened the door, "It's been a long night and even a longer day. I'm going to call it quits. That alright with you?"

Ryan responded, "Yeah, go on home. This is far from over. There are probably a lot more long nights ahead of us."

Mark entered the room, "What do you mean this is far from over? I thought we came to the conclusion that this was just two guys trying to move up in the ranks by getting rid of Rhino and the Marello family found out and took Silinger and Marino out?"

"No!" Ryan jumped up from his chair. "That's the conclusion you came up with, and I'm not buying it. There are too many holes in that theory, too many questions that still need to be answered." Ryan sat back down behind his desk.

As he sat there leaning back and running his hand through his hair, he closed his eyes and all he could picture was the bloody, lifeless body of Rhino. It made him bang his fist on his desk so hard it sent his desk lamp crashing to the floor where it shattered. "This shouldn't have happened."

"What shouldn't have happened?" Mark asked.

Oops, he'd thought out loud in front of Mark, "Nothing. Go home. I'll see you in the morning."

Though Mark left, Ryan knew he wasn't going home, not that he really cared at this point. As Ryan tried to figure out how he could possibly share with Michael about his need like he did with Rhino, he remembered the manila envelope in the bottom draw of his desk. He opened the drawer and pulled it out.

As he looked at it he recalled Rhino's exact words: "If anything happens to me, and I mean anything, and you know that I never had a chance to talk to Michael, please make sure that he gets this tape. I am putting my trust in you. Make sure you convince him to watch it."

Ryan put the envelope back in the drawer and shut it. How would he ever accomplish that?

* * *

Michael entered the hospital ICU. There was no one in the waiting room. Was he on the right floor? Someone tapped his shoulder. Michael turned around so fast he almost knocked the cup of hot tea out of Elizabeth's hand.

"Sorry," Michael said. "Hello, Elizabeth, right? Do you know where my sister is?

"Yes, it's Elizabeth, and yes, I do know where your sister is."

Feeling terrible, Michael replied, "I remember. Sorry, I have had a lot to deal with in the last twenty-four hours. I hope you will excuse me."

"That's very understandable. I hope I didn't scare you."

Michael looked around for Sue, "Look, excuse me, but do you know where she is?"

Elizabeth put her hand on Michael's shoulder, "She is in with your father. They are not even supposed to be letting family in right now, but your sister stood firm and demanded to see him."

"That's Sue. Never tell her she cannot do something. She will go out of her way to prove that she can," He finished with a smile.

Elizabeth smiled back. Once again, Michael was impressed. He was not what one would call a "ladies man;" although, he knew he was handsome. He used his charm instead of looks to get what he needed. Yet, there was something about Elizabeth that made him take notice, but he didn't know what it was. It made him want to talk to her.

When she offered a chair for him to sit, he accepted. "So, where is everyone else?"

"Sue sent them all home. After the doctor came out and said that all looked good, Sue insisted everyone get some rest. They all left rather quickly. It seemed as soon as the last person left that the doctor came back and told Sue about your dad's stroke and resulting coma. It really scared her, and she gave me her cell phone so I could call you. I hope you didn't mind."

Michael could just sit there and wonder what it was about this woman that made her stand out above all the others. He never wanted to get close to anyone because of what he was involved in and whom he was involved with. A woman could become a weakness and a potential tool against him. Whether as a pawn or as bait, she could make him stumble, falter, and put his and even her life in jeopardy. For that reason, he never allowed the pleasure and luxury of closeness nor the warmth or the love of a woman to become a natural occurrence in his life.

Now sitting in the waiting room alone with Elizabeth, Michael longed for companionship. Maybe it was because his father was in serious condition or perhaps it was because he had lost his best friend when his brother was killed. Whatever the reason, sitting with her in the quietness of the waiting room made him feel more at ease than he had at any other point during the last twenty-four hours.

Michael looked at Elizabeth, "How long have you been up here?"

She was just swallowing a mouth full of tea, and when she opened her mouth to answer, a little spilled over her bottom lip and down her chin, "How embarrassing." She wiped the excess tea off her chin. "I really don't know. I haven't kept track, which is perfectly fine. My friend needs me here, and I'll stay as long as she wants."

"You have your life and things that need to be done. Yet, you choose to put all that aside for someone else? Someone who is not even family? Why?" It didn't make any sense. Did she have an ulterior motive, or did some people just have genuinely pure hearts like hers?

"Because Sue is going through a rough time, and I want to be here to support her in anyway that I can. She may need a shoulder to cry on or someone to pray with her. I just know that if I was having a tough time, there is nothing like a good friend who is there for you."

Elizabeth took another drink of tea, "Do you have a close friend who is always there when you need them?"

What was she trying to do with such a question? "I have a lot of people who are close to me for different reasons. I do not think any of them are close enough that I would want or need them around me when I am in a crisis, or as you put it, need support. I can take care of myself and the needs of my family. I can handle any situation that may come up, like right now for instance."

He planted his hands on the armrests of the chair, "I am able to handle myself in this very complicated time in my life. As you are aware, I just lost my brother, my father is in a coma, and I have different arrangements that have to be made on both sides of those issues. I realize there are going to be family needs, and I have already addressed them. As you can see, there is no one here to offer a shoulder to cry on or to pray for me. I do not need the help of anyone. I can take care of myself and my family alone."

She set her tea on a magazine table, "Sue said you were one who can stand alone and that you hold family very high on your list. I admire that about you. I wish my father had cared that much about his family like you do. He was more into what was important to him and what was on his agenda. If anything were to disrupt that, he would go ballistic. So, I basically started to become self-sufficient in different areas of my life. I made some stupid decisions and some bad mistakes, but I have learned from them. I walked alone for a long time and came to a point where I just felt so cold and empty, kind of like a lost soul out of place."

Her words about being empty resonated with Michael. That was how he felt a couple of hours ago. In fact, he still felt that way. Now, Elizabeth was saying the same thing.

"But, I found comfort and help with Jesus." She took a single breath before changing the subject, "So, how long do you think Sue is going to be in there?"

Michael looked past her and at the door that led into the ICU, "I have no idea, but knowing my sister, I will have to go to her before she will leave our father's side. I need to go see her and my dad; I do not mean to be rude."

Elizabeth smiled, “You are far from rude. I completely understand. I’ll just get another cup of tea, and you tell Sue I’m out here if she needs anything.”

As she got up, Michael also stood. As he walked toward the door, he stole a glimpse back toward Elizabeth and tried to clear her from his mind. What was it about her that made him get pleasure from her company? As he walked through the ICU entrance, her words about feeling cold and alone reminded him of his own feelings.

He walked into his father’s room. Sue put her arms around him and started to cry. Michael held her, surprised by how easy it was for his tears to start as well, “How is he doing?”

“No change. He just lies there. He doesn’t respond. All you hear is the stupid beeping from these machines. It’s driving me crazy.”

Michael held his sister tighter, “Well, Sis, Dad just had a stroke and is now in a coma. I am not trying to sound cold or mean, but when someone has had a stroke, all they do is lie there. When was the last time the doctor was in to see him?”

Sue backed away, “It’s been about an hour. Where have you been all this time?”

“Between talking to the police, making funeral arrangements, and taking care of some business, I have been busy. Everything is taken care of for Nick’s funeral. It will be at the Restful Hills Funeral Home.”

“Is there anything that I can do?” Sue asked, composing herself.

“I have taken care of everything. All I need you to do is show up, and we will be able to honor Nick and give him the respect that he is due.”

Michael sat next to his motionless father. The grey hair and wrinkled features seemed to be exaggerated. Michael's father was in his mid-seventies, but he had aged well. It was hard to pick a definite age. "He looks so old, so frail, so weak, so…vulnerable," whispered Michael.

Leaning against Michael for support Sue said, "It's going to be tough on him when he finds out that Rhino is dead and he wasn't even able to go to his own son's funeral."

That thought took Michael by surprise. He took Sue's hand and held it tightly. She kissed the top of his head, "I love you."

Michael refused to look up at Sue so he could hide his tears from her. It felt good to have her there, and her words gave him a sense of security he never felt before.

They both held each other and cried.

16

RYAN MARTIN WALKED into his house. Out of habit, he dropped his keys on the hallway table and put his badge and gun on the top shelf of his bedroom closet. There they would be out of the way without the fear of an accident. His home was a simple three-bedroom ranch on a nice size corner lot. Because he worked for the city, it sat inside the city limits of Pine Bridge.

He walked down the hallway and yelled, "What are all the lights doing on?" He stepped into the kitchen where his wife, Colleen, stood at the stove putting dinner together. He stepped behind her, wrapped his arms around her, and kissed the back of her neck.

She flinched, "Stop that!" She was pretty and petite with shoulder-length red hair and bright blue eyes. She also had a sense of humor that Ryan cherished. "You gave me goose bumps all down my arms. You can't do that!"

"Yes I can! You're my wife, and I can kiss you whenever I want." He kissed her on the neck again which made her squeal and start to laugh.

"You better stop it, or your dinner will burn."

Ryan stepped back, "Kristine home?"

"Yes, she is. Why do you ask?"

"It was a rhetorical question. I know she's home. Every light in the house is on!" "Kristine!" He folded his arms, "Can't you make sure she shuts off lights when she leaves the room? Her bedroom light, the bathroom light, the hallway light, and the family room light are all on."

Colleen waved a spoon toward the hall, "But the hallway light isn't on."

"That's because I just shut it off!" He cupped his hands to his mouth, "Kristine! Get in here!"

"Now Ryan, don't yell at her."

"Don't defend her. She is a straight-A student, has the fashion sense of a super model, but has no common sense! She can learn to turn off lights."

"Hi, Daddy," Kristine walked into the kitchen, set her book down on the counter, and gave Ryan a peck on his cheek. Even though she was eighteen-years-old, she still called Ryan "Daddy." He loved it, even though it sounded juvenile.

"Where did you just come from?" asked Ryan.

"Out of the family room. Why do you ask?" replied Kristine.

Ryan stopped himself from smiling, "If you were in the family room, then why are the lights on in your room, the bathroom, the living room, and even the hallway?"

Kristine turned and peered out of the kitchen, "The hallway light isn't on." Colleen snickered behind him.

"The hallway light isn't on because I shut it off. I'm tired of trailing behind you and shutting lights off. The switch goes in two directions, up for on and down for off. You seem to know only one direction. Be responsible and shut off the lights!"

"What is the big deal?" Kristine huffed.

"The big deal is that you don't pay the bill. You want to start? I'll make you pay one percent of the bill for every light you leave on. How's that sound?"

Kristine rolled her eyes, turned to walk away, and muttered, "Whatever."

Ryan stopped her with a hand on her shoulder, "Don't walk away from me and say, 'whatever.' You know better than to talk to me like that. If I thought it would do any good, I would ground you to your room, but that's where you spend most of your time anyway. Maybe I shouldn't allow you to do school work. How would you like that?"

Kristine planted a hand on her hip, "That would be stupid."

"Well, I need to do something to make you learn to shut lights off, and if that would teach you, then why not?"

Colleen stepped between them, "Kristine go to your room, but first, shut off the lights in the family and living room." She then turned Ryan around and nudged him toward the kitchen table.

"Why must you always push her buttons?"

"Why do you always come to defend her?" Ryan countered.

They just sat there and looked at each other. Then, Colleen smiled at Ryan, and they both started sharing about each other's day. Ryan asked where Rae, their other daughter, was.

"She went to a concert with some friends," Colleen answered.

"What concert?"

"You don't want to know."

Ryan tensed, "How can we have we two completely different daughters?"

"We have two different daughters because otherwise life with them would be very boring. This way it's challenging," Colleen laughed.

"It's challenging alright," Ryan finished as Rae walked in.

"Hi guys," Rae kissed Colleen and gave Ryan a hug. Rae was two years older than Kristine and often exercised her adulthood freedom of independence from mom and dad. Though her parents did not always agree with her decisions, she was never rebellious.

"What are you doing home? I thought you went to a concert?"

Rae scanned the contents of the refrigerator and turned to face her parents opening a can of pop, the reward for her hunt, "I didn't agree with who they were going to see, and I didn't like the traveling situation. So, I decided not to go."

Ryan smiled at Colleen, "Well, what a surprise."

He stood to give Rae a hug, but she leaned back, "What do you mean by that?"

Colleen said, "Don't start now."

"What I mean is that usually you do things that make me wonder what you're thinking," Ryan sat back down.

"Well, Dad, maybe you need to have a little trust in your older daughter. You did teach me well you know, and I did listen to your teaching even though you may think I just blew you off. I have a level head on my shoulders. I wish you would just trust me to make smart decisions when needed."

As Rae said this, she turned to go into her room. Colleen and Ryan both cringed at the sound of the door to her room, as it slammed shut.

"Well, you're two for two," Colleen told Ryan.

"Guess I'm just letting the job get to me, especially today," Ryan said.

"What happened?"

Ryan grabbed the can of pop that Rae left behind and took a drink, "Remember when I told you about Nick Marello?"

"The one called Rhino?"

Ryan nodded, "Well, early this morning he was killed. We have an idea who did it, but not quite sure on why. About six miles west, we found two more bodies. These men were employed by Titan, which is ran by the Marello group. They had a gun that we feel was the weapon used to kill Rhino, but with those two also dead, we have a bunch of questions and not many answers."

Colleen grabbed Ryan's shoulder and squeezed, "Didn't Rhino just get saved?"

"Yeah, about two weeks ago, and when I tried to tell his brother earlier today about it, he just about took my head off. Then, I remembered the manila envelope in my desk and the request that Rhino asked of me."

"That being…"

"That if something happened to him, I would make sure to give the envelope to Michael and say anything that would make him read the contents and view the tape. After today, I don't know what to say or do."

Colleen leaned in and rested her head on his shoulder, "Well, why don't you give it to him when you go pay your respects?"

"Thanks for the idea, but I can't show up there for two reasons. First, Michael would automatically get defensive. He would probably have one, if not two, of his bodyguards escort me off the property. Second, if he did allow me to talk to him and I was to hand him the package with all the other agencies watching him, it would appear that I was either paying him off or giving him information. With the investigation of the murder of his brother going on, I don't want to mess that up for two reasons…"

Colleen placed her hand over his mouth, "Must you always have more than one reason to do anything?"

"Please listen to me and take this seriously," Ryan pleaded. "I believe someone close to both Rhino and his brother are out to take over Titan. It's just an early hunch but one that I can't ignore. Also, I want an opportunity to comply with Rhino's wish to get that envelope to his brother and hope and pray that Michael will see his need."

Colleen kissed his cheek, "Pray about it. God will give you something, a door will open, and He will make a way."

"You're right," Ryan stood up to give her a hug. "Let's get our girls and have dinner."

* * *

After Sammy got off the phone with Moe, he called Willy to be sure he was still on the same page as the rest of them.

"Don't forget Michael came in and basically forced us to sell our businesses to him and promised to share the wealth. Well, at the start, he was sharing, but the funds don't seem to be coming in like they used to. Now, he's more concerned about being influential in the workings of the city and having contacts everywhere that benefit him while we are moved to the back row. Because of that, our financial situation suffers."

Willy said, "Wait a minute. I'll have to defend Michael about that. Don't forget that we all earned an immediate profit of $10 million, and that made us all very rich, very fast. Then he also let us continue to operate and take all the profits while he took all the headaches."

"Yes, I understand that, but when we all agreed to form Titan, we said we'd look out for what was best for all of us. Michael is being very selfish now, so we suffer." Sammy reminded Willy, as he reached into the fridge for a beer.

"He isn't making any more money than we are."

Sammy cracked his knuckles, "This may be true financially, but with all the influence, connections, and power he is obtaining, he could have enough to take over the whole operation and end up leaving us out in the cold."

"That's right. I've even heard him say that the money takes second place now and that grabbing the power and getting things done his way is a bigger high."

"There ya go," Sammy nodded. Willy was still with the plan, unlike Paul. "If Michael calls, just play along with what he wants done, and we will see what the next move should be."

He hung up and then called Moe to report on Willy. He also told Moe that they should probably wait to do or say anything until they hear from Michael, which might not be until after the funeral.

"We need to be very careful the next couple of days. Knowing Michael, he will be watching every move everyone makes. That means he will be watching us, also. The best thing we could do is to make Michael think we are with him, and when we make him feel comfortable, then we will go in for the kill."

Moe agreed, and they both hung up at the same time. Sammy had a smile of satisfaction and accomplishment. Their plan was working perfectly.

17

IT WAS ONE of the longest weeks in Michael's memory. The funeral for Nick went smoothly. He had called the rest of the men from Titan and asked that they not attend the wake or funeral because of the press, the police, the FBI, and whoever else may be there. He wanted the family not to be disturbed by outsiders and wanted to give them a quiet and respectful funeral for Nick.

The press was still there; however, with Michael's connections and with a small army of bodyguards, they kept at a respectful distance. The story hit the papers with full force, because of who was involved, and the impact it would have on the city, the story appeared above the fold in the local paper. The fact that there were no other suspects as well as two other bodies found six miles from where Nick was shot was in the paper every day. Even the national paper mentioned it in brief. It was also on the network's news cast on a daily basis.

Michael now sat at his desk, going through the events of the past week. He ran everything through his mind and could reach only one conclusion.

Steve killed Nick.

But why? Why would Steve kill his mentor and father figure? Was it an attempt to take Titan away from Michael ordered by the rest of the group? Why would Titan want Nick dead? That was simple. If it was a play against Michael, Nick would have to be eliminated to have any chance of coming after him. But why Steve?

Nick was killed in the garage, and Steve had gunpowder residue on his hands. Steve acted on his own, but why? There was no power struggle between Paul, Sammy, Moe, or Willy, unless the struggle was to team up against Michael and take away what he had built.

The reason Steve came to Michael's office the day his dad had his heart attack was a key piece of the puzzle that he needed. But, the scenarios that came to mind either didn't make sense or didn't fit in this puzzle. He looked through Nick's personal effects that Detective Martin had given him. The one thing that also did not fit was the fact Nick had a Bible on him.

Why did Nick have a Bible? Was it his? If so, was he reading it? Why? The notebook that had, "NEED TO TALK TO MIKEY," in big red letters perplexed him, too. What did Nick need to talk about? *Why did he not talk to me?* It was over a week that Nick entered that in his notes. Why did he only try to get a hold of him once by leaving voicemail?

Michael grew overwhelmed. When the phone rang, it made him jump. He picked up the receiver.

"Mr. Marello, Detective Ryan Martin, do you have a minute?"

Michael sat there, thought for a moment, and then concluded whatever information the detective had might help him figure out what happened to Nick, "Yes, Detective, I do, but that is about all

I have. Have you found out anything that will tell me who killed my brother?"

Martin cleared his throat, "As a matter of fact, I have some information that tells us what we believe to have happened. We found the bullet that killed your brother. How descriptive do you want me to be, Mr. Marello?"

"Do not worry about me, Detective. I can handle whatever gory details you want to share with me about my brother's death."

"Well then, after the bullet passed through your brother's head, it ricocheted off the cement and lodged in one of the wooden support beams along the south wall. After ballistics tested the gun that was found in the duffle bag on the bridge next to Marino's body, we could confirm that the gun was the one used to kill your brother. Now, I've already told you that we tested Steve Silinger's hands for gunpowder residue and that confirmed that he had recently fired a gun. There was no such residue on Kevin Marino's hands, which leads us to believe that Silinger was the one who shot your brother."

Michael allowed all of the information to register, "So, what are you telling me, Detective? Case closed?"

"Well, Mr. Marello, unless you have anything else to tell us, I really don't know where else to go." Martin waited for a moment, "What I would really like, Mr. Marello, is if you could come down to the station and answer some other questions that may help us continue the investigation. Also, I have another item that belonged to your brother; you can pick it up when you come down."

"Detective Martin, you can just go ahead and mail that to me. I have no desire to come down there, and I believe I can take care of finding out anything else about my brother's murder."

"Look, I don't want to trust this personal item to the postal service," he said. "It will only take a minute for you to come pick it up."

"What is so personal about the item, Detective?" Michael inquired.

"It's a manila envelope with a video tape that your brother requested I get to you if anything happened to him."

"What is on the tape, Detective?"

"You know, Mr. Marello, I'm really not sure. But, it must be of some importance if your brother gave it to me. He knew I would make sure you got it."

Michael squeezed the phone tightly trying to subside the anger growing within, "Let me get this straight. You have something that my brother felt was very important for *me* to have? He gave it to you to give to me? Why is that, Detective?"

"I can't answer that. All I know is I want to carry out a good friend's request."

"A good friend? *You,* Detective? My brother thought of a cop as being a good friend? That is as strange as trying to figure out why my brother was killed in the first place."

"Look, Mr. Marello, I don't want to debate whether you feel that your brother and I were good friends or not. All I want to do is get this to you because your brother asked me to. So, you call me when you can swallow that pride and come down to pick this up," Detective Martin hung up the phone.

Michael added more questions to the already mounting pile. What was in the envelope? Why did Nick give it to a cop? Why did Detective Martin consider Nick to be a good friend? While the pile of questions grew, the answers did not.

* * *

Ryan hoped his last statement would bruise Michael's ego and make him want to come and get the tape. The knock at his door disrupted that thought, and he focused on his visitor.

Captain Altman walked into Ryan's office and stood in front of his desk. His broad shoulders and five foot ten inch frame made him look bigger than he was.

"What case are you working on?" Altman asked.

"The Marello shooting."

"May I ask why? Isn't that a done deal?"

"No, sir, I don't think it is. There are too many loose ends."

"What are you talking about? It's an open and shut case according to Capwell. He feels that it was two soldiers fighting for power, and they took out Marello then fought and killed each other. Sounds good to me."

"Well, sir, I don't think so. I feel there is more to it than that. Besides, like I told you before, I don't trust Capwell. He's a womanizer and a drunk. He gambles all his money away. I don't like his conclusion, and I feel he is trying to close a case that needs further investigation."

"Is that so, Detective? What gives you the right to judge a man's private life? As long as he does his job, I couldn't care less what he does on his own time. I don't have the time or the manpower to waste on a case that is going to come up empty. If Capwell is right, we'll let the Marello's fight it out between them. If innocent people get involved or hurt, then we will step in and come down hard. Until then, the case is closed! Got it? I don't want another man-hour wasted on this case. Period!"

"But, sir..."

"Forget it. You're not going to talk me into giving you anymore time or men to look into a case that has basically been solved. Move on to something that needs your attention. Now!"

"That's fine. I will just do some investigating on my own time."

"I don't think so. This case is closed."

"You just told me that you didn't care what a person did on his own time. So, if I want to use my own time to investigate this further, I will."

"That decision is yours, Detective. But, if it starts to interfere with your normal caseload, I will have you demoted. You understand? You're messing with a very powerful man, and I'm not talking about Marello," Altman walked out, slamming the door behind him.

What made the Captain point out how powerful he was? Was it a threat? Was he usurping his authority, or was he just being cocky? Either way, it bothered Ryan.

18

DOMINIC'S PHONE RANG, and he immediately stopped his searching of Titan's files. He recognized Luther's number. He hoped it would be the call he was waiting for, the call that Luther had found out something, the call that would start the revenge he was so desperately ready to carry out. "Talk to me."

"I met up with this drug addict who goes by the name Spider. He's telling me that there's this prostitute who's in bed with a cop, no pun intended. The cop's name is Capwell, and he has the goods on her. She wants to get out from under him in more ways than one."

Luther paused for a moment and waited for a response. When there wasn't one, he continued, "My source told me that in one of his encounters with this prostitute they shared some drugs. My source also told me she shared how this Capwell guy is bragging that he's helping take down the Marello empire and how there is going to be a blood bath because of it. Capwell told this street creature that if she ever said a word about it, she would disappear."

There was still silence on the other end of Luther's phone. Then, Dominic finally asked the question, "So, what are you going to do next?"

"As always, verify the information, double check if there are any loose ends, and if so, tie them up. Set a time and place, make sure there is an alibi, execute precisely to the plan, and go back and make sure there's no trail."

"Call me when it's done!" Dominic hung up.

Luther knew the drill. He had done it before, and it was always done to perfection. With all the right connections and all loose ends always taken care of, the investigations would end up going nowhere and after so long, would be deemed, "case closed." In order for him to accomplish the task at hand in the short time he had, he thought out his plan before he moved on it. He already had the okay from Dominic to take out Capwell—whoever he was. He had to get to this girl and get her to give up Capwell.

Luther waited outside the Hidden Agenda for a couple of hours. It had been early evening when he met with Spider; and as the hours went by, this girl, Joy, would be leaving to start her night-time prowl of the streets looking for lonely men and frustrated husbands. Businessmen from out of town thought they had a right to show off their virility to a woman they could just leave behind and would extol to all their male counterparts their successful business trip by adding another notch to their belts.

As the hours went by, Luther watched the different patrons come and go. Joy left, heading east on Jefferson Street. No customers followed her out. She walked a block to Ottawa Street and turned north. Luther jumped from his car and jogged two blocks east. Then, he turned north and sprinted up two blocks to cut back west toward Ottawa Street.

He came to an alley between an auto parts store and a dry cleaner. He knew that with the high heels Joy wore he'd be way ahead of her. He stood there between the buildings slowly catching his breath and waited. Luther was not out of shape, but with the five-block jog and his adrenalin pumping, he was a little winded. He steadied himself, wiped the sweat from his brow, and waited. As Joy passed, Luther let her know he was there.

"Pssst, hey baby, you looking mighty fine tonight."

The sound first startled Joy. Then, she shifted into business mode, "Hey sugar, you want some of this?"

"Come 'ere, baby, and let me check out the merchandise."

Joy stepped into the darkness of the ally, and when she stood next to Luther, she had to strain her neck to look up at his face. Luther wanted them both to stay in the darkness of the alley so that no one would see them together. He grabbed her by the arm and started to walk to the other end of the alley. Joy started to protest. Luther stared at her and put his finger to his lips.

"Shhh!"

"What are you, a cop?"

"Shut up! Just walk with me, and you will like what I have to offer."

"I like what I see already, honey. If you got the cash, you will like it, also, darlin'. But, I ain't into no rough stuff, and you are hurting my arm. So, let go," Joy tried to release herself from Luther's grip, but all Luther did was squeeze harder.

"Ouch! You're hurting me!"

"I said shut up and calm down. I told you if you wait a minute you would like what I have to offer." They got to the other end of the alley, and Luther stopped. He looked straight down into Joy's eyes.

"Rumor has it that you are being controlled and squeezed by a cop by the name of Capwell. That true?"

"Maybe, what's it to you?"

"What if I told you that if you help me, I would make sure that Capwell never bothers you again?"

"And just how you going to do that? You a pimp?"

"You don't need to worry about that. I just need to get him somewhere out of here, and I need you to help."

"What if I don't want to help?"

"Then, you'll have to deal with him by yourself for a long time."

"I can take care of myself. I can handle that woman-chasing, no good, two-timing, little piece of—"

"That's not what I hear. From what I understand, he's got the goods on you, and you can't do anything about it. I can help you with that."

"What? Just because you think you're a big guy, you can take care of a cop? This guy has got connections man. He has people that can make you and I both disappear. You can't stop that. I can't stop that. That's why he's got me where he does, and if you aren't careful, you can be gone, too. Now, stop all the talk. Do you want some of this, or are you going to talk all night?"

"Listen little lady, and listen good. I will make sure that you will not have to worry about this cop after tonight. This I promise you. Not only that, but after tonight, you won't be on the street anymore either. You help me, and this is yours."

He pulled a wad of money from his pocket, "There is ten thousand dollars here. You help me get this cop, and it's all yours. That is just the start. Like I said, after tonight, you'll be off the streets for good. The cop will be gone, and everyone will be happy."

"Let me see that," Joy reached for the money. "How do I know this is real?"

"You probably couldn't tell if it was real or not. So, I wouldn't worry about that, not when you need to worry about this cop."

Joy started to count the money and purred at Luther, "Just what is it you need from me?"

"Ah, ah. Not just yet, missy. First, you have to agree to help," He took the money back. "Then, I will let you count it, but you will only get a thousand first. I will pay you the rest after I take care of the cop."

"Fine, but you promise that you will get the cop off my back and that I won't have to be on the streets any more, right?"

"That's a promise. After tonight, you won't have to worry about that cop, and it will be the last night you will be out on the streets."

"What do I have to do?"

"Just be yourself. When he meets with you tonight, tell him you have a surprise for him, something new and exciting. First, make sure he is feeling good and loose. Have him drive you to the old abandoned Jefferson Mall. Pull around to the back on the south side of the mall. Have him pull to the edge of the parking lot. Sit there, and do whatever it is you do to make him happy. When you're done, just tell him you want to sit there and just be alone, away from all the crap on the streets. As soon as he starts to pass out from the alcohol, reach over and give him a kiss on the cheek. As you do that, reach toward the lights and flick them on and off. I will take it from there."

"So, I go back to the bar, take him to the old mall, and after that, I won't need to worry about him or need to be on the streets anymore?"

"That's it. If you tell him anything about our little arrangement, I guarantee you will never be seen on the streets again. You think this cop is bad? I will be your worst nightmare. I've got nothing to lose, and it won't hurt me at all to take care of you," Luther's voice was so chilling that Joy just stood there open-mouthed.

"Now, close that pretty little mouth of yours, and let's go through what it is I want you to do."

After several minutes of Luther reminding Joy of what would happen if she went against the plan, Luther was sure she knew better than to turn on him and that she would carry out her end of the deal. He handed Joy a thousand dollars and reminded her she would get the rest at the end, "One more thing I want you to do."

"What is it?" She sounded frustrated.

"Do you have a cell phone?" Luther asked Joy.

"What do you think big man? A working girl needs to stay connected these days."

"I want you to call the Hidden Agenda and tell Big Jacks that you want to talk to Spider."

"What for?"

"Just do it. When Spider gets on the phone, tell him you want to meet him after the bar closes. Tell him to meet you here. Now call," again Luther made sure to sound very chilling. Joy called the bar and asked for Spider.

"Hello."

"Spider, its Joy"

"Hey Joy, what's up beautiful?"

"I want you to meet me after the Agenda closes. I will be lookin' for a fix and a little lovin'. How bout it? You up for that?"

"Sure sassy, why not now?"

"I have a few things to take care of first, and I know you usually leave before the bar closes. So, I wanted to get in touch with you before you left."

"No problem, baby, where do you want to meet?"

"Meet me in the alley between Zarelli's Auto Parts and Martha's Cleaners."

"You got it beautiful. I'll see you there."

Joy got off the phone, "You're not going to hurt Spider are you? He just called me beautiful, and he can't wait to see me. In fact, maybe when I get off the streets, Spider and I could hook up for good. I would like to see that happen. So, you don't hurt him, okay?"

"Let me see your phone," Luther demanded.

"I need my phone! You can't take it! What if I have a client call?"

"You don't need to worry about any other business except the business at hand. Now, give me the phone," Luther grabbed it from her before she could resist.

"What are you going to do with it?"

"Not to worry, I will give it back to you after we conclude our little deal."

"And Spider?"

Luther did not respond. He wanted the phone to make sure Joy didn't call or tell anyone where she was or where she would be going. He wanted the events to unfold without any interference. He didn't want any innocent person to get in the way. Those who would be eliminated tonight would all be necessary to protect Dominic, Michael, Titan, and himself. The plan was set.

"What time do you and this Capwell usually meet?"

"After nine, why?"

"I want you to show up late, maybe only five to ten minutes."

"He'll be upset if I'm not there. Big Jacks don't like it when Capwell gets mad."

"I could care less if Big Jacks gets upset," Luther smirked. "I want Capwell to be upset. He won't think straight and will be driven by emotions instead of common sense. He'll be easier to persuade when making decisions based on anger. Just show up late."

Luther walked back to his car, which he had parked across from the Hidden Agenda and waited. An hour passed, and a car pulled up to the front. Luther watched as the guy got out of his car. When he went to enter the Hidden Agenda, he bumped into Spider who was leaving.

"Look out you low life," Luther heard him tell Spider almost pushing Spider to the ground. "Get out of here before I bust you for loitering."

"Yes sir, yes sir, yes sir, Mr. Capwell. Sorry, sorry, sorry, Mr. Capwell," Spider averted the guy and ran off.

Luther knew his target and left to execute his plan.

AS MARK STEPPED into the bar, he scanned the occupants for Joy. He spotted Big Jacks behind the bar and walked over to him. Big Jacks was talking to a brunette at the end of the bar.

"Hey there, Mark, old buddy, what's new?"

"Give me a shot of Ouzo," Mark demanded.

"Just one?"

"Taking it a little slow tonight. Have you seen Joy?"

"She was in a little earlier and then went out. Probably went to drum up some business. She called here looking for Spider."

"Who's Spider?"

"Aw, just some junkie. Joy has been nice to him a couple of times, and he has returned the favor."

"Shot number two please."

"So much for taking it slow," Big Jacks poured Mark another shot. Mark threw the Ouzo down his throat and then threw his head back. Even though Mark could not stand black licorice, the Ouzo's effect on his body made him excuse the taste.

"One more, please," Mark requested.

The third one went down even smoother than the first two, and Mark started to feel the effects of his nightly routine.

"So, you say she was here earlier and then she called here looking for some guy named Spider? What'd she want him for?" Mark's words slurred. "I never heard her talk 'bout him before. Who the heck is he? Why isn't she here where she's supposed to be, waiting for me not calling some guy named Spider?" Mark really felt the alcohol now.

"Settle down, Mark. I'm sure she is gonna show up soon. She knows better than to leave you hangin' man."

"She better know by now, that's for sure. Now give me another hard one, will ya? And follow it with a beer chaser." Big Jacks poured the fourth shot and then went to the tap to dispense the beer into the mug.

"Alright, that's it. She better show up before I finish this beer, or I'll shut you down for the rest of the night. You know I can do it, so you better hope she shows up soon."

"Wait a minute, man. I have no control over where she goes or who she sees. To shut me down just because your woman stood you up just ain't right."

"You big, toothless, no good punk. You aren't going to tell me what's right and what I can and cannot do. I will shut you down in a heartbeat. I'll take away your liquor license, and I'll even plant some drugs in here so that you're put away for a long, long time. I might even tell them you're nothing but a no good pimp, and that you run all the whores in this city. I can make your life miserable. Don't you ever forget that. I will have nothing but a smile on my face when I put your no good—"

"You're not gonna put anyone in jail," Joy came up behind Mark, threw her arms around his neck, and gave him a kiss on the cheek. Mark smiled as he saw the relieved look on Big Jacks' face.

"So, where have you been?" Mark said.

"I am a working girl don't you know? I was out trying to make a living with what I got."

"Who's Spider?" Mark asked.

"He's just some guy that I see every once in a while. You know, when I need a little somthin', somthin'. That's all. He's nothing to worry about. Just some junkie."

"You know I don't like it when you do drugs. If I have to, I'll bust ya if you can't stop. I don't want people to think that I support that habit. I hate drugs, and you know it. So, if I catch you with or hear that you have been with this Spider character again, I'll kill him. Then, I will come looking for you, and you'll wish that you had never met me. You got that?"

Joy took her hand and caressed Mark's cheek, "Yeah baby, I got that."

Mark grabbed Joy's wrist and squeezed so hard she let out a scream. Everyone in the Hidden Agenda stopped and looked in his direction.

Big Jacks reached over the bar and grabbed Mark's shoulder, "Dude! Everyone's watchin' man!"

While still squeezing Joy's wrist, Mark reached for his gun. He pulled it out so quickly that before Big Jacks knew it Mark's forty-five automatic pressed against his forehead, "Back off big man, or I'll blow your brains out all over the mirror and all over this bar!"

Big Jacks let go of Mark's shoulder and backed away. Mark then put his gun to Joy's forehead, "Now, who's Spider?"

"I told you, he's just some junkie that I get a fix from and in return, I fix him. If you know what I mean?"

"That's all he is?"

"Yes, that's it. I promise."

"You know that if you're lying to me I would have no problem pulling this trigger and ending your pathetic life right here in this dump in front of all of these other pathetic low-lifes."

Mark relished the full effects of his drinking, and it felt good to have the power that he did. No one in the bar would stop him if he were to pull the trigger. If he did, no one would turn him in. They would go along with whatever story Mark would tell the cops. They knew that he was one cop you never turned on.

Everyone in the bar watched as Mark continued to press the gun against Joy's forehead, and several turned away. Instead, he pulled the weapon away from her forehead and then leaned forward to kiss it.

"Now, that's what I like. You need to tell me the truth at all times. Because you know what happens when you lie, right?"

Joy didn't move. Didn't speak. It was too long of a wait for Mark. He backhanded her across the face, "Right?"

"Yes," was Joy's reply.

"That's the answer I was looking for. Big Jacks bring the little lady her favorite drink. I'm buying."

Big Jacks had not moved since he had backed away from Mark's gun. He stood as if he was frozen to the floor. That is until Mark yelled, "Now!" Big Jacks grabbed a bottle of vodka and poured it into a glass along with some club soda and a twist of lime. He brought it over to Joy and set it down. "Go ahead baby, drink up," Mark told Joy.

Joy took the drink and emptied its contents into her mouth. She finished the drink in one swallow.

"Now, that's the Joy I know. No hard feelings right?"

"There are no hard feelings. I'm sorry if I made you think I was giving my love or allegiance to someone else. Let me make it up to you. How about we try something new and different tonight? I got some place special I want you to try. We have never been there before, and I know we won't be bothered."

"I'm game baby. Let's stay and have a couple more drinks. Then, we'll take off. How's that sound?"

"Anything you want is fine with me, baby. I just want to make sure you don't drink too much and end up falling asleep."

"You don't need to worry about me. The wife's been very cold lately, so I am in need of some lovin'."

"Now, that's what I like to hear."

Mark ordered another round for Joy and himself. They sat there for another hour, drank, laughed, and did some making out. By the time they were ready to leave, Mark was in the mood and was like putty in Joy's hand, "So, sexy, where is this new place you want to take me and have your way with me?"

"The old Jefferson Mall. The parking lot in the back. There is never anyone there, and we can have fun either in or out of the car. What do you think about that?"

"I like that. Let's go," Mark grabbed his keys.

* * *

Luther parked two miles south of the mall. Because of the industrial heritage of the city, there were various abandoned railroad tracks, which the city had turned into walking trails. Dominic shared with Luther that Titan, along with the city, was a big contributor in an effort to use the land instead of letting it just sit there and go to waste. Luther also used the trail when he needed to. The trails were closed at dusk, so at the hour Luther walked down this particular trail there was no fear of being seen.

He stopped about a thousand yards from the parking lot. He wore hospital scrubs, a hairnet, and rubber gloves. So that there would not be any recognizable footprints, he even wore the booties over his shoes. He did not want any chance of DNA or clothing fibers to be left behind at the murder site. He used the same routine with each job. Tonight would be no different.

The headlights shined as they rounded the empty mall. Luther did not move. He just waited for the signal. After what seemed like half an hour, the lights finally flashed on and off. Luther cautiously made his way to the car. As he got closer, he saw Joy pulling her top on and Mark leaning on the driver side door.

Luther jumped into the back seat, reached into Mark's jacket, and retrieved his forty-five. He pulled the chamber back, which placed a bullet into the barrel. That brought Mark to life.

Luther shoved the forty-five into Mark's mouth.

"What are you doing?" Joy shouted.

Mark's eyes widened, flicking from Luther's face to the gun and back. Luther pulled the trigger. The sound was deafening as Joy screamed and put her hands over her ears.

The back of Mark's head exploded all over the inside of the car. Blood splashed onto Luther and Joy. She could not stop screaming.

"Shut up!" Luther screamed.

"What did you just do? I didn't know you were going to kill him. If I had known that, I would have had nothing to do with this. I'm not a killer. I'm not going to jail for killing a cop.

Luther wrapped Mark's hand around his own gun.

"Hey, can you hear me? Don't just ignore me. Hey, did you hear me?"

Luther lifted the gun, and pointed it at Joy, "I promised you that after tonight this piece of dirt would not be a bother anymore. I also told you that after tonight you would no longer be on the streets. I'm just keeping my word."

She screamed, but the sound of the gun going off made it look like she had her mouth open but nothing was coming out. The bullet hit her in the chest. It blew a big hole as it entered and left an even a bigger one when the bullet exited. She sat there in complete silence, her mouth still open.

Luther dropped Mark's arm; the gun was still in Mark's hand. Then, he took the remaining nine thousand dollars and Joy's cell phone and shoved it in her purse. Luther did not want to welsh on their agreement. Besides, it would look good for Joy to have that amount of cash on her.

He got out of the car and jogged back down the trail. He had parked his truck in the lot of one of the warehouses owned by Titan. When he got to his truck, he stripped off the scrubs. In the back of his truck, there was a garbage bag and a five-gallon bucket of water. He spread the scrubs out over the tarp that he had laid in the bed of the truck. He then stepped into the bed and washed himself with the water from the bucket. He had a washcloth and some soap. With the tarp covering the bed of the truck, it caught any dripping water. When he finished, he slipped on a pair of jogging shorts and a tank top.

Luther then took the scrubs, along with the washcloth and soap, and shoved them, his socks, and boots into the garbage bag. Next, he wrapped it all in the tarp.

After cleaning up and burning the evidence, Luther felt bold and knew he had one more job to do. Why wait? He'd take care of Spider next. He drove back to the Hidden Agenda and parked across the street. He got out of his truck and walked the same route he jogged to meet Joy in the alley. This time though, he would meet with Spider, just as Joy had asked him to. When Spider got to the mouth of the ally, Luther told him to step into the darkness.

"Where's Joy? She's suppose to meet me, not you."

"Careful, Spider, no need to get all bent. I told Joy to call you. This way no one knows our business. That's how you like it. At least, that's what you told me, right?"

"Right, right, right. What kind of business do we have?"

"You don't remember? I owe you something for the information you gave me earlier, remember?"

"Yes, yes, yes, now I do. You got some stuff for me, do ya, do ya, do ya?"

"Ray, I got some dynamite stuff. It will take you where you have never been before."

"I like, I like, I like! Call me Spider though, not Ray. I weave a web of rumors, and they all get caught up in my little web. Call me Spider."

"Ok, Spider, come on back here. I'll give you the treat."

They walked to the back of the ally. Every other step, Spider looked over his shoulder. Luther reached into his pocket and pulled out a vial of clear liquid. Spider saw it, and a smile came across his face.

He reached for it, and Luther said, "I want you to try it here for me. My guy tells me it's the best. I want to make sure it is worth the money I paid."

Spider reached into his army jacket and pulled out a pouch. He opened it, and Luther saw all his tools of the trade, the junkies' necessity for getting a fix. He pulled out a syringe, a spoon, and a lighter. He wrapped a rubber band around his bicep and pulled it tight. He then reached for the vial. He was about to pour the contents into the spoon when Luther stopped him.

"It's already been cooked. It's pure gold. That's what he told me."

"Ooh, pure gold, I can't wait to feel that running through my veins. Let me fill it up."

"You go right ahead."

Spider filled the syringe about half way. He flicked the end of the needle and pressed the plunger a little to get any air out of the needle. He stuck it in his forearm and released the rubber band from around his bicep. As the syringe emptied, the smile on Spiders face turned to horror. He looked up.

Luther watched with a smile, "Sorry, my little eight legged wanna-be. I had to tie up all loose ends. You were dangling out there, so I had to cut you off. Arsenic is worse than the drug of choice. Sorry!"

Spider collapsed, his body convulsing.

Luther walked away.

20

THE PHONE WOKE Ryan Martin out of a much-needed deep sleep. Colleen stirred next to him and grumbled, "Hurry up and answer it."

As he reached for the phone, he knocked it off the night table. It stopped ringing. He grappled for it in the dark. He could hear the voice on the other end repeatedly ask, "Hello? Is anybody there?"

He lifted the phone from the floor and put the receiver to his ear, "Hello?"

"Detective Martin, are you there?"

"Yes, I'm here. What do you want? It's four-thirty in the morning."

"Detective, this is Officer Lansing. We need you to come down to the station. We have a dead cop found with a prostitute. It looks like he shot her and then killed himself."

"What's the officer's name?"

"Mark Capwell."

Ryan felt like he was punched in the stomach, not only because a cop had been shot but the fact that it was Capwell told him that the retaliation might be starting. "Where was he shot?"

"Out behind the old Jefferson Mall," Lansing responded. Ryan was silent for so long that Officer Lansing said, "Sir, did you hear me? Captain Altman wants all detectives at the station A.S.A.P."

"Right, I'll be there as soon as I can," Martin hung up.

"Is everything all right?" Colleen asked.

"Yes, go back to sleep." He got in the shower to try and wake up. He turned the water to cold. He was not at all upset when he heard that the cop who died was Mark; he never did like or trust him. It bothered him that he felt nothing for the loss of a human being, especially one who may have stepped into eternity, separated from God. *God, forgive me for my coldness.*

After the shower, he dressed and went downstairs to grab something to eat. When he walked into the kitchen, both Kristine and Rae were up and sitting at the kitchen table waiting for the toaster to finish.

"Good morning, girls."

"Good morning, Father," Kristine said.

"Hey, Dad," Rae peered into the toaster.

"What are you girls doing up so early?"

"Neither one of us could sleep," Rae said.

"We were both hungry, so we thought we would grab something to eat," Kristine finished.

"What's your excuse?" Rae asked.

"I got a call. There is a dead cop, and it looks as if he was doing something other than police work, which is probably why he's dead right now. It's my job to investigate and figure out the who, what, and why part of it."

"Sounds like a lot of work, Daddy," Kristine kissed him on the cheek.

"Yeah, Dad, go get 'em cowboy," Rae winked.

"Thanks, girls. Have a great day," Ryan walked out the door.

"You, too," they answered in unison.

As Ryan got to his car, he thought about Mark. He remembered what Mark had said when he was looking at the lifeless body of Rhino. Would Ryan feel that way when he saw Mark's body? He got in his car and decided to bypass going down to the precinct and head straight to the old mall.

* * *

Dominic rose early and sat at the kitchen table watching the small television on the counter. The morning news report of a dead cop was all over the screen. The reporter was on the scene, and in the distance sat a car with a yellow tarp over it.

"We are live outside the abandoned Jefferson Mall where this morning, the police are investigating a double homicide. We have heard an unconfirmed report that one of the victims is a police officer. We have not heard anything on who the other victim is. We will be here live most of the morning with any other further developments. Reporting live from Jefferson Mall, I'm Lisa Williams. Tony, back to you in the studio."

"Thank you, Lisa. In other news, former all-state football star, Ray Welleden, was found dead this morning in the alley between Zarelli's Auto Parts and Martha's Cleaner's—an apparent victim of a drug overdose. Police say that the two scenes are not related..."

Dominic shut the television off. As he got up and slid his dish in the sink, his cell phone rang, "Talk to me."

"Have you seen the news this morning?"

"Yes, I have."

"Ok, just wanted to know."

The line went dead. Dominic closed his phone, and a smile came across his face. Luther did his job and didn't leave a clue. If Dominic were to ever run the Titan business, Luther would be his right hand. He sat there for a moment and thought about what to do next. *What would Michael do?*

* * *

Michael turned off the news and sat at his desk. He ran different scenarios through his mind and still concluded that it had to be an inside job. The pieces just did not fit. *Who did this, and why did they do it?* Michael's phone rang.

"Hello."

"Michael, its Paul. Listen, I know that you have asked us to keep our distance until the investigation settles down a bit. I have something I need to share with you, and I can't say it over the phone. I would rather do it in person."

"Paul, you know my door is always open for you. Come over whenever you feel like you can make it."

"I would rather meet at the golf course if you don't mind?"

"That would be fine. You tell me when, and I will be there."

"Let's say about nine tonight. Will that work for you?" Paul suggested with a small quiver in his voice.

"Yes, that would work out great, Paul. Just call me if anything changes."

"I will Michael. You be careful. See you at nine."

Michael hung up the phone. Paul's last statement seemed strange. Michael knew that with the death of his brother they all needed to be careful until they figured out who was responsible, but to hear it from Paul was out of the ordinary. He looked forward to their meeting. Whenever Paul needed to see him, it was a major concern.

Michael returned to the work on his desk. The computer screen had a list of names and companies that Titan had worked with. To the right, it listed the CEO and president of each one. With each file, there was a secondary file attached to each company that listed all financial transactions. A small icon next to each one had either a smiley face or an angry face. If Michael's files were ever searched, he would tell those investigating that they represented good or bad business dealings with those companies.

The real reason for the icons was that they contained hidden files. All Michael would have to do is double click on the icon, and it would open up a whole different set of files. Instead of double clicking left, he'd double-click right. Then, it would ask for a password. Michael and Dominic were the only two who knew of these secret files. These files contained every transaction Titan made, legal or illegal. It listed all those who were bought off from the city government. It held the names of every employee who ever worked for Titan.

It also had information on the corporate structure of each business and information on each employee's background, from work records to personal information. Michael knew how much they owed and who they owed it to. That's how he became so powerful.

As he went over the list, he methodically eliminated names of those he knew would not be coming after him or who would not try and take Titan away from him. The list dwindled quickly. Even after Michael bought someone out, he still treated everyone fairly, from upper management to those on the shop floor. He even had a list of all the union presidents and shop stewards who were in charge of the labor force at some of the businesses that Titan had acquired.

As Michael scanned the files, he noticed a new entry next to Salluci Construction. It had an angry face beside the company name. That change was made a week ago, and he didn't make it. That meant that Dominic was in the file and found something that made him question Salluci Construction. He dialed Dominic's number.

"Yes," was the typical response Michael got when he called Dominic.

"Dominic, I am going through the company files, and I noticed you made a new entry next to the Salluci business. There any reason why you did that?"

"Yes, I was doing some research for a restructure of the chain of command, and I noticed a name I thought I heard you talk about, someone in your past. I can't think of the name right now. It just didn't fit. After the death of Rhino, I just forgot to mention it to you. I will come by and look at the file and see if the reason for the change will come to me."

"Make it tomorrow sometime. I just got a call from Paul, and I am going to meet him at the course at nine," Michael continued scrolling.

"Anything I need to know about?"

"Not really sure. Paul did say something a little strange. He told me to be careful. That is not normally the way Paul would end a conversation."

"After what has happened the past week, I don't think it's strange at all. He's just looking out for you," Dominic said.

"You are probably right. It was just strange to hear him say it."

"Maybe, it was because a cop got killed. I don't know."

"What? A cop was killed?" Michael stopped scrolling.

"Yeah, I thought that was why you were calling."

"And why would I be calling you about a cop being killed?" Michael stopped for a moment. "Dominic, this conversation ends now. I want you to meet me at the course at eight thirty. We will talk before I talk to Paul."

"Yes, sir."

Michael hung up. He knew better than to discuss anything over the phone. He also knew that Dominic would not discuss the situation any further until he talked with him, but deep down inside, he knew that Dominic had something to do with the death of this cop. He gazed at his computer screen.

* * *

Dominic tried to remember why he made the changes to the file. What had he found, and what particular meaning did it have? He left his apartment and headed toward the heart of the city. He was scheduled to meet with Luther to go over the job. Now, he had to think of what it was that made him change the file, why Paul wanted to meet with Michael, and how he was going to explain to Michael why he had the cop killed.

* * *

Ryan Martin pulled in to the back of the old mall. There were cops all over the place, helicopters in the air, and television crews trying to get whatever information they could. He left his car and was surrounded by reporters.

"Detective, is it true that one of the dead bodies is a cop?"

"No comment."

"Officer, is it true that there is more than one body?"

"I said no comment."

"Detective Martin, I am Lisa Williams from the local station. We have heard that this may be a retaliatory move for the murder of Nick Marello, also known as Rhino. Is that true?"

"Look, as you can see, I have just arrived on the scene. I have yet to talk to the officer in charge. I have no idea who the victim or victims may be. So, at this time, in response to your entire line of questioning, NO COMMENT! Now, get out of my way."

Ryan shoved past the reporters and walked up to the car. He lifted the yellow tarp and took in the scene with some animosity. Not only was he upset at the reporters, but he was also disgusted to see two lives blown apart by violence. He looked at the male first. It was definitely Mark Capwell. The back of his skull was missing, and there was blood all over. The female was unknown to Ryan. He dropped the tarp back down, stepped away from the car, and quietly told his fellow detectives.

"All right, listen up everybody. I have an ID on the male victim. It is a police officer. In fact, he is a detective. The victim's name is Mark Capwell. He has been shot through the head. It looks like a suicide. I have no clue who the female is. Run her prints through BCI and let me know what you find, Officer Lansing!"

"Yes, sir!" Lansing responded with a salute.

"Get in touch with Capwell's family. I don't want them to hear this over the air waves."

"Detective, do you think that this was a hit by the Marello family?" Lansing asked.

"We will see what evidence we come up with and where it leads us. Until we have a solid confirmation, it looks right now to be a murder and suicide. We're not going to stop the investigation. We're going all out. We need to know if this gunshot was self-inflicted or if someone else pulled the trigger. Get me everything on the girl. If she has a cell phone, I want the call logs. She looks to be a hooker. Pull her sheet and see where she has been. I want anything that seems out of the ordinary to be brought to my attention. Remember people that this person is one of ours, so let's get it right."

Ryan's phone rang. Being in the middle of a murder investigation, Ryan knew he should answer it, but he chose to ignore it. He went around to the passenger side of the car, and as he was sliding on a pair of rubber gloves, his phone rang a second time. Again, he ignored it. He decided to open the back car door. He didn't want to disturb the placement of the female victim. By this time, the sun was up, and the car was full of sunlight. Ryan scanned over the interior of the car.

There was blood splattered everywhere. It was on the roof of the car, the back window, and the back seat, but wait…an area of the back seat had no bloodstains. There were stains on either side of the spot. It looked as if someone or something had been there when the blood splattered and was then removed. Or maybe it was a person who did the killing and then left. Ryan made a mental note of this and jotted it down in his little notepad. Again, his phone rang. This time, he chose to answer it.

"Detective Martin."

"Where are you? Did I not tell you to get down here? We have a dead cop, and I need you to get on this right now!" Captain Altman screamed into Ryan's ear.

"I'm already on the scene," Martin said in his defense.

"Why are you there? You were told to come down to the station, not go to the crime scene. Do you ever follow orders?"

"I don't need this Captain. I'm here, and I want to find out what happened as soon as I can."

"Why is that, Detective? I thought you didn't care for Capwell too much?"

"Captain, my personal feeling about someone does not change the fact that we have a dead cop. Whether I like the cop or not, it is my duty to investigate and see if I can find out who may be responsible, period. If he took his own life, that's something I have no control over. But, there is another victim here, and if a suicide did take place, then we also have a murder. If not a suicide, then we have a double homicide and twice the amount of work. I didn't want to waste any time going to the station first and thought it best to get to the crime scene as soon as possible. Now, if you have a problem with me doing my job, then either take me off the case or fire me. If not, then just let me do my job and try to find out what happened here."

Ryan waited for a response, but one did not come. He put his phone back in his pocket and returned to the search of the car. The female victim's purse rested on the front seat between both bodies. Martin grabbed it and stepped back from the car. He set the purse on the roof of the car and rummaged through it. He ended up turning it over and poured out its contents.

"We can rule out robbery," Ryan yelled out. "We have what seems to be about ten thousand dollars in cash."

"Now, I know a hooker doesn't make that kind of money on the streets of this city," came the response from a young, tall detective Ryan did not recognize.

"Who are you?" asked Ryan.

"Detective Anthony Vallencia," He extended his hand.

Ryan shook it while he tried to figure out who this was, "So, why are you here?"

"Captain Altman sent me down. That's why he wanted you to go to the station so that proper introductions could be made. I was just upgraded to detective, and since we lost one of our own, he wanted to put me with you so that we would work together and solve this crime soon."

Ryan continued with the search of the purse, "Ok, we have a cell phone." He tossed it to one of the evidence technicians, "Find out who she last called." Next, he pulled out her license, "We have a name of our female victim. Her name is Joy Samuelson. Run it through BCI, see if the prints match the name."

"Where do you think she came up with that kind of cash?" Anthony wondered.

"I got no clue," Ryan responded.

"You don't think she got it from Mark do you?"

"With the type of life Detective Capwell led, I don't want to talk bad of him, but there is a strong possibility that she could have got it from him. I will leave it at that."

"Do you think someone may have wanted Mark dead?"

"I'm sorry, Detective, what was your name again?"

"Anthony Vallencia, but you can—"

"Let me guess, Tony, right?" Ryan answered sarcastically.

"Yea, Tony, how'd you guess?"

"I've been a detective quite a while. Comes with the territory," Ryan finished.

Officer Lansing made a muffled laughing sound.

"Oh, I get it! I'm the new kid in town, so let's have some fun with him. I get it. Let me just say, Detective Martin, I'm here, and you'll just have to deal with it. We can both work together and use our energy to try and solve this case, or we can stand here and act like little kids in a school playground. The choice is yours, but let's remember why we are here. Got it?"

Ryan stopped looking at the evidence and slowly walked over and stood face to face with Vallencia, "Oh I got it. You don't need to worry about me. I will do my job and solve this case. You need to just keep your mouth shut and come to the understanding that you, my friend, work for me. I'm the lead detective on this case, not you. You need to learn to listen. I don't like the fact that I have to babysit a newbie. The fact you showed up unannounced and expect me to welcome you with open arms just because Captain Altman sent you is a little naïve on your part. Let me do my job, and we will see where it leads, okay? Or, you can take your badge and go home because you are on my playground. You got that?"

Detective Vallencia looked a little sheepish, "So, Detective, what do think happened here?"

"I'm not going to assume anything, but the people who Capwell hung around with could have had a reason for doing this, too. We are just going to have to do our job and see where the evidence takes us."

"Are you saying Mark was a bad cop?"

"I am not going to label a cop good or bad. I didn't like his way of doing police work or how he handled his private affairs. If what he did or didn't do or how he handled himself makes you want to label him a bad cop, that's up to you. I have a dead cop and a dead female. All I want to do is find out what happened and who's responsible, okay?"

"Yes sir. Have you come up with anything yet?"

"Well, it bothers me that there is a spot in the back seat that has no blood splatter on it," Ryan pointed to it.

"Do you think there was someone in the back seat?"

"That's my initial conclusion. But, how could they have gotten to Mark's gun and also shoot the girl without a struggle?"

"Won't an autopsy find out if maybe both victims were asleep? Maybe the one responsible snuck up on them while they were asleep."

"Could be, or maybe it was a setup. Maybe the plan was to kill Mark. Maybe that's why she had so much money on her person. Maybe the killer decided they wanted no witnesses, so they shot the girl as assurance of their anonymity. Maybe they left the money as a decoy to throw us off the trail."

"That's a possibility, Detective. So, where do we go from here?"

"We will have to wait for the autopsies and a background check on this Joy Samuelson. Then, we can see where the trail leads. Until then, you talk to the officers who are searching the trail and those in the field. See if they have found anything."

Ryan took his phone from his pocket and called his wife, "Hey, baby, looks like it's going to be a long day. I can't really tell you why or what, but it will be a while."

"It's all over the TV. You looked good on the camera."

"Thanks, sweetheart. Listen, say a prayer for me. I have a feeling that this may be the start of that blood bath I told you could happen."

"Really, why?"

"Just a gut feeling. I'm going to give Michael Marello a call."

"Do you think he had something to do with this?"

"Well, that is going to be my excuse for calling him. I am also going to remind him that I have a package his brother left for him. Maybe, I can get him to come down and pick it up. Listen, I got to go. I'll call you later. I love you."

When Ryan got off the phone, he saw Captain Altman talking to the new detective. Ryan walked up to Altman and told him what the initial investigation had turned up.

Detective Vallencia stepped to the side but hovered.

"I understand that you think that Mark was murdered and that Michael Marello could be behind it. What are you waiting for? I want him arrested and charged!"

"I never said that Michael Marello was responsible for this. Where did you get that?"

"Anthony informed me of your findings."

Vallencia leaned in.

"I never implicated anyone. Whatever Detective Vallencia told you, came from his own conclusions, not mine. I have nothing as of yet linking Marello or anyone from Titan to this crime scene. I have two bodies and a theory of what could have happened. It's all speculation, nothing solid. Anthony had no right telling you any of this."

The young detective moved quietly away from the both of them.

"Don't go turning the blame on him. I asked a question, and he answered to the best of his ability. Now, if you think that Marello had any involvement at all, I want him brought in and questioned," Altman rebuked Martin, shoving his finger in his face.

"I will go over the evidence when it is all gathered together. Then, and only then, will I bring in any suspect for questioning. You know as well as I do that if we bring in Marello on a hunch or trumped up charge, his lawyer will have him out so fast the ink on the arrest warrant will still be wet. Let me do my job and train the rookie right. If Marello is guilty, we will bust him and make it stick."

Captain Altman stared at Ryan for a minute. Then, once again, he pointed his finger at him, "You mess this up, and I'll have your badge." He turned and walked away.

21

PAUL MADE SURE everything was running smoothly for Titan. With all the moves that Michael wanted to take place after Rhino's death, the possibility of a glitch was very real. Money and products were moved. Warehouses were emptied, and soldiers were dispatched to the street. There was the small possibility that a new cop wanting to impress the brass would see the action on the street and make an arrest. It was Paul's responsibility to assure that everything ran smoothly while in defense mode. He knew Michael was very confident in his ability to handle the task.

Paul was nervous. He had set a meeting with Michael, but not until late in the evening. He wanted to be sure everything was in place and that he had protection for himself. He had no other family. The more he thought about it, Michael was the closest to family he had. Yet, after tonight, Paul wouldn't have any family. He might not even have his life. He understood that, but it lay heavy on his conscience that he was partly responsible for the murder of Rhino.

Murder.

It sounded so cold, yet the rest of the men felt it was necessary for the protection of Titan. Paul, as usual, was too nervous to speak how he really felt.

How did he feel? He felt the move was too abrupt and not thought out. Even though Paul questioned the action, he decided not to say anything because he knew Sammy would hurt anyone who voted against the execution of Rhino. That sounded so much better than murder. But, it was murder—murder of a good friend's brother. No matter how Paul tried to condone it or explain it away, the truth was that Rhino was dead, and Paul was guilty.

How would he start the meeting? Maybe, he would start out by saying, "Michael, I'm so sorry." Or perhaps, he would say, "Michael let me explain myself." Whatever he came up with would not matter. As soon as Michael heard, "I'm responsible for the murder of you older brother," it would not matter what came out of Paul's mouth. Paul began to cry. Should he go through with the meeting or save his own life and just cancel? He could not live with himself with this eating at his heart. He had to tell Michael, and he would tell him tonight.

* * *

Sammy, Willy, and Moe sat together in Moe's car in the parking lot of the Wooded Hills Country Club.

"I called you here for a reason," Sammy started. "As you know, we bugged Paul's phone. In all honesty, Willy, we bugged yours, too. Moe and I knew that neither Paul nor you were in favor of the hit. We had to protect ourselves. We felt one of you would contact Michael. Now, we know. Paul has set up a meeting with Michael at nine. We can't let that meeting take place. Do we agree?" Both Moe and Willy nodded their heads.

"Where is the meeting going to be held?" Moe asked.

"Right here at the club," answered Sammy.

"We can't get rid of them here. We need some place neutral," Willy said.

"I agree. I have a plan that will take care of Paul before he even gets here, and it will appear to be another hit at Michael," Sammy resisted the urge to rub his hands together. "It will actually look like an accident, so no one will think anything about it. Once Paul is gone, we will have no other obstacles in our way. We will be able to take Michael out, take over Titan, and run it the way it should be run. We will make ourselves a lot of cash, with no one to stop us."

Moe asked Sammy, "What about Dominic?"

"He's just a punk kid. He has no smarts whatsoever. With Michael gone, I'll just crush him like a bug. I'm not afraid of him."

* * *

Dominic met up with Luther for an early dinner at Stan's. Stan's was well known for its grilled steaks. The atmosphere was very masculine with thick wooded chairs and tables, dim lighting, and huge brick ovens in the middle where all the steaks and chops were grilled to perfection. It was a place Titan used to entertain guests and finalize business deals. They always sat right in the middle at one of the larger tables. When a business deal was being brokered and then finalized, Michael liked to show off his latest accomplishments. Stan's was one of the few places Michael would be so arrogant and show off his influence and power.

"So everything was taken care of?" Dominic asked.

"I handled it all. I think the results speak for themselves." A waitress came over to the table to take their order. "I'm buying," Luther demanded.

"Be my guest, friend. But, after what you did for Titan, I should be buying for you."

"No need for that. I was more than happy to help business run smoothly for you."

Luther looked at the waitress in her cute little uniform and smiled, "Well, cutie, my friend and I will have the Basil Hyden Bourbon Tenderloin Tips with garlic mashed potatoes and a spinach salad."

"Can I start you out with a cocktail?" The waitress blushed as a smile crossed Luther's face.

"Yes, as a matter of fact, we are celebrating the execution of a deal, so please bring us a bottle of your finest Riesling."

"I will be right back, gentlemen."

Dominic laughed at Luther, "What are you doing?"

"Nothing, she's kind of cute. Maybe, I'll give her my number. She can call me when she gets off."

"Listen, I have more important things for you tonight."

Luther dropped the smile, "What is it?"

"Paul called Michael today, and he wants to meet with him tonight at the golf course. Something just doesn't feel right. Apparently, Paul told Michael to be careful. I think he knows something that he just ain't tellin'. I'm supposed to meet with Michael at eight thirty at the course. I know he is going to ask me if I had anything to do with the business we took care of early this morning. I can't follow Paul to make sure he is not bringing some kind of surprise for Michael. I will be there when Paul comes in. It's before then that I'm worried about. So, that means no womanizing tonight. I want you sitting in front of Paul's place and following him to the meeting with Michael. Got it?"

"What are you going to tell Michael when he asks?"

"The truth. When he hears the reason why, I feel he will understand and will be glad I took care of it."

The waitress returned with the wine and poured two glasses. She then turned and walked away looking over her shoulder and winked at Luther. Luther just shook his head, "Not tonight," Dominic warned Luther, "just business and only business tonight."

* * *

Detective Martin thought he would give Michael Marello a call to see what kind of response he would receive. The phone rang as he put it to his ear.

"This is Michael Marello."

"Mr. Marello, Detective Martin, do you have a minute?"

"Yes, Detective, I do, but only if this is in connection with the death of my brother."

"Well, in a roundabout way."

"Well then, my time is contingent on just how much you have to tell me."

"Let me just say that we are investigating the death of a police officer. Maybe you know something about that?"

"All I have heard is what is on the news. From what the news is saying, the cop killed his girlfriend and then took his own life. Sounds pretty pathetic to me."

"Me too, Mr. Marello. It's just that the officer who died was involved in your brother's case, and I thought—"

"You had a case on my brother? You never told me that. What kind of case are we talking about?" Michael's voice had an edge to it.

"Just the usual. This cop was tailing Rhino to keep an eye on his movements and associates."

"What for, may I ask?"

"Come on, Mr. Marello, you know that we are always watching Titan Inc. to make sure everything is legit."

"Obviously, it must be. You have yet to find anything illegal."

"No sir, not yet. But, that doesn't mean you're clean. That just means you know how to wash and clean."

"What are you saying, Detective? Are you calling me a crook?" The last word came out as a shout.

"Not at all sir. I was just calling to see if you had any information for me on the dead police officer." Maybe Ryan could smooth this conversation out a little. He must remain calm.

"No, Detective, I do not. So if that is all you needed—"

"One more thing, Mr. Marello, I want to remind you of the package I have here from your brother. Could you come down and pick it up?"

"As a matter of fact, Detective, I have a meeting tonight. I will pick it up on my way."

"That would be fine, Mr. Marello. I will be looking for you," Ryan said a small prayer of thanks. He would be able to fulfill Rhino's request.

* * *

Michael waited for Dominic. The package he picked up from Detective Martin sat on the conference table. He was checking the tape that was already in the video recorder. He usually would check it every five days. With all the happenings going on over the last seven days, he was a little late in checking.

He rewound the tape. The first image was of the cleaning people. It was timed at five thirty in the morning. Michael fast-forwarded to the next image, which was of more cleaning people. Again, he pressed the fast-forward button. He stopped it when he saw people sitting around the table. Michael rewound the tape. First, he recognized Sammy and Moe talking. The date was on Monday. Willy then joined, and soon, Paul was there. Michael could not remember calling this meeting.

They all sat at their usual seat and waited. They must have been waiting for him, but then, Steve entered the room.

"What are you watching?" Dominic asked from behind him.

Michael shut off the tape and turned to Dominic. He asked him straight out, "Did you have anything to do with the death of that cop and his girlfriend?"

"Why do you ask?"

"Because if you did, you must have had a good reason, and I would like to know what that reason was."

"I will not let you know what I was or was not involved with. If I tell you anything, then you become an accomplice to whatever I share with you. You never wanted to get your hands dirty, so let me keep them clean. I will say this—no mistakes were made."

"You got all this confirmed?"

"Yes, there was nothing left behind. The cops will end up with no evidence."

"Why did you not try to get more information from the cop, like who he was working for and what part he had in Nick's death? According to police, they believe Steve Silinger is responsible for Nick's death. You needed to connect the dots, not destroy the puzzle."

"I'm sorry. I thought I was doing something to avenge Rhino's death."

"You were thinking with your heart and not your head. I understand. You left no trail, so we are clear. The only thing is we still are not sure why Steve killed Rhino."

They both sat at the conference table. "What time is it?"

"Five after nine," Dominic answered. Just then, his phone rang, "Talk to me, Luther." Dominic's eyes flicked to Michael, "What?"

Michael heard chattering on the other end, but the words were too muffled for him to make them out.

"How? I thought you were following him?"

Michael waited patiently as Dominic listened for a long time. "You're ok, right?" Dominic asked.

Michael raised an eyebrow.

"Okay, keep me updated." Dominic hung up and then turned to Michael, "Paul was just killed."

Michael got a sick feeling in his stomach, "How?"

Dominic repeated the whole story, "Luther was very detailed in his description of what happened. I had Luther tail Paul. I wanted to be sure he was not setting you up. When Paul left, Luther waited about two minutes before he followed. Since Luther knew where he was going, he didn't need to keep a close tail. He came up to some traffic that was moving very slowly, so he backed off and turned the corner. Luther knew he would catch them a couple of blocks down. Paul was passing the slower cars, and as he went past the final car, it swerved into his lane. It clipped the rear corner of Paul's car. Paul lost control and crashed into the ditch."

Dominic looked at his hands, "Then, his car exploded."

As Dominic continued the story, Michael grew sicker and sicker.

When Dominic finished, he asked, "What should I do?"

Michael sat there motionless for what seemed like a minute. He then walked over to the video recorder and pressed play. The image on the TV screen once again showed the board of Titan minus Michael. He was still wondering why Steve was there. Then, Michael froze. He watched the screen like a hawk. There was no sound. But, as Michael watched, he could tell what was happening. The group was commissioning Steve to take out Rhino.

"What are you watching?" Dominic asked again.

Michael turned to Dominic, "I'm watching the group—*my* group—order the death of your father."

"What? How can you tell?"

Michael proceeded to go through the tape and pointed out the different body language, the anger, and the pictures of Rhino placed in front of Steve on the table, "Watch Steve's emotional response. See the sweat on his brow and the uneasy twitch in his face? He is trying to make them believe he can handle the hit. The final telling point to the whole deal is when they all hug Steve at the end of the meeting. That is Steve receiving the blessing from the board."

"What about Paul?" Dominic said.

"Watch," Michael told Dominic. "Paul completely abstains from the conversation. He did not agree with the order to take out Rhino."

"So, you think Paul wanted to meet with you to explain what happened?"

"Yes, and on his way, they had him taken out. That was the way Bruce Trait tried to have me killed twenty years ago."

"Who?"

"Bruce Trait."

"That was the name I saw in the Salluci file."

Michael stared at Dominic silently.

"Remember when you called me earlier today about changes in the Salluci file? I told you a name stuck out that made me question why it was there. Bruce Trait was that name."

"Why was the name there?"

"I was back tracing just to be up to date and to tie up any loose ends like you taught me. At one time, Trait Enterprises financed Salluci Construction. The name Trait stood out to me, and I couldn't remember why. Now, I remember."

Michael's mind raced and so did his heart. The anger started to stir. Those he had trusted, those he had called friends, and everything he thought he had control of was now in question. Whom should he put his trust in now? Who was his ally, and who was his enemy? Who was really in control?

His phone rang, shattering the silence. It was Sue, "Michael! Daddy just died."

22

DOMINIC TRIED TO catch Michael as he collapsed. He half-dragged Michael into a chair.

"Michael, are you ok? What is it? Talk to me."

"Everything has changed. I have no idea who to trust. Those closest to me have turned against me. They killed my brother and one of my best friends. What I thought I had control of I may not have any control at all. My father just died. My world is falling apart right in front of me."

That last statement Michael made took Dominic by surprise. He had never seen Michael so helpless.

"Did you just say your dad died? My grandfather?"

"Yes, that was Sue on the phone. She was hysterical. I need to call her back."

Dominic handed the phone to Michael. As he did, it rang.

"Sue? I am so sorry. I dropped my phone, and the battery got knocked off. Did I hear you right? Did you say that our father died?" A pause. He listened, nodded, and then ran a hand down his face. He motioned to Dominic to get him some water. "Hey, baby sister, how are you holding up?"

Michael grabbed the water from Dominic, "I know it is hard to believe. We will get through this though. We are a strong bunch, and we will bounce back. Listen, I am here at the golf course with Dominic, and I am going to have him drive me home. I will begin to make arrangements from home. If there is anything at all you need, call. If I do not answer, Dominic will, and he will see to it that whatever needs to be done gets done."

Michael looked at Dominic who nodded his assurance.

"I have to be off the streets for a couple of days. There are some things I need to take care of before the funeral, and it will be easier for me to do it from home. Do not worry little sister; you are not going to lose me. I will call soon."

Michael got off the phone and looked at Dominic, "Get the tape from the VCR and grab that package off the table. Call Luther and have him choose the men he would trust with his own life. Have them placed around my house and Susan's. Call the funeral home in the morning and make arrangements. Now, get me home."

* * *

Once there, Michael set up a TV and a VCR in his office. He told Dominic to take his laptop and download all of Titan's files to his computer. This way, he would have access to all of Titan's files without having to leave his office. Michael set up a war room, and he worked on a plan to defend and retaliate. He wanted to be left alone. Dominic seemed to have read Michael's mood and left the room.

As word got out of the death in Michael's family, the calls started coming. Even though it was late at night, the calls came with well wishes and support. They came from other businesses and local officials and even from the office of the mayor.

Dominic screened all calls, and those he got from reporters, he just hung up. The next call was from the police.

"I'm sorry, but Mr. Marello is not taking any calls right now."

"I'll take the call Dominic," Michael said as he reached for the phone. Dominic's eyebrows shot up, and he handed over the phone. He was surprised to hear Michael as he entered the room. He knew that Michael would be distraught, but he did not realize that he would be willing to talk to the police

"Hello, Detective Martin, is there something I can help you with?"

"I need to discuss the death of one of your partners." Michael was well aware of the death of Paul Delemonni, but he let the detective continue.

"Detective Martin, what is it you need that is so important that you need to call so late?"

"Mr. Marello, I am sorry to bother you at such a late hour. I had no idea of your personal loss, my condolences."

"Thank you, what is the real reason for your call, Detective?"

"I'm sorry to have to inform you of other tragic news. From what I understand, you are already aware of the death of your business associate, Paul Delemonni. May I ask how you already know this when it happened less than two hours ago?"

"Detective, do we have to go through all of this again? If you know so much about Titan as you say you do, then you should also know that I have just as many ears and eyes out on the streets as you do. Some of them may even work for you."

Michael was letting his arrogant side come out. He also wanted Ryan to know that he really did not have the time to waste on information he already knew. Michael needed to get off the phone as soon as he could so that he could start the arrangements, not only for his father's funeral but also his revenge and retaliation. It would take all of his concentration. He was not sure yet how he would carry his plan out. All he knew was that it was going to be brutal.

"Detective, I want to help in any way I can in finding out what happened to Paul Delemonni. But right now, I have a funeral to arrange and other plans that will take up the bulk of my time. If there is anything I can do, please let me know."

"Michael…I mean…Mr. Marello. You stopped by earlier and picked up a package. I was wondering if you had a chance to look at its contents."

"Detective, my father just died. My very close friend and business partner was murdered. I have not had time to look at the package. If and when I do, why would I tell you anything that my brother personally left for me? I need—"

"Who said anything about Mr. Delemonni being murdered?" Martin interrupted.

"Detective Martin, I need to attend to more pressing matters right now. Let me just say this—for someone who says he knows so much, you seem to have no clue as to who I am or what you are getting caught up in. My advice to you is to find another city to fight crime. You are not going to do it here. I do not need you or the police or the law for that matter. I will take care of things the way they need to be dealt with. This is not a threat or promise; this is fact, Detective. If you want to retire happy, then do not get caught up in what is coming. It may go deeper than you want to find out. If you dig too deep, you may just not make it to your retirement. Goodbye, Detective."

Michael hung up the phone and turned to Dominic, "We have a lot of work to do."

When digging through the files, Michael found that after he'd stolen the business from Bruce Trait, Bruce had other holdings Michael was not aware of. Salluci Construction was just one of many. A distant cousin of Trait's, who was outcast from the Salluci family, owned it. Sammy was being mentored by Bruce, much like Dominic was mentored by Michael. The only thing Michael could come up with was that over the years Sammy and Bruce had built a network inside of Titan—a network that, when it was expanded, would take him down and Titan. It would be destroyed. The best and only way to let their plan unfold was to get rid of Nick. Paul must not have been completely on board, so they eliminated him also.

They had bigger inside connections than Michael thought. He was not sure how deep, but he knew that in order to cover up Nick's death or at least try, the connections had to be deep. Michael's questions and concerns returned, flooding his mind. *Who can I trust, and who is really in control?* He needed to know because he felt he was not in control, and it was imperative to get that feeling of control back.

23

MICHAEL SAT IN the quietness of his office as morning light invaded the darkness. The only existing sounds came from the ceiling fan and early morning birds. Files were put in their proper drawer. He had stopped looking at them and shut the computer off. What would happen next? In some ways, he had control. In his mind, he was like a writer who could make the next chapter in his life a happy one or let it crash down with a tragic ending.

Right now, his life was crumbling all around him—a life that for the most part was filled with lies, blackmail, betrayal, deceit, corruption, scandal, and even death. Was all the power and money worth the seclusion? Did all the influence and people in the right places really make him feel immortal? Would seeking revenge change the ending and make it happy?

Michael looked out into the morning light and thought of Nick. Now death, because of the life Michael lived, touched him personally. Without Nick in his life anymore, everything felt out of place. That thought made him remember the conversation he had with Sue's friend, Elizabeth, in the waiting room at the hospital. Elizabeth had shared with him a time in her life when she walked alone and how she felt so cold and empty. The exact words she used were "a lost soul out of place." That was just how Michael felt at that very moment. In the early moments of daylight, Michael wept.

* * *

Captain Altman burst into Ryan Martin's office screaming more obscenities in one sentence than Ryan could ever remember hearing. Ryan did his best to calm him down.

"Don't tell me to settle down, Detective. Do you realize what the body count is up to with this whole Marello case—a case you told me to give you a little leeway?"

"Yes, sir, I do. Three."

"Well, Detective, I count six."

"Six?"

"Yes, six," Altman finished tossing three files onto Ryan's desk.

"You can't really count Capwell and the girl. Yeah, maybe Delemonni, but the investigations on those three are not complete."

"Are you telling me that you don't think there's a connection between Marello and Delemonni? A business associate of Michael Marello's winds up dead a week after the death of his brother, a cop who was working the Marello case is shot in a questionable situation, and you think they have no connection, Detective. Who are you trying to kid?"

"Captain, I have connected the same dots. It just seems that there may be something in those connections that doesn't make it that simple. I have my doubts. One of those connections is a cop that is known for the associates he deals with. That is one of the biggest doubts I have.

"Are you saying that Mark was a dirty cop?"

"I have told you many times how I was very uncomfortable with the way Mark handled himself as a cop. Did his actions dishonor the badge? Maybe, maybe not. We'll see what the investigation brings out. Was he dirty or not? You might not believe this, sir, but I hope he comes out clean. But my gut tells me otherwise. Look, in a couple of days, we honor one of our own. Let's not stir up anything that might smudge his badge, not before the family has time to mourn."

"Well, how about this, Detective? I want you and your investigation to take a look at the possibility of Michael Marello being responsible for these murders."

"Captain, are you serious?"

"Yes, I am. You have a problem with taking orders?"

"Are you ordering me to turn this investigation toward making Michael Marello a suspect in six murders?"

"No, what I am telling you to do is look at the probability that he could be involved with them."

"You do realize that doing this will make him responsible or at least involved in, as you put it, the death of his own brother. Are you nuts?"

"Watch it, Detective. What better way for him to cover it up then to have his brother killed and then begin to wipe out the rest of his associates and take over complete power."

Ryan stood there for a moment. Captain Altman's idea of a motive was not too far-fetched. Michael was a very power-hungry individual. He craved it like a drug. Ryan also remembered the last conversation he had with Michael and how Michael warned him about getting in too deep. Was it possible that Michael was so power hungry he would have his own brother killed?

Yes.

Did that happen?

No, it did not.

Could there be an internal power struggle at Titan that involved Michael and other members of his group? Yes. Could Nick have known about that without telling Ryan? Yes. Maybe that was the reason Nick was going to give up names to Ryan. He did tell Ryan that his biggest concern was for his brother's safety. Ryan wished he knew what was on the videotape that he gave to Michael. It was something Nick was emphatic about making sure Michael got a hold of.

"Martin, are you with me here?"

Ryan straightened in his chair, "Yes, sir, I'm here. Just running all that information through my head."

"So then, you will look at that angle?"

"Yes, sir, I will add that to the investigation, run it through, and see if it is plausible."

"Thank you. Will you be at the funeral?"

"Yes, sir"

"Good. I'll see you there."

"Yes, sir."

Captain Altman shut the door as he left. Ryan tried to remember all the different talks he had had with Nick. He could not remember anything specific about an internal power struggle. All he could remember was Nick worrying about Michael's safety. Now with the death of Paul Delemonni, it seemed very likely that there could be a war between the members of Titan. These were all very powerful men with numerous connections. This could end up like a mob war before it was done.

* * *

Dominic knocked on Michael's door.

"Come in."

"Sorry to bother you Michael, but I was wondering if you needed anything."

"Come in Dominic. Sit here a minute and listen to what I have come up with."

The majestic feeling in the room and the fact that he was there in Michael's office almost made Dominic want to bow. So much power and decision making was done in this room. Deals that changed people's lives and changed this city were conceived in this room. He wanted to be a part of that someday. It felt so good to be so close to so much power. "Here is what I have come up with so far. Sammy Salluci and Bruce Trait are related through marriages that go so far back it is not worth wasting time or breath. Let us just come to the conclusion that they are now our enemies. I was going through Rhino's notebook and found a couple of interesting entries."

Michael stopped for a moment and frowned at Dominic, "Why are you looking at me like that, Dominic?"

"You just called Nick, Rhino. You haven't done that since before his death."

"Caught up in the business end of it I guess. Anyway, there are a couple of marks Nick made that got me thinking he knew something was not right. Whenever there is an entry with Sammy's name, up above it are two little initials—*b* and a *t*. That tells me Rhino had connected Sammy to Bruce Trait. Now, I have not figured out the why or how. This notebook does not go back to a time when it was put into question. Nick kept notes for only six months. After that, it was all entered in his mind, and he did not need notes. Unfortunately, I do not have Nick's mind to recall why the entry was made in the first place. But, I have come to the conclusion that Sammy Salluci is no longer a friend."

"So, when do we eliminate him?" Dominic asked.

"I have taught you to not react, but to act. Because you reacted, there is a dead cop and our only connection to who else could be behind this. Also an innocent girl's life was taken. You know that I hate it when innocent people become statistics. The police will be watching and listening. We need to be sure and swift."

"You're right, Michael. I'm sorry."

"It is time to share with you some more information on how I started Titan. You need to be fully informed because what could be happening means you need to know it all for your protection and mine."

As Dominic sat down, he tried not to let Michael see how anxious he was to hear more of Titan's history. His desire was to learn everything he could to help Titan stay strong and to make Michael proud. He listened with intent.

"After searching and realizing what Bruce was doing, I decided to put my plan of becoming a powerful figure in the business world into action. I copied all the files to a disc. I came up with a simple proposal. The information that I had was clearly detailed with names, dates, and numbers—how Bruce, with illegal practices that included fraud, was robbing each of his business associates, customers, and sales staff. It was time for Bruce to retire and leave the business in his protégé's capable hands. That, being me."

Michael looked over Dominic's shoulder. Dominic followed the gaze to a picture on the wall. "My plan was to purchase the business for $1 million, which at that time was worth over $40 million. I told Bruce that after five years the information that I had would just disappear if I did not hear from him again.

I sent a letter with hand-picked details of his fraud to each of his four business associates that cleverly laid out the rest of my plan. I let them know that I was obtaining the Trait Bindery at a rock-bottom price under the circumstances. Now, they all had an opportunity to strengthen their individual businesses and make a ton of cash in the process.

"I would mortgage the business to take out a $40 million loan. I would give $10 million to each associate and run all five businesses as one conglomerate. In exchange, after three years, I would take over all five businesses. At that point, I would be sole owner, and they would work for me and receive attractive compensation packages. The fact that each man would receive $10 million and retain ownership of their respective companies for the next three years was very appealing. They all agreed and signed a contract making me the sole proprietor of what would become Titan Inc. To finalize my plan and put it into action, I just had to actually take over the business from Bruce."

"Let me guess. You're telling me all this so that I know just who might be my or our enemies," Dominic cocked his head.

"Absolutely! It's imperative that we always know who can and who will try to take what we have. There is an old saying that says "nothing is ever passed down, it is always taken." What is happening right now is because of what I did in the past. You need to know that past to protect your future. For instance, not everyone was that eager or that happy about the venture. Moe has always been a little bitter and jealous that I bought his company and then tripled its profits. But he does not have the guts to try and take over Titan. At least not on his own. Willy is too much of a simpleton and a follower. He was the easiest to bring into the fold. Paul was the most devoted. That leaves Sammy." Michael stopped and stared at Dominic.

"Well then, please continue," Dominic encouraged.

"That morning I walked into the plant holding a navy duffel bag and headed straight to Bruce's office. Although his secretary tried to stop me, I just waved her away and barged through the door. Bruce stood and asked what I was doing there. As he continued to ask, I second-guessed my plan…only for a minute, mind you. Then, I told him that we had a problem."

"Bruce was a very imposing individual who could take control of any given situation. He would counteract any opposition from a person and then trample over that individual instantly. If I showed any kind of weakness, he would use that to his advantage. Jerry was the same way. If I learned anything from Bruce, it was the way to be intimidating. As I stood there, I gained more confidence and started to head towards Bruce's desk."

It was exhilarating hearing Michael tell his story. What power. What strength. Dominic soaked it all in.

"Without a word, I brought up all Bruce's past dealings on the computer screen. Bruce was a naturally angry person, and whenever he got angry, he lost all business sense. Remember that, Dominic. So, he made a quick decision and sold me the company to save his own skin."

"I stayed calm and assured him that no one else knew…except for his four business associates that he'd been stealing money from and the two detectives out in the parking lot. I was covering all my tracks. Two old friends from high school were on the local police force and would turn the other way for a case of beer."

He chuckled, "I told Bruce the duffle bag held one million dollars in cash. I reached into my back pocket and pulled out a thick packet that I dropped on the desk. My calmness was driving Bruce mad. 'This is a contract,' I said. 'Sign it, take the money, and run, and then you are free to go.' I could tell by the look on his face that he wasn't used to my authority. The longer I was in control, the more confident I became."

Dominic practically bounced in his seat, "What did Jerry do?"

"Jerry hated the plan. Bruce seemed to take it pretty calmly and made sure Jerry was on board. Bruce just looked in the duffle bag, signed the contract, and changed my life forever. He made Jerry leave with him, but not before Jerry whispered to me, *'This isn't over yet.'*

"So, did Jerry ever go through with his threat?" Dominic asked while trying to hide the smirk that was starting to appear on his face.

"This will continue a little later," Michael said rather sternly. "Right now, we need to make sure that what you put into motion earlier is not going to come back and create more of a problem for us."

"My intention was to—"

"We cannot change what has happened. We can, however, change the course of direction. We need to try to find out who all is with Sammy; it may be the entire board. For now, I want you to call the funeral home for me. We will talk again."

Dominic called the funeral home and began arrangements for Michael's father's funeral. It was just over a week ago that there was a Marello funeral at the same place, and the woman in charge recognized the name. She told Dominic not to worry. She would take care of all the necessary arrangements. He then called Luther to see how things were running on the streets.

"I want you to go by the Salluci Construction office and destroy it," Dominic told Luther.

"Which one? There are four throughout the city."

"Do all of them at the same time. I really don't care how you do it. Just do it! Tell the people you use that they will get paid off with drugs. Enough drugs they can sell on the street and make a very handsome profit."

"What if there are people in the office?"

"That's good. That will even send a louder message."

"And what message is that?"

"That they need to be careful. It's hard to know the devil when he looks like your best friend."

* * *

Michael soaked in the quietness of his office. The fan was still going, but the morning chirping had stopped. He ran through everything again in his mind....his discussion with Dominic. He needed to call Sue to see how she was feeling. For a brief moment, he evaluated his life. He had hurt a lot of people. People had lost everything on decisions he made. Even though he was never directly involved or ever wanted to be involved in certain decisions, he knew that people had been eliminated because of Titan.

Michael never knew of names or dates, how or whys. He never wanted to be part of that. In his head, that made him innocent of any person's demise. He made sure he was never placed in that loop. He never wanted to be able to be convicted of murder. So, he made sure whenever discussions started to go there, he would stop them and then leave. That was one way he would keep his conscience clean. He never could be convicted of crimes he knew nothing about.

But sitting alone in his office did not make the guilt go away. He now was aware that Dominic was involved in some manner with the death of a cop and a prostitute. That did not sit well. It made him angry, and he hoped Dominic would be more rational and not make decisions without thinking of the consequences.

* * *

Elizabeth walked into the kitchen. Sue had been up for a while, made a pot of coffee, and was cooking eggs and bacon. The kids had already eaten and were out in the backyard playing. "Sorry I slept so late."

"Don't be silly. I would be making breakfast for the kids anyway."

"Well, I could have helped you."

Sue transferred the bacon to a plate with a paper towel on it, "You just being here is a huge help. I'm definitely going to need it the next couple of days."

Elizabeth poured herself a cup of coffee, "Not to worry. I am right here and will help any way I can."

"Do you really mean that?"

"Of course I do, Susan. You know I will do whatever needs to be done to help you." Elizabeth grabbed Sue's shoulder.

"Have you thought much about talking to Michael?"

Her hand slid off Sue's shoulder. "I knew you were going to ask me that."

"So, does that mean no?"

"What that means is I am still praying, but I do feel that God is opening Michael's heart to Him. You're right. We seem to be very comfortable with each other, and maybe God can use that to draw Michael to Himself."

"That's so good to hear. I hope you're right." Susan dished eggs onto Elizabeth's plate. "What are you thinking about?"

Elizabeth grinned, "Michael. He is a very handsome man. You can just tell He owns a room whenever he walks into it. He has a swagger about him that would make people notice him and would draw a smile from most any woman."

"Elizabeth, are you attracted to Michael?" Sue asked with a big smile.

"I love his devotion to family," Elizabeth told Sue as they both smiled.

"Are you thinking what I am?" Sue started to laugh.

"You mean when I told you I thought that Michael was endearing?"

"Yes!" Sue yelled out, and they both started to laugh. Just then, the phone rang. "Could you please get that for me?"

"Got it! Hello?"

"Hello, Elizabeth? Is my sister there?"

Michael—a voice she didn't mind hearing on the other end. "Yes, Michael, she is, but she is in the middle of cleaning up breakfast. She asked me to answer the phone."

"Well, that is nothing new," Michael chortled.

"What's so funny?"

"Nothing, I just think it is great that you are always there to help my sister. It is very endearing."

Now, it was time for Elizabeth to laugh.

"Okay, what did I say?"

"Nothing it was just something Sue and I were talking about. That's all. Here's Susan."

Elizabeth handed the phone to Susan and went to sit down at the kitchen table. She enjoyed being around Michael. He has such charisma and charm in his voice. She would not want to get involved with him unless he changed his ways, but maybe God *did* want to use her in Michael's life to introduce him to Jesus Christ.

She felt like she needed to pursue it, not only for herself but maybe for the opportunity to introduce Michael to a forever friendship with God. When Susan got off the phone with Michael, she would tell her.

"All right, Michael, I will be there. Okay, here she is," Susan handed the phone to Elizabeth. "He wants to talk to you."

"Hello?" Elizabeth shrugged while looking at Sue.

"Elizabeth, I was wondering if you would like to join me for dinner one of these nights."

"Um, sure. Okay, yes, I would like that."

"Quick question, even though I think I already know the answer. Will you be at the funeral?"

"Yes, I plan on being there. I want to always be there for Sue and also for you."

"Great! Perhaps later that evening you would like to join me for dinner at Stan's?"

"I would love to."

"Great! I will be looking forward to our time together, and hopefully, you will be also."

"Yes, I am looking forward to it. Okay, bye," Elizabeth hung up the phone and turned to face Susan who had a tear in her eye. "Is everything okay?"

"Yes, everything is fine. It's just that I can see God working and answering prayer and strengthening my faith. It's so exciting."

"Well, this will make you even happier. I think you're right. I think God may want to use me to show Michael His love, and I want to be used by Him to do just that."

"I figured that out before you did."

"Oh, really? And how did…" Elizabeth stopped herself, and they just both started to laugh at each other.

24

DOMINIC KNEW THAT with the order he gave Luther, Luther would use street gangs to make it look like a turf war. Dominic would plant the money he used to pay off each gang to once again make it appear that gang rivalry had caused it. Michael would not want anything to happen before his father was buried tomorrow.

Two of the most notorious gangs were on the north and south sides of the city—Satanic Disciples on the north and Lords of the Southside on the south. If handled right, there would be no way to link Dominic or anyone else to this retaliation. It may open the streets up to a gang war, but the innocent casualties would be worth the risk. Any death would be necessary. Plus, it would look just like Dominic wanted it to look, gangs killing each other over property they never really had control of to begin with.

Dominic hated gangs, so anytime he could use them for his dirty work the better. Who cared if they went to jail or wound up dead? They were garbage anyway. Michael never wanted to work with or be associated with any gang. Dominic had always thought it as cheap labor at no cost to Titan.

Luther could handle the job. He did a good job getting rid of Capwell with no ties, so Dominic would not be the least bit worried. What he was concerned about was Michael. Michael said not to retaliate against Sammy, at least not yet. But, Dominic couldn't wait; he wanted payback now.

* * *

Sammy sat at his kitchen table and sorted out what to do next. The death of Michael's father was the best thing that could have happened. Michael's mind would be on the funeral, not business. This made it even easier to continue their plan and to help build a line of defense. Something did trouble Sammy though. He needed to find out what really caused Capwell's death.

He knew that Capwell was involved with that prostitute, so it was no shock to find him dead along with her. It was just too clean. Too clear-cut. Almost like a setup, but who could have accomplished that? If Michael was in the dark, then he would not know about Capwell. No one else involved in the plan knew of Capwell being on their side. So, who was responsible? Maybe the booze and the debt got to Capwell, something snapped, and bang!

Maybe.

Or did Michael know and was planning a retaliation of his own? Sammy went through the list. Capwell was dead. Steven and Kevin, the only two involved in the actual death of Rhino, were dead. Paul Delemonni, who knew of the plan but had turned against the group, was eliminated. There was nothing to link Sammy or the rest of the group to Rhino or Paul's death. So, who could possibly know?

Sammy had covered his tracks. He had also learned from Michael to tie up all loose ends, and as far as he knew, they were all tied up.

* * *

It was a cool start to the day. The grass was wet with the morning dew, and the sun was blinding as it shined brightly in the blue sky. Michael and Susan agreed that the funeral for their father would be a private affair. Michael didn't want to make a spectacle out of their mourning. Besides, with the cops still investigating Nick's death and reporters always asking questions, it was simpler to keep it private. Michael didn't want anyone from the Titan board there either, not only because of the news coverage, but because he could not trust any of them.

Family once again surrounded Michael with comfort—something he never experienced before. This brought joy at a time of great sorrow in his life. He hated being alone. The loneliness he once cherished now brought on doubt, confusion, and memories of adventures he had with his older brother when he was a child. Being alone also brought pain and regret. The pain of losing his older sibling and the regret over the life he'd lived was responsible for that pain.

As Michael stood by his father's casket, Susan walked up, "How are you holding up?"

"I feel the love and support of the family, and it is bringing a comfort that is making this a little easier to handle. How are you doing?"

"I don't like this. First, it was Rhino, then Daddy. I don't want to lose you, too, Michael."

"Well, Sis, I have no plans of leaving any time soon."

"But because of the life you live..." Susan stopped herself and then smiled, "I'm glad to hear that." She gave him a hug.

Elizabeth stepped into the room as Susan and Michael stood at the casket. Michael had seen her several times before, and he could still not figure out what attracted him to her. But, when he saw her on this day, he knew. There was something about the way she handled herself. The confidence in her step, assuredness in her approach, and humbleness in her character drew him, not to mention her beauty. Her brown eyes just seemed to have a brightness about them that said *I am content*. Her brown hair accented her soft cheeks, and her smile lit up her face.

She hugged Susan. "I'm so sorry for your loss." Shortly after, she turned to Michael, grabbed his hand, and told him the same thing she had told Susan. Then, she took a seat.

Other family members arrived to pay their respects and condolences, but Michael stole a glance toward Elizabeth. He was fixated on her appearance. What was it about this woman that was so hypnotizing?

Tommy, Michael's second cousin, walked up, "Michael, if there is anything you need or something I can do to help, please let me know."

"Thank you, Tom. You and your family being here is more help than you can ever imagine. Seeing all the family here showing support for Susan and myself is greatly appreciated."

"Family always comes first, Michael. You should know that."

"It is more evident to me now that I have ignored family and the benefits of that closeness."

"What better time, Michael, to get reacquainted than starting now?"

"Thank you, Tom. I will look forward to it."

Michael always held family close. The problem was his family consisted of his dad, Nick, Susan, and Titan. Now, Michael's dad was gone, and his brother had been murdered. Those at Titan were responsible and could not be trusted. All he had left was his little sister. He knew he needed family and the closeness of it.

As Tom walked away, it opened the door for other family members to approach Michael. It made for a time of refreshing conversation and laughter—getting caught up in what was happening in other family member's lives. The only drawback of this was that it made it hard for Michael to see Elizabeth. He felt bad that she sat by herself most of the time. Some of the time Susan would sit with her, but even then, she was always smiling and seemed to be watching Michael as often as he would watch her.

As Reverend Simmons walked up to Susan to pay his respects, she reintroduced him to Michael. Reverend Simmons was about the same age as Michael. He was six-foot-two, partially bald, and had a beard. Michael was slightly surprised by that. It just seemed to Michael that it was out of the ordinary to see a man of the cloth with facial hair. Then again, the pictures always portrayed Jesus with a beard. The reverend's wife was with him, and she also had more fashion sense than Michael always pictured. Her hair was shoulder length instead of tied up in a bun. Her dress was just below the knees and very trendy. She wore just the perfect amount of makeup and looked more like a professional instead of the wife of a pastor.

They were both very pleasant people who showed true compassion and sorrow for Susan. There were also several other close church members that Susan had asked to be allowed to pay their respects. They too did not fit the picture Michael had always painted in his mind of what church people would look like. They showed Susan and him compassion and support.

Why would they do that? Strangers showing love, support, compassion, sorrow, and unselfishness didn't make any sense.

"Michael, I am so sorry for your loss," Reverend Simmons extended his hand.

Michael shook it. Ah, there it was—smooth skin and a light squeeze. This reverend had not worked a hard day in his life. No surprise there.

"Thank you, Reverend. I really appreciate the support you have given to Susan and myself. I understand the support for Susan being a member of your congregation, but I am stunned that you and the members of your church are showing me that same love and support."

"Michael, we are told in Scripture to love one another and to love our brother as we love ourselves. I am happy to hear that Christians are practicing what they are told to do in the Bible. You know that in the short time your father was awake from his coma I talked to him about that same thing. He also was surprised to see love given by strangers. I told him about the love given by Jesus and how He gave it to everyone."

Their conversation was interrupted as other family members were coming in to pay their respect. The reverend told Michael that if he had time later maybe they could talk. Michael acknowledged that but knew that would probably not happen. Later, he was going to meet with Elizabeth. He looked forward to that. As the service was about ready to start, Michael walked up to her, "Would you sit with us?"

"Of course!"

Everyone was seated, and the room quieted as Reverend Simmons stepped to the podium. He shared a couple of Scripture verses and talked about Michael's father's life. Michael did not like it when other people talked about his father, but as Reverend

Simmons spoke, the words seemed to penetrate Michael's heart. The Scripture that he shared pierced him deep in the bottom of that inner empty place.

"In Scripture, we are told, *'What does it profit a man if he gains the world but loses his own soul? The things of this world are nothing.'* In the world today, we are told that whoever has the most toys wins. We are told we deserve things we cannot afford. We place ourselves in position to owe money for things we can't and won't take with us. The material things that matter so much to us and we hold on to with all our might will not matter in eternity. What *will* matter is the one thing we can take with us…"

Material things were what Michael's world was all about. All the position and power, money and influence, this was his world. Did he gain all of this for nothing? Were people's lives torn apart because of his world? Did people lose everything and did some even die because of his world? He began to shake. Susan laid a hand on his arm, but Michael began to shake even harder.

He couldn't escape the thought that many of the things he had gained were because others lost. The faces and names flashed through his mind. Dates and meetings, conference calls, and those closed-door meetings he never took part of were too numerous to remember and to count. The list went on, and the shaking got stronger. As the Reverend continued, so did the list. Then, it was as if someone grabbed a hold of Michael's heart and squeezed. It took every breath out of his body. Nick, Rhino, his older brother—the one who watched Michael's back and protected him, the one who would take a bullet for him not just because of the lifestyle Michael lived but would do that even when they were kids—was gone. Because of the life Michael chose and involved Nick in, he was murdered. Because he wanted power and influence, money and recognition, his big brother was killed.

Because Michael was selfish, his brother was dead.

The more Michael thought on this he began to cry. He had everything, and Nick was dead. What did that all mean? It meant that his closest friends and allies had turned on him. They were the ones responsible for Nick's death. Not Michael. Michael had everything worked out, and he and Nick had need of nothing. That had been ripped away from him now. Yes, the life he lived was in some part responsible, but the fact was and is that his closest friends had turned on him.

They are the ones who will pay for this. He would see to that. The shaking stopped.

"He gave His life for us in the sacrificial death on the cross. Let's not forget that," Reverend Simmons' voice shook Michael from his thoughts. "He gave everything so that we could be with Him in Heaven for eternity. Without the shedding of blood, there was no remittance of sin. His death was necessary. His death brought forgiveness, and that is what Ben Marello grasped before he passed. He realized that a loving God provided a way to heaven and that death was necessary for forgiveness to be offered. That was the death of God's only Son on the cross. Please don't forget that. If you take anything away from this day, please remember that Jesus's death upon that cross was necessary, and because of that, a gift is offered to all of us. Ben took that gift and now according to the Word of God is in heaven. That's the faith we as Christians should hold on to. Let's pray."

As Reverend Simmons prayed, Michael pondered those final words of the message. His dad was in heaven because of a gift given to all. That seemed a little too easy. Michael loved his father but knew of a past that was not heaven-worthy. Once again, this talk of heaven, Jesus, and forgiveness was something Michael could not get a handle on.

After the memorial service, Michael thanked Reverend Simmons and his wife for the message and the support. He told them, along with all those who were there, that there would be a luncheon at Stan's and everyone was invited. As the last of the family left, Michael approached Susan, "Why didn't you tell me Dad became religious?"

"Michael, I know how you feel about religion and me talking to Daddy about it. I just didn't want to deal with you jumping all over me about it, so I just kept it to myself."

"I have nothing against religion. I just knew Dad was not in the best of health for you to be talking about heaven and hell. His heart could not take that kind of stress."

She folded her arms, "Michael, let me assure you that there was no stress. Daddy was very calm and relaxed when I talked to him. He sat there and listened to Reverend Simmons, and when Reverend Simmons finished, Daddy had tears in his eyes. It was then that he accepted Christ."

"That is where I get confused. Why does a person have to accept—" His cell phone rang. He turned away from Susan and Elizabeth and answered. He talked in a low harsh whisper. "Where are you?"

"I had some business to take care of," Dominic responded.

"All your business needs to stop. You need to honor your father and show respect, not be out there conducting business."

"That detective is sitting outside the funeral home. Want me to take care of that?"

Susan and Elizabeth eyed him. He hushed his voice even more, "Now is not the time. Remember, I told you to have patience. We will deal with it at the right time and only then."

"You know something needs to be done sooner rather than later," Dominic reminded.

"Just meet me at Stan's. We will talk there." Michael slapped his cell phone closed.

"Who was that?" Susan asked.

"Dominic."

Susan and Elizabeth looked at each other and just shrugged their shoulders. Michael retrieved their coats and purses, and they left the funeral home in silence. There was not going to be a burial at the cemetery. They had decided to have their father cremated. As they got in the car and drove away, Michael noticed Detective Martin sitting in his car across the street. Dominic was right.

Michael looked in his rearview mirror. Martin pulled out behind them.

They drove for several blocks, and finally, Michael got angry. He called Dominic. "Where are you?"

He was two blocks away as he too was headed for Stan's. Michael told him what he wanted him to do. Michael drove around the block and came up to Jefferson and Ottawa. As the light turned green, Michael went straight instead of turning left. As he went through the intersection, he swerved to the left into a parking space. The person in the car immediately behind him and in front of Ryan Martin beeped his horn and yelled some profanity at Michael. In order for Detective Martin to avoid rear-ending the car, he had to slam on his brakes. Dominic swerved his 1968 Nova right in front of Martin's car and jumped out.

Dominic stood in front of Detective Martin's car. Michael slowly got out of his car and walked up to the detective. He looked at Dominic and told him, "You may leave." Dominic reluctantly got in his car and drove away, tires screaming. Michael leaned down into Martin's window and asked, "Is there something I can help you with, Detective?"

"No, Mr. Marello, just out for a morning drive. Beautiful day isn't it?"

"Yes, it is. It would be even better if you were not following me."

"I have no idea what you're talking about. I'm just out for a drive," Ryan responded sounding defensive as he put on his sunglasses.

"Well, if that is the case, Detective, I will just say this. And, since it is just you, me, and your car, I will be frank. Get off my back. You just go back to your desk and shuffle some papers, drink some coffee, and eat some donuts. When I am done, you can come pick up the pieces."

"Mr. Marello, you'd better let the police handle this. That way, no innocent people will get hurt."

Michael leaned closer to Ryan Martin and in a cold and deliberate tone said, "Not to worry Detective. There will be no innocent victims. They will have deserved to die. I will see to that."

"Mr. Marello, are you telling me that—"

"What I am telling you, Detective, is get out of my way and let real justice take its course. Good day, Detective."

Michael stood up, turned, and walked back to his car. *He could have me arrested, but my lawyer would have me out before Martin finished the paper work.* What did Ryan take from the conversation? Michael didn't care. *He must know that I know who was responsible for Nick's death.* If that was the case, Michael did not regret how the conversation went. He wanted the detective to know that the person or persons responsible would be handled in a way Michael wanted it to be handled. He headed back to his car.

* * *

Dominic was happy to see that Michael was ready to confront the detective. He was sure Michael was getting ready to retaliate and wanted the cop off his back. He called Luther and told him to meet him behind the casino that sat on the river. There, Dominic and Luther would finalize their plans for payback against Sammy Salluci.

Dominic did not have to wait long for Luther, "Is everything ready?"

"All the players know what to do and are waiting for the go-ahead."

"Michael wants me to meet him at Stan's."

"Does Michael know what you're doing?"

"I will inform him if he asks. If he doesn't, then we'll see how he responds to the news when he finds out."

"What about the payoff?" Luther said.

"You know how the payoff works. You pay them just like you paid Spider."

25

BY THE TIME Michael arrived at Stan's, everything was ready. As always, he had the center of the dining room. All close family members were already there and so were Reverend Simmons and his wife. Michael was very happy to see so many people there.

Dominic wasn't there yet. That bothered him. After confronting Detective Martin, Michael figured that Dominic would head straight for Stan's. He must be up to something.

Susan leaned toward him, "May the Reverend give thanks for the meal?"

"Yes, that would be fine, but I want to say something first." As everyone chose their seat and waited for the food to be served, Michael stood at the head of the table. "Before we are served, I want to express my deepest thanks for all the support and love you have shown to Susan and me. It has been a difficult two weeks in our lives, and we know that in some ways it has affected your lives also. Taking time out of your busy schedule and making this time a priority really means the world to us. Also, let me say this, I need to make a point of reconnecting with most of you. I have let the joy of family slip away, and the benefits of that have eroded, too. It is my fault, and I blame no one but myself. I wish to apologize for the distance I have created. I am learning that seclusion has more disadvantages than advantages. So, while we take the time to remember, may it also be a time of renewing. Hope you enjoy the meal."

Just as Michael finished, Dominic walked in. As everyone sat back down, Michael left the table and met Dominic half way, "Walk with me." Michael could hear Reverend Simmons pray as he and Dominic walked down the hall towards the men's room. "Check it out."

Dominic stepped into the restroom, and he smelled vanilla and ceramic. He looked at the two stalls and the three urinals and found them to be unoccupied. He stepped back out and turned towards Michael, "What's the deal?"

"You tell me."

"Tell you what? I got nothing to tell."

"Where have you been? I left you long before now. You should have been here waiting, but when I got here, you were nowhere to be found. Where did you go?"

"I had some things to take care of before I got here," Dominic responded as he checked his appearance in the mirror.

"What kind of things?"

"What's with the third-degree?"

"I need to know what you are planning," Michael said as he grabbed Dominic's shoulder and turned Dominic to face him.

"Why?"

"Because after the meeting I had with the detective and what I said to him, anything else that might happen may just point in our direction. And, we cannot have that. Not now."

"What was it you said?" Dominic asked with earnest.

"I told him to move out of the way and let real justice take place."

"Boy, am I glad to hear you say that. I already have a…" He trailed off.

"You already got what? Did you not just hear me say we need to wait so that it does not point back to us? You cannot go off half-cocked and do something where innocent people could get hurt. You know I hate to have innocent people involved. Whatever it is you have set up, you need to put a stop to it now!"

"Sorry, Michael, can't do that. You've always taught me that once a plan is in place don't stop it or get in contact with those who are connected. So, it's not wise to try and stop it. You taught me to tie up all loose ends, make sure the trail has no leads, and if there are leads that they point in a different direction. Trust me; there are no leads. You taught me well."

"What I also taught you is respect. If this gets back to us, I will not be able to avenge my brother's death."

Dominic pressed a fist against the wall, "Avenge your brother's death? It's been over two weeks, and you haven't done anything. You keep telling me wait. Well, I'm tired of waiting. Rhino may have been your brother, but he was my father! Those responsible have to know that they will not get away with this. Don't you realize it's perceived that you may be in over your head by doing nothing?"

"Well, we are not sure who all is involved in this. You may eliminate a key piece to the puzzle, but then what?" Michael responded forcefully.

"Have a little more confidence in me please! No one is going to get eliminated. I'm just sending a message, that's all. That's more than you've done!"

"You better watch it. Let me do this the way I feel is the best way to handle it."

"You can't do anything if you're standing around doing nothing. I'm sorry, but I can't let you know anything. That will just make you an accomplice, and the less you know the better. All I'll tell you is that Sammy will know that someone knows he is responsible, and you are that someone."

"I am asking you to put a stop to this. I do not want innocent people getting hurt."

"Boy, you have no confidence in me at all do you? Don't you think I listen when you talk? I know exactly how you feel about innocent people. When this takes place, there will be no victims. That's it, only a message."

Michael was frustrated and yet admired Dominic's refusal to stop whatever it was he had planned. He liked the determination in Dominic's eyes, but at the same time, he feared it. He was built like Rhino, only taller, but he had the rock star look of his uncle—chiseled cheekbones, curly jet-black hair, and olive colored skin. Nick had that same look, and he had become a killing machine with no feelings for anyone but Michael, Susan, and himself. That was all that ever mattered to Nick. He did not want Dominic to turn out the same way. Once again, Michael could see that the life he chose also affected all those closest to him.

"Come sit and have a bite to eat," He took a step toward the door.

"Sorry, but I can't. I got business to attend to. You go back to the table, and as you told that detective, let real justice take place," Dominic left Michael standing by the men's room speechless.

Michael returned to the table of family and friends and tried to ignore the thought of Dominic and what it was he had planned.

The thought easily escaped his mind as he enjoyed the meal and the company.

* * *

Dominic left the restaurant and called Luther.

"What do you need, man?" Luther answered as always.

"Are we all set?"

"Waiting for the word."

Dominic held the phone tightly to his ear, "You got the word."

"Did you talk to Michael?"

"Yes, he isn't too happy, but he knows."

"So then, he's okay with it?"

"No, he's not okay with it, but I don't care. If he wants to sit on his hands and do nothing, fine. I'm not going to. You go ahead and do what I want you to do."

"Dominic, are you sure you want to do this without Michael's blessing?"

"Luther, there haven't been too many times that I've told you to shut up, right?"

"Got it. Say no more man."

"Good, I'll watch the news in the morning. Don't call. If the job is done right, I'll hear about it on the tube."

Dominic put his cell phone in his pocket and debated whether to go back inside Stan's and apologize to Michael, but he decided not to. *Michael's not right. There is something about him that is changing. He is not the same.* He got in his car and drove downtown.

* * *

Detective Ryan Martin arrived at the precinct and went straight to his office to call Colleen. He had not been in touch with her all day and wanted to let her know he was okay. He had made a promise to her that if there would be long periods of time that they did not speak, he would call her first chance he got to let her know everything was fine.

"Well, Big Guy, about time I heard from you. What's up?"

"Aw, this and that. Thought I would call you and let you know I miss you and look forward to seeing you," Ryan shuffled through some files on his desk.

"Do you really miss me? I don't think you do. I think you call just to make me think you miss me," Colleen's smile transferred through her voice.

"Well, when I get home, I'll be happy to show you how much I miss you. How about that?"

"Hmm, sounds like a plan; when do you think you will be home?" Her voice echoed as if she were in the kitchen.

"I got a couple calls to make and a couple of reports to fill out, so I should be able to cut out of here in an hour or two. How's that sound, Baby?" Ryan frowned looking at the pile of reports piled on his desk.

"That sounds great. I'll be waiting."

"I'll be there soon beautiful. Bye, Baby," Ryan hung up the phone and leaned back in his chair. A knock at his door interrupted his focus. As he turned to see who it was, Captain Altman stepped into his office.

"Well, Detective, that is so sweet you and your wife making plans for later. Or was that your wife? Don't answer that; I don't care. What I do care about is how you are coming along with the case on Michael Marello?"

"Still trying to logically think it through. I still can't buy the idea that Michael Marello would have his own brother killed to take over Titan Inc. all for himself. I mean let's face it. He started it and for all intents and purposes, it's his anyway. So, the reasoning behind your theory really makes no sense, Captain. That's where I'm having a hard time getting behind your theory. It just logically does not make any sense."

"Well, how about you wrap yourself around this, Detective? Arrest him!"

"On what charge? What grounds do I possibly have to arrest Michael Marello?"

"We have covered this. We arrest him for the murders of Paul Delemonni, Nick Marello, and Mark Capwell."

Ryan stood from his desk, "Captain, I just don't see that as a logical—"

"Forget your logic! I am ordering you to arrest Michael Marello for the murders of Paul Delemonni, Nick Marello, and Mark Capwell. You remember Capwell right, Detective? He was your fellow officer that was killed in the line of duty, the one we just buried. Oh, that's right, you really didn't like Capwell. You thought he was a dirty cop, didn't you? I remember. Maybe that's why you're so reluctant. Could that be the reason, Detective?"

"Captain, I resent that statement. I always honor a fallen officer, no matter how I personally feel about them. As far as arresting Marello, there is no evidence linking Michael Marello to these crimes. All you have is theory, and you will never get a judge to issue a warrant on theory."

"I have a judge waiting to hear my theory, Detective; you don't have to worry about that. All you have to do is pick up the warrant and serve it."

"You have a judge who is going to issue a warrant on a theory? What judge is going to do that?"

"As a matter of fact, I do, and that judge will be more than happy to support my theory. I have talked to the judge about this. I was assured that when I call the warrant would be issued for Michael Marello's arrest, so I am going to make the call. You head on over there and pick it up, and we'll serve it today."

"Captain Altman, sir, can we at least wait a couple of days? Today, Michael Marello is burying his father. It would look pretty cold and heartless on the part of the police department to arrest him right now."

"You don't think he's a flight risk?"

"He has no idea that we are even looking at him as a suspect. Why would he be a flight risk?"

"True, I will give you a couple of days, but if anything happens before you arrest him, I will expedite his arrest. You got that?"

"Yes, sir. Oh, and Captain, off the record, if you ever imply in any way that I may be having a relationship with someone outside my marriage, you will regret it! Got that, sir?"

Captain Altman slammed Ryan's office door, and Ryan plopped into his chair. He leaned back and ran his fingers through his hair. Why was Altman so emphatic on arresting Michael Marello? Ryan's phone rang, and the officer at the desk informed Ryan that there was a reporter wanting to know if he could ask a few questions.

"A few questions about what?"

"Something about arresting Michael Marello for the murders of Paul Delemonni, Mark Capwell, and his brother, Nick Marello."

"Tell them wherever they got their information it's false. Don't say anymore than that."

"Yes, sir."

When Ryan hung up his phone, again the questions raced through his mind. Why was the captain in a hurry? How did the reporter hear that they were looking at arresting Michael Marello? Maybe Capwell wasn't the only cop he needed to worry about. He would personally keep tabs on Michael to make sure he would not run once word got out that the police were looking at him as a suspect. It would not take long for the word to get out on the streets. Ryan called Colleen to let her know that they would have to put their plans on hold.

* * *

Everyone but Susan, Michael, and Elizabeth left Stan's. Michael still basked in the enjoyment that came from being surrounded by family. He was going to make a point of keeping in touch with everyone. Susan would be his connection as she was always close to family and knew how to get a hold of people. Michael was still concerned about Dominic and what his plan was, but he didn't let that dampen his anticipation of dinner with Elizabeth later that evening.

He was looking forward to not being alone anymore. The life he had made for himself was not bringing the satisfaction he once cherished. He was a very proud man, and his accomplishments were numerous. That was what he had to prove not only to himself but also to others—that he was somebody and had made it. But, the lifestyle he was so proud of caused the death of his older brother. He cringed.

"Lunch was so nice," Susan said. "Thank you for planning it all, Michael."

"Listen, Sis, I know that you have always been concerned about the life that I live. I just wanted you to know that there are some things that I need to take care of, and after that, you just might see a different kind of person."

"What are you saying, Michael?"

"I have been taking inventory of my life and all those that are a part of it. Nick is gone and so is Paul. With dad passing, I just think I need to prioritize things a little differently, reconnect with some people, and stop being so reclusive. Keeping to myself is something that brings an inward pain. Being around family and the love that is felt is something I really enjoy. I want to make that the priority."

"It's so good to hear you say that. What do you think, Elizabeth?"

"I think family is something that we should always hold on to. The bonds are strong and hard to sever. We should all work at being there for each other. I think it's great."

The lighting in the restaurant highlighted Elizabeth's face in a way that made her look stunning. Michael was speechless for a moment as he fumbled with his words. What was it about this woman that he was so drawn to?

"I agree with that," was Susan's response.

As the three of them headed for the coat room, Michael took Elizabeth aside, "May I pick you up at six?"

"That would be perfect."

"I would like you to be able to try the dinner menu here at Stan's. They have great pork tenderloin."

"Sounds delicious," Elizabeth said.

"Perfect then, I will see you at six."

Michael helped Susan and Elizabeth into their coats. The fragrance of Elizabeth's perfume was almost intoxicating. Michael was again perplexed at the effect this woman had on him. He could enjoy having Elizabeth as a part of his life, but because of his lifestyle and the danger associated with it, he'd never had a woman in his life. And, he definitely would not want to place Elizabeth in any danger.

"What a gentleman. Thank you."

"No problem, ladies. Listen, Elizabeth, if it would not be to bold of me to intrude on your time, would you mind taking Susan home? I have to stop by the country club and check on a couple of things. Then, I need to stop by Titan and pick up some papers."

"Michael! That's just rude! Don't make Elizabeth drive me home. I'll run around with you."

Elizabeth held up her hand and smiled, "Susan, it's not a bother, and it's not rude. I have no problem with taking you home."

"Are you sure?" Michael said.

"Yes, I'm sure. You go take care of business, and I'll take Susan home. Just make sure all your business is done and you're not late for dinner. I will be waiting."

"A little sassy are we?" Michael said.

"I just don't want to miss a free meal," was Elizabeth's response.

All three of them broke out in laughter as they stepped out into the crisp afternoon air. As they walked down the sidewalk, a black SUV turned the corner with tires screeching. The windows on the SUV were all tinted black, and you could not make out any of the occupants. As soon as Michael heard the tires screaming and saw the black tinted windows, his heart started pounding.

There was going to be a hit.

26

MICHAEL'S MIND RACED. How is he going to protect both Susan and Elizabeth, let alone himself? As the speeding vehicle approached them, Michael noticed the back window start to roll down. *Here it comes. This is why I do not want people I care for to be too close to me. They are innocent of this lifestyle and should not be a casualty because of it.* Then, Michael's mind once again was filled with the many lives that were changed and lost because of his life. Now, could it be that Susan and Elizabeth were also going to be added to that list?

Michael could see the barrel of a rifle protrude from the open window. He instinctively stepped in front of both girls and heard the sound. "BANG! BANG!" Then came laughter from little kids with big grins on their faces as the SUV continued to fly past them down the street.

"That's not too safe. They are driving way to fast," Susan said.

"And, those kids should be in seatbelts, too," was Elizabeth's response.

Michael stood there, and all the outside noise vanished. He could not hear Susan or Elizabeth. The noise on the street seemed to disappear. The realization of his own mortality became a reality. Death, for once, was something he now feared. In all his life, he had never feared it, even with the death of his brother and father.

His life was surrounded with corruption and death. The death of others, he was now sure of, was necessary to obtain all his power. What power? That power has no power over death. That power did not save Nick. That power did not save his dad, and his power would not save him. Death was now something that was very real and fearful for Michael. As he stood there in the middle of the sidewalk, he was silent and could not seem to move.

Then, the fear of death was soon replaced with anger. He was not responsible for the death that had entered his life, but former close friends were. The ones that he had entrusted so much to had turned on him. Soon, the noise of the city and the voices of Susan and Elizabeth could once again be heard. Michael turned to look at both of them, "You two be careful. I have business to take care of."

He turned and walked away. Susan tried to get his attention, but Michael continued to walk toward his car and reached into his pocket for his cell phone. He tried to get in contact with Dominic, but there was no answer. As he opened the door to his car, he stopped to look back at Susan and Elizabeth. He smiled and waved goodbye. He got into his car and drove off.

As Michael drove, he clenched the steering wheel. Now, whom could he trust? The one he trusted the most was dead, and the others had turned against him. All he had was starting to mean nothing. He drove in the direction of the country club, making a mental list.

First, he was more than positive that the rest of the Titan board ordered Nick's death and had Paul Delemonni taken out. No one from Titan had called when Michael's father was in the hospital. They were all too eager to avoid both funerals, and though it seemed strange to Michael at first, he now understood. Looking at the videotape, it was definitely a hit ordered and was given to Steve to handle. When Steve came to Michael's office, he was coming for permission to carry out the hit. That still haunted Michael.

As the list grew and the events of the past two weeks filled Michael's mind, the anger grew and so did the confusion. All the thoughts of the loss of his father and brother, the betrayal of those at Titan he held close, the effect Elizabeth was having in his life, and what Dominic may be planning mounted, making Michael feel nauseous.

Then, Michael remembered the words Reverend Simmons spoke at the funeral, "What does it profit a man if he gains the whole world, but loses his own soul?"

Michael was not sure what the last part of that sentence meant, but he definitely started to wonder if what he had was profit. Nick was dead; there was no profit there. Michael used influence, power, and money to get what he wanted. There was no profit in that.

His mind was filled with all the possessions he had and how he actually obtained all of them. The thought was making him feel sicker. He pulled off the side of the road, got out, and vomited. He got back in his car, grabbed a napkin out of the glove box, and wiped his mouth. He then grabbed a piece of gum.

He hated how he was feeling, and he was sure that all of these emotions had been brought on by the failure of those he had held so close.

Michael pulled his car back onto the road and headed toward Wooded Hills Country Club. He was now making a different list. Moe, Willy, and Sammy were at the top of that list. They would have to pay for what they had done. For the first time in Michael's life, he was able to justify having someone killed. Someone was going to pay for the loneliness and insecurities Michael was feeling. Someone was going to pay for killing Nick. Michael would make sure of that.

27

SAMMY, MOE, AND Willy sat around the conference table at the Wooded Hills Country Club. Sammy made sure that the course was closed to the public so that they could meet without fear of being overheard. The room was filled with smoke from Willy's cigar, and a drink sat before each man. How should Sammy start? Before he had a chance, Willy spoke up.

"So, how do you know that the police are going to arrest Michael for his own brother's murder?" Willy rolled his cigar between his fingers.

"My source at the station—and believe me it's a good one—has told me that within the next couple of days they are going to issue a warrant for his arrest," Sammy paced back and forth, trying to clear the air as he paced past Willy.

Moe was downing his second beer, and after draining it, slammed the bottle down on the table, "Doesn't get any better than that!"

"What do you mean by that?" Willy exhaled a plume of smoke.

"What I mean, my chubby friend, is we are in the clear. Once they arrest Michael for the murder of his brother and Paul, then we got nothin' to lose." Moe got up and headed toward the beer. He slapped Willy on his belly as he passed. "Lighten up big guy. Have another drink and join Sammy and me in the celebration."

"What celebration? Don't you two realize the connections Michael has and the powerful attorney he uses? They aren't going to be able to make those charges stick, and you know it. I think it's too early to celebrate anything," Willy crushed out the cigar.

Sammy leveled a gaze at Willy, "You're not getting cold feet are you? You know what could happen if a person gets cold feet, right?"

Moe laughed, "Yeah, just try asking Paul what happened when he got cold feet. Oh wait, you can't. He's dead." Sammy joined in the laughter.

"I don't know what you two are laughing for," Willy grumbled. "This is serious. Michael has connections and very powerful ones. He hasn't even let us in on all his connections."

"That's right!" Sammy slammed his fist on the table. "There are a lot of things Michael kept from us that we had a right to know about. But no! He was mister big stuff and untouchable, while he left us out in the open and unprotected. Since Paul was the only remaining member who was reluctant to go along with our plan and Capwell is dead, we could easily tell Michael whatever we wanted. Heck, we could even go along with Michael and just go into protective mode. We could just let things run their course and wait for a better opportunity to take Michael out. That was my plan from the beginning. Michael thought too small for the huge operation he controls. Well, controls for *now*. When I execute my plan, Michael will be left with nothing. He'll be lucky to escape with his life."

The more Sammy played out that scenario, the happier he became. He stopped pacing and took a drink, "At whatever point in the future that happens, the police would just think the same people who killed Rhino, Steve, and Kevin caused Michael's downfall."

Moe nodded, but Willy still seemed doubtful.

"You got that right," Moe finished his third beer.

"Fine, Michael may not have told us everything, but so what. He has made all of us very rich, and we all live a comfortable life. So, what's the big deal?"

"The big deal is, my round friend, we want more. We want to make the decisions. Why does Michael have all the power to say what we invest in and what property we buy or take over?" Moe said.

Sammy tried to reassure Willy as he sat back down in front of him, "As far as connections go, I have a couple that Michael is not aware of, and they're going to help convict Michael of these murders. Then, we'll be able to run Titan the best we feel is right."

"I got that. I'm on board with that. I just think we are underestimating Michael's ability to control his own destiny," Willy started puffing a new cigar.

"Believe me, Willy, Michael has no idea the power that's against him. God can't even help him with this," Sammy once again tried to clear the air from Willy's fresh cigar.

"That's absolutely right," Moe slurred after his fourth beer. "Rhino can't help him…cause he's dead, and his best friend Paul—bless his little pea pickin' heart—can't help him cause… well…he's dead, too. God just better step out of the way, cause nobody can stop this train that's rollin' now," Moe spoke with a confidence that made Sammy laugh out loud.

The three of them sat there and finished making plans of what to do with Titan once Michael was out of the way. Sammy was confident, but he knew Willy still had his doubts. That was something that Sammy may have to deal with in the future. For now, they continued to celebrate.

* * *

Michael again tried getting in touch with Dominic, but Dominic was doing what he was supposed to do—not be in contact with anyone if there was a job planned. Michael had taught him well—*too* well. He needed to talk with Dominic about the future of Titan. Michael would not be able to run Titan the same way anymore. There would have to be a new board in place, and the old one would have to be eliminated.

As Michael pulled into the parking lot at the country club, the sign said the course was closed to the public for a golf outing.

The board was meeting.

He pulled out of the parking lot, drove a quarter mile down the road, and pulled into the grounds keeper driveway. He sat there and waited. It was about half an hour later when he first saw Willy drive by. Then, he saw Sammy and Moe driving together. Tightening his hands against the steering wheel, he pulled out behind them.

Should he catch up with them and confront them? Or should he make them pay? Then, the idea hit. He could avenge his brother's death the same way they took Nick's life. Again, Michael tried to get in contact with Dominic as he turned the car around and headed home.

* * *

Dominic sat inside The Old Keg enjoying a cold beer, as he waited for his pizza. He had ignored his phone, and in fact, after the second time Michael called, he just shut it off. He was mad at Michael and his reluctance to do anything in retaliation for Rhino's death. There was something different about Michael, and Dominic could not quite put his finger on it. He didn't like it.

"Would you like another beer?" The pretty young waitress asked.

"I sure would little lady. What time do you get off?"

"I'm married handsome, sorry. Hit on someone else," She started to walk away.

"So, what does that mean? You must have liked the come-on; otherwise, you wouldn't have called me handsome."

"What that means is I'm committed to my marriage, and if you're looking for a little fun, you should look elsewhere."

"Well good for you. I like to hear people who are committed to something. You just can't trust if there is no commitment. I mean, I had an uncle who was committed to something he held close to his heart. Now, I just don't know. I'm beginning to wonder if I can trust him. You stay committed to your marriage. I applaud that. Good for you!"

"Right. I'll get that beer for you."

Commitment—that is what Michael had always taught Dominic. Respect and commitment. What happened to all that? It seemed as if Michael had forgotten about it.

Where was the commitment to Titan Inc.? Where was the respect for his brother? By doing nothing, there was a lack of respect. Dominic was not going to let the death of Rhino go unanswered. He was committed to that whether Michael was or not. After tonight, Sammy would know that he had been found out. He would pay for killing Dominic's father.

As the waitress returned with Dominic's beer, he stared at her, "Are you sure I can't persuade you to have just a little bit of fun?"

"You're a pig you know that? I said no. No means no, period! Got that?"

"Good for you. Yes, I got that. I'm sorry, and I'm glad you're staying committed. We need more people like you. Would you please bring me my check?"

"But you haven't even got your pizza yet."

"I know. You and your fellow workers enjoy it on me. By the way, just for my own record, what's your name?"

"Lee Ann."

"Well, Lee Ann, it was nice having a conversation with you. Now, if you could bring me my check please."

As she brought the check to Dominic, he paid in cash and left behind a $200 tip. As he was walking out of the restaurant, Lee Ann followed, "Hey, thank you. This is way too much money."

"It was well worth the price. It was good to see someone who sticks to her guns and really believes in something. Use that money to buy yourself something that husband of yours will enjoy. I'm sure we will see each other again. I like the food here. I'll be back."

"Thanks again."

As Dominic got in his car, he made a mental note of the time and day. At some point, he would drop by again to see Lee Ann and find out how committed she really was. He liked her a lot, and maybe, it would be just another notch in his belt.

* * *

When Michael got back to his house, he went directly to his office and sat down in front of the television. He noticed the tape on the coffee table that he had picked up from the detective. Maybe he should watch it. Then, he turned his focus to the tape already in the player. He turned on the power to both the TV and the VCR. He watched the tape over and over. The body language was unmistakable. This was the planning and ordering of Nick's death.

Michael's anger rose each time he watched the video. By the look of the tape, Sammy was the one leading the meeting. Moe was second, then Willy. Paul sat there and had no contribution to the meeting at all. *That* was the reason Paul was murdered. Michael finally turned off the tape and tried Dominic one more time. It went straight to his voicemail.

Michael lay down on his couch. He needed to rest, especially before taking Elizabeth out for dinner. He drifted off almost instantly, back to a time that brought a smile to his face. They had just moved in a new neighborhood. As the truck with all their belongings pulled into the driveway, he and Rhino jumped out of the back.

"Go open the garage door," Dad said.

As they raced to the garage to see which one would be first, Rhino let up just a little so that they would both get there at the same time.

They both reached down for the handle and lifted the door. There, standing alone in the garage, were two brand new bright shining Schwinn bikes. Rhino's was a red three speed, while Michael's was a green standard bike. They both jumped on them right away forgetting about all the stuff that needed to be unloaded.

"Go have fun and be safe," Dad waved.

They rode around and explored the new neighborhood. They found a street that ran downhill. It was one of the tallest hills that either one of them had experienced. There were not streets like this in the old neighborhood. Michael was a little reluctant to challenge the hill. Two lines of trees made a canopy over the bottom of the hill so you really could not see what was at the end.

"You go first," Rhino challenged.

"No way, you go first."

"How 'bout we go at the same time?"

Michael was also a little doubtful about that. Many times in their young lives Rhino would encourage Michael to try something new and exciting with him. However, Rhino would often leave Michael to do it alone, while Rhino watched rolling with laughter.

"Come on. I'll go with you I promise. We'll explore the new neighborhood together."

"Sure, I've heard that before."

"No, really. On the count of three, we'll race down the hill."

"Alright," Michael said.

Rhino began counting, "One, two, THREE!"

Michael jumped on his bike and raced down the hill. The wind made his eyes water, and he saw that he was flying alone. As he reached the bottom of the hill, there was a single set of railroad tracks that headed west into the train yard that was just on the outskirts of the neighborhood. Michael tried applying his brakes, but because of the speed, he ran over the bumpy crossing, tossing him from his seat and back down. He was able to stay on his bike; but when he came back down on his seat, he landed awkwardly, and the pain took his breath away. Even though he knew Rhino could not see what had happened at the bottom of the hill, he heard Rhino laughing at the top of the hill as he yelled out, "Sorry buddy, you had to be the first. I had to make you go first. Watch out. Here I come."

Michael heard those words, but he also noticed a train engine and a caboose coming around the small bend just before it crossed the road. Michael screamed at Rhino to stop. Rhino was screaming and laughing so loud he did not hear. Just before the train reached the street, it blew its whistle, and Rhino heard it. But, it was too late to stop. Instead of just coasting, Rhino peddled faster.

Michael yelled, "Stop! Stop! Don't try to beat it! Rhino stop!"

The bike was traveling so fast that Rhino's feet fell off the pedals. He crossed the tracks, and the engineer blew his horn.

Michael jolted to a sitting position, the dream dissipating. His heart pounded, and sweat lined his forehead. He hated falling asleep. It was getting bad whenever he was alone especially with the thoughts and memories of Nick and the fact he was now gone.

Michael got up to get ready for the dinner he had planned with Elizabeth. He was looking forward to spending time with her. It would definitely be better than being alone. He needed to ask her some questions about the differences between her and his sister. There were some questions that he needed to ask her about some of the things Reverend Simmons said. Michael for some reason, was more comfortable talking to Elizabeth about these things than his own sister. Why was that? Those questions, along with how he was going to make Sammy, Moe, and Willy pay, made for a very confusing ride to pick her up.

When he got to Elizabeth's apartment, they met out front on the sidewalk. Elizabeth wore a little black dress with spaghetti straps, black high heels, and a very small thin necklace that did not hang too low. The shawl was wrapped around her but left her shoulders exposed. Her hair was a shining auburn brown, and her makeup made her eyes sparkle. Michael had never looked at her the way he did tonight. Elizabeth was simply gorgeous. She took his breath away.

He opened the car door, and she got in. As she sat down, her dress rose up exposing her knees and thighs. She immediately pulled her dress back down to cover them up. She looked at Michael and smiled—an embarrassed smile. As Michael walked around to the other side of the car, he thought to himself how classy she was; he liked the conservative style she had. It was not a far drive to Stan's. There was a little small talk, but Michael did not want to get into anything until they were at the restaurant. When they arrived, Stan himself greeted them.

"Good evening, Mr. Marello. The usual table?" Stan turned to summon a waiter.

"You know what, Stan? We are going to be a little different tonight. Give us a quiet booth for two, out of the way."

"No problem, Mr. Marello. Leo will show you to your private booth."

"Thanks, Stan,." Michael placed a $100 bill into his palm.

When they got to their booth, Leo made sure it was to Michael's approval. Michael told him it was just fine and to bring them a bottle of their best Riesling. As Leo left, Michael slipped him a $20 bill. When he returned with the wine and poured it into the glasses, Michael tipped him $50.

"Are you trying to impress me with all this cash flying around?" Elizabeth said.

"Excuse me. No, I just feel that good service needs to be rewarded, and the more you reward it, the better service you get."

"And, what's with the private booth? Either you are embarrassed to be seen with me or you think that if you flash enough cash that maybe you can—"

"I am not embarrassed to be seen with you at all, and I am not planning on trying to get anything," Michael insisted, sounding a little defensive.

She blushed, "Michael, I'm so sorry. I know that you're not like that. I just put my foot in my mouth. Can we start over?"

"Yes, we can Elizabeth, and let me start by saying you look very attractive tonight. I would never be embarrassed to be seen with you."

"Well, thank you, Michael. You're looking like your usual handsome self."

"Hmm, I had a difficult time on deciding what to wear. Obviously, I chose right."

"Yes, you did. You look very dapper."

"Dapper? Please do not let my sister ever hear you say that. She would die laughing."

That put a smile on Elizabeth's face, and she proceeded to tell Michael about the time she had used the word *endearing* to describe him. They both laughed.

"I do think your devotion to family is very endearing. It's good to see you're willing to spread it out to your extended family. We all need that," Elizabeth told Michael.

"But, it bothers you the way I flash money around."

"I really am in no position to judge you, Michael."

"No, I know. It's okay. The reason why I wanted a private booth is to talk to you about some things."

"Really, like what?"

"It has to do with the money thing really. I have a lot of money, and I thought I had happiness. But, now that Nick is gone, I have come to learn a couple of other things. I question whether or not it is all worth it."

"Is what all worth it? The money or the power?"

"Both. I mean neither one. Neither the money nor the power was able to stop my brother from being murdered. In fact, it may have caused it. As I look back on the way I have accomplished and accumulated my wealth and power, I ask myself about how many other people have lost loved ones? How many have lost a brother or a father? How many people have had their lives ripped apart financially in order for me to obtain and grow? It has really been a burden, and the more I am alone, the more those thoughts just seem to invade my mind."

"Michael, there is nothing wrong with having money. But, I will say this. How we have obtained it, as you have said and what we do with it after we have it, could be wrong in God's eyes. Remember what Reverend Simmons said about it? What does it profit a man if he gains the whole world…"

"…but loses his own soul," Michael finished. "Yes, I remember that. I understand the profit part. I mean let's face it. I have made a profit. My problem is that I am not sure what the last part of that means?"

"Jesus taught in parables and used metaphors to teach the Jewish people. He said in one parable that it's easier for a camel to go through the eye of a needle than a rich man to get into heaven. What He means is that the things on this earth will not mean a thing in heaven. It's not the one with the most toys who wins, and we can't buy our way into heaven."

"So, does that mean because I am rich I will not be able to get to heaven?"

"No, it doesn't mean that. There is only one way to heaven."

"Yes, I know. I have heard many times about a free gift, but I cannot understand how Jesus would do what he did and not get anything in return."

"Oh, but He did. He brought glory to His Father and gave each one of us an opportunity to spend eternity with Him. We need to see that without the shedding of blood there is no forgiveness of our wrongdoing, there is a life separated from God, and an eternity in a Godless hell. We all deserve it. The Bible tells us that all people are sinners and fall short of God's glory. I am no different than you. I am a sinner saved by grace. That's it. It's that simple. Nothing special about me."

"Well, there is something special about you. You are different from Sue. You are not judgmental or condemning. Whenever she would talk to Nick or me, she would just sit there and point out all the wrongs we were doing and how we needed to turn from our way of life. She was like some of those preachers you hear on TV who bang the lectern and wave their Bible at the camera. I keep telling myself that I want no part of that."

"I know what you mean, but a person does have to come to a place in their life where they have to either accept or reject. God gives us a choice. Hopefully, we make the right one."

"What is the right one?"

"For me, it was coming to the conclusion that when I leave this world I want to be able to stand before God and for Him to say to me *'well done my good and faithful servant.'* So, I accepted His free gift. For others, they choose not to accept. It's totally up to you."

"Thank you. What you say makes a lot of sense."

"I'll pray that God will help you make the right choice."

He lifted his wine glass to her then took a sip. "I just know it is a lot easier talking to you than to Susan."

"Michael, Susan is worried and concerned for you, that's all."

Leo brought the pork tenderloin to the table. He poured Michael more wine, and Elizabeth chose water. They sat there the rest of the evening engaging in light-hearted conversation just getting to know one another better. By the time they had finished dessert, it was well past ten. They had been at Stan's for over three hours, and the time flew by. When they left, Elizabeth sat next to Michael on the way home. She pressed her shoulder against his during the short ride.

Michael's mind raced, filled with the evening's conversation, the beauty of Elizabeth, and the dream that he had earlier that afternoon. What was it Dominic had planned? Deep down inside, Michael, in a small way, hoped it would send a strong enough message.

The talk with Elizabeth about eternity made things a little clearer, but he still had questions. Next time he was with Elizabeth, he would ask more.

They turned down Ottawa street and passed one of the Salluci offices. Gang signs marred the front of the buildings. That was strange. Usually the gangs didn't mess with anything protected by the Marello organization. Was this part of what Dominic had in the works? He questioned the intent of what Dominic may be planning. He also evaluated what type of person he really was. If Elizabeth knew the *real* Michael…

He would make sure she never saw it.

28

THE NIGHT AIR was cooler than usual, and Elizabeth found it warming to lean against Michael as he drove. Michael's Lincoln had that new car smell that she just loved. She had enjoyed her time with him at dinner and learned that he was a very devoted man in whatever he was involved with. Though Susan and she had joked about it, the truth was that Elizabeth found a lot of endearing traits in him. When that word crossed her mind, it made her giggle.

"What are you laughing at?" Michael said.

Oops. Had she actually laughed out loud? How embarrassing. "Oh nothing really, just something we talked about earlier. I had a nice time getting to know the private side of Michael Marello."

"Well, I just wanted you to see that I am a normal person, not the mean and ruthless character that some people think that I am."

"Did you ever think that maybe who you hang around with helps to feed that perception?"

Michael was silent for a moment. Had she overstepped her bounds and made him angry? "I'm sorry."

"No need to do that," Michael told her. "There may be some merit to what you just said. For the last couple of days, I have…" He glanced out the window and took a deep breath, "When I tell you this Elizabeth, it is something I have never shared with anyone, and it just boggles my mind why I feel comfortable sharing it with you. But, I have questioned all my motives and actions that I have made. Some of them are out of necessity, some are because of pride, but most are out of selfishness. I have built an enterprise upon the failures of others, and I have been the one who made them fail. I have walked on people's backs, and in the process of that, I have ruined many businesses and many lives. I have gained because of what others have lost." Michael stared straight ahead.

He passed her street and now rerouted to head in the right direction. She watched familiar neighborhoods zip by and said while not looking at him, "This is my place."

"Listen, I am sorry I bored you with the problems of my life," Michael pulled to the curb.

"Don't apologize. I had a great time with you. You are a very gentle man. I can see that in you. Others might just see the business side of you, but after spending some time with you, I see a different Michael Marello than they see. You got a good heart. I see a very compassionate man who cares very deeply for whatever it is you hold close to that heart. I know that the last two weeks have been very straining for you. I'm sure you have dealt with every emotion possible, and yet, you find time to be a gentleman and a friend. Thank you for the dinner and the conversation. I hope we can do it again soon. Good night."

As Elizabeth opened the door to the Lincoln and the soft dome light illuminated the interior, it at first blinded Michael. Then, when his eyes adjusted, he was once again taken by her beauty.

"Let me walk you to the door."

"No need. It's not that far. I will be fine. It has been a long day for you. You go home and get some rest. If you ever need someone to talk to or maybe someone to take to dinner, just call. Good night."

Michael waited until she was inside. She turned to wave and then closed the door. Michael started the car and drove home. Different scenes of life attacked his mind. Elizabeth was right when she said that she was sure he'd experienced every emotion possible. The emotion that he was experiencing the most and the one that was attacking him now was anger. He was afraid that he had said too much and now Elizabeth was either scared or repulsed to be with him. Again, the life he chose would keep him distant from someone who he would not want to get hurt.

He cared deeply for Elizabeth. He would not want to involve her into that lifestyle at all. He already may have said too much, and now, she may want nothing to do with him at all. Maybe it was time to change that lifestyle. Maybe once he took care of Sammy, Moe, and Willy, he could run Titan differently. Maybe with Dominic's help, Titan could help people instead of ruin them.

Maybe.

First though, there would have to be more loss before there could be gain. Sometimes a loss was good if in the end it was a greater gain. This would be a worthwhile loss. Not only would he not have to answer to any of the Titan board about the changes he would make, he also would be avenging his brother's death. That would be the greater of the two gains. Revenge!

More death before new life—new life for Titan and a new way of life for Michael. There would be a benefit from death. Maybe Michael didn't gain from the death of Nick. Maybe there was no benefit from his dad passing away, but there would definitely be a benefit from the death of Sammy, Moe, and Willy. Revenge is sweet when a positive outcome follows.

He was not only angry with the three remaining Titan board members, but he was also angry with himself. There was no way he could involve Elizabeth with his world. She was too sweet and innocent. He was becoming more ruthless as the thought of revenge answered all his problems. Michael would never let Elizabeth see how cold a human being he could be.

It was true that throughout his rise to prominence others lost everything, and it never bothered him. He was also aware that when those meetings took place of which he was never a part of, people lost their lives. Michael knew about them deep down inside, but again, the gains were worth it. He could never let Elizabeth know that, even though he now knew that death would be a great gain.

Was he really personally planning revenge? That used to be Nick's job. That part of the so-called business Michael never wanted to be a part of. Now, he wanted to take part first hand. He would want to see the look on their faces just before they took their last breaths. Michael wanted Sammy, Moe, and Willy to feel just like Nick did before he was murdered. They were going to pay with their lives. This was the part of his life that he could never let Elizabeth see or become a part of. That made him angry. That made him confused, but it didn't change the conclusion. There would be more death—necessary death.

That last thought hung on Michael's mind. Necessary death. Is death or was death ever necessary? Sure, in war, they were told casualties were necessary. Out on the streets, gang violence often took innocent lives. Was that death necessary? Was death necessary in Michael's life?

Michael used to be able to filter all the different thoughts he had, file them, deal with them, and come to conclusions about them. Now, they just flooded in and piled up. He could no longer delete or clear his mind of them. That would bring more anger. This thought of necessary death could not be deleted.

Then, one of the statements Reverend Simmons made at the funeral snapped into Michael's mind. He said that the death of Jesus was necessary for forgiveness to take place or something to that effect. So, death could be necessary if the outcome was better. That thought played in Michael's mind for a moment, and then, he was able to file it away. Murder was wrong…but this time, it was necessary. Period.

* * *

Dominic looked out of his apartment window and saw the sky ablaze as the flames glowed off the overcast sky. A smile came across his face. Luther had been successful. Revenge felt sweet.

But Dominic wasn't done yet.

* * *

Sammy Salluci was on the phone and was furious, "I don't care how you find out, but you need to find who is responsible before the sun rises. You got that?" He slammed the receiver into the cradle of the phone. He then picked it up and threw it across the room. It smashed into a vase of flowers sitting on a table in the entry way of his house.

His wife, Helen, came running out of their bedroom. "What's the matter, Sammy? Why did you just destroy our phone and my flowers?"

"Because someone just fire-bombed my life, and that doesn't make me very happy. Okay?"

"Fire bomb? What'd ya mean fire bomb? I don't understand."

"What I mean is that someone set my four office buildings on fire, and now I have no business at all!"

"Who would do something like that to you? You are such a good man."

The phone rang, and Sammy went into the kitchen to grab the one on the wall. "What?"

"Sammy, who is it?" Helen asked.

Sammy waved her off and listened to the voice at the other end. "Go ahead."

"It looks like there may be the start of a cross town gang war. Two members from both the Lords of The Southside and Satan's Disciples are dead, and their bodies are burning as we speak."

"I don't buy that," Sammy finally said. "The street gangs know better than to mess with anything that is controlled by the Marello organization. Why just my business? Why not any of the others? I don't believe it's the work of street gangs. Keep me informed. Find out who!" Sammy hung up the phone.

"What'd they say?" Helen said.

"They think there is a gang war brewing and that each gang made a move on the other to try and take over territory that the other gang claimed to own."

"But, you have always told me that because of who Michael Marello is that the gangs don't mess with his organization, right? You need to call Michael and let him know."

"As soon as I get all the facts on who is behind this, I'll call him. Not yet though. I have a feeling someone else is responsible, but I won't be sure until I get all the info."

"You should call Michael right now. He has been good to us, and he can help."

"No! I'm not going to call him!" Sammy screamed.

"Sammy don't be a—"

"Don't be a what? Don't be a fool? Let me tell you something. You have no idea what you're talking about or what I should do. I know exactly what is going on, and I know exactly how to handle it. As soon as I find out who did this, they will pay with their—"

"Sammy! You're not going to—"

"Shut up! I will do what I have to do to protect my interests and my family. Now, go to bed. I don't need you hanging on me when I have things to take care of. Go on. Get out of here!"

As Helen walked down the hall to their bedroom, Sammy watched her and shook his head in disgust. Why did he ever marry such an old frumpy woman? Why could she not be youthful and exciting? Maybe he would change that after he took over Titan. There would be a lot of changes once that happened.

He walked into his family room, turned on the TV, and sat in his favorite chair. The thought of getting a cold beer entered his mind, but he brushed that away and turned to the news channel. The local stations were full of either infomercials or old movies. He turned on the cable news network to see if there were any reports on the fires. One channel reported how gang violence had erupted. Sammy listened intently to the report.

"There are several businesses burning at this hour, Charlie, and now, we have just learned that firemen found two bodies in the Salluci Construction office building on Ottawa Street. That is on the south side of the city. There are three other fires burning at this hour. They are on the north, east, and west side. We have been told that those are also Salluci Construction offices. The reason why police feel that this is gang related is there was gang graffiti sprayed on all of the buildings. Even though all four are in neutral territory, police feel that the two opposing gangs are trying to gain new territory and are sending a message to the other. Reporting on the fires burning throughout the city, I'm Brad Seeman. Charlie, back to you in the studio."

"Thanks for that report, Brad. In related news, police are also reporting that there may already have been retaliation by both gangs. Police have found two burning cars. Both cars are at the old drive-in theaters on both the east and west side of the city with two bodies in each one. All four victims have been murdered. The wounds of each victim are a message to the opposing gang. That is why the police fear a gang war could erupt. In other news, unions are gaining strength..."

Sammy turned off the TV and called Altman at the police station, "You don't believe that this is a gang thing do you?"

"No, I don't. It's too clean. The retaliation was too quick, and the fact that they were both at the drive-in makes no sense either. The only thing that makes me think that it is gang-related is how each one was executed. Two were shot in the head, and two had their throats slit."

"I don't care if they were hung upside down. Don't be stupid. This is a message from Michael Marello. He knows that he is being targeted."

"How would he know that?" Altman asked

"I don't know and don't care. I want him arrested now!"

"Don't push. Everything is in place. We just have to worry about how much Marello knows and how he found out."

"He's going to pay for this. You know as well as I do that two people were found at one of the fires. We can now pin a murder charge on him, right?" Sammy mused lighting a cigar.

"Yes, we can, which would be a reason to expedite his arrest."

"Well, you be sure that that happens. Do your job and do it right, and our plan will still work."

"Don't press your luck, Sammy. I know what to do. It'll get done, and you'll have control. But, don't ever tell me how to do my job!" The line went dead.

Sammy may have pressed too much, but if Michael was out of the way, the takeover would be quicker and smoother. If Michael was responsible for fire-bombing his business, Sammy wanted him to pay, especially for the deaths of his employees. That was another concern for Sammy—who was in his place of business after midnight?

Sammy made another phone call, "I think we need to meet. All of us."

"Do you really think that's necessary?" Altman asked on the other end.

"If we don't, it may wreck our whole plan. We need to send Michael a message, and it needs to be a strong one. In fact, let's meet in a half hour."

"Are you crazy? It's after nine o'clock. This will not make points for you. This just—"

"Stop talking. Do as I tell you and let me worry about the repercussions," Sammy hung up his phone, and Helen called out from the bedroom, "Was that Michael?"

"No! Now shut up and go back to bed!"

29

THE BLUE WILLOW was Sammy's favorite restaurant, and he loved to eat there when under a lot of stress. It was practically empty at ten o'clock at night. Moe and Willy were already sitting when Sammy walked in. He reached the table and surveyed the room.

"What are you looking for?" Moe asked.

"Just making sure I wasn't followed. How about you two?"

"We arrived at the same time, and the parking lot was empty," was Willy's response.

The waitress came to the table and asked Sammy if he wanted anything to drink. "Yeah, I'll have a gray goose martini and bring me a bowl of pasta and meat sauce."

"Eating this late at night is not very healthy my friend," Moe warned.

"Yeah, I know, but I can't show up at the Blue Willow and not have a bowl of their pasta. It's a weakness."

"So, why the urgent meeting?" Willy went quiet as he saw Captain Altman walk in. Altman saw them and proceeded in their direction.

"Gentlemen, this is an awful late time to be meeting," Altman said.

"We know, but it's a necessity. Have a seat," Sammy said.

"Why didn't you tell us that we were all going to meet?" Moe said.

"All of us? You mean—" Willy was cut off mid-sentence.

"Yes, Willy, all of us. I didn't tell you because I wanted it to stay secret for a reason. We need to make a decision about Marello, especially after what he did tonight."

Judge Paige Monroe was the next to arrive, and she didn't take the time to make herself look presentable. She had no makeup on, and her hair was tied back in a ponytail instead of flowing over her shoulders as it usually did. She had on a pair of gray sweatpants and a white blouse. She looked at the four men at the table, "Was this really that important that it couldn't wait 'til it was at least light out?"

"Just take a seat and shut up!" The voice demanded coming from behind Paige.

Bruce Trait stood behind her, smoking his customary pipe. His six-foot stature made him seem more in control than the others. He went around and shook everyone's hand. He came back around and sat down with the other five.

"Sammy has a good reason for calling this meeting. He is under the impression that Michael knows that we are trying to take Titan away from him, and because of that, Michael is starting to retaliate. I agree with him. If you didn't know, all of Sammy's businesses were fire-bombed. They say it was gang related, but both Sammy and I feel it was too clean to be the work of gangs. These gangs are nothing but inexperienced hoodlums who could never pull off a job so clean."

The waitress came with Sammy's martini so Bruce and Paige each ordered one, too. Bruce continued the meeting, "If we are right and Michael knows, we need to move quickly. How soon can we have him arrested?"

"I told my lead detective that I had a judge willing to write up a warrant. As soon as she does that, I can have him arrested." Altman stared down Judge Monroe.

"And why haven't we written the warrant yet?" Bruce asked as the waitress brought the other two drinks.

Paige took a drink and swallowed hard, "Because he hasn't asked."

"Well, I'm asking."

"Then, when I get to my office tomorrow morning, I will issue it, and you can go and pick him up. How's that sound, Captain?"

"That would be just dandy—"

"Enough!" Bruce slapped his hand on the table. It quieted Paige and Altman and made all five of them jump.

Sammy loved that type of authoritative display. Michael will have no chance against Bruce.

"I have waited over fifteen years for this take over. I have kept silent and in the shadows just to wait to avenge my son's death and to rightly take back what Marello took from me. I don't want the two of you and your childish bickering to mess up any plans. So, just agree to do your part, and let's get it done."

Willy glanced around the table. "I don't know… Call me dumb or stupid, but why is this judge on our side again?"

Sammy shot Willy a look who in return shrugged.

"That's okay Sammy. I am happy to share with everyone my reasons for joining the group," Paige downed the rest of her martini. "Because of my connections with Michael Marello, I have made a name for myself in the judicial realm. But after I was used and the compensation stopped, I felt it was time for payback. That young Dominic thinks he is a ladies' man and can do what he wants to a woman. Well, his world will come crashing down once Marello is taken out. I will see to it that he pays for every count you can pin on him. Besides, rumor has it that I am being considered for the state supreme court, and what has been offered me is much better than what I got from Marello." Paige brushed her hand across Bruce's.

That small act of affection bothered Sammy. He couldn't have Paige getting in the way. She could always be eliminated if needed.

"So, now that we know what needs to be done, let's not mess it up. I have a future state supreme court judge, a police captain, and with the three remaining members of Titan, that gives me enough power and connections to take down Michael Marello. When that happens, we will all make a lot more money," Bruce raised his glass in a toast.

The waitress brought another round of drinks, and as they were toasted, Bruce once again spoke, "One more thing. I don't know what it means or if it means anything, but one of my guys told me that this Dominic was up in Chicago talking to Vincent Garvallenci."

"Isn't he the head of the Chicago mob?" Sammy asked.

"Yes," Bruce answered.

"Well, why would he be talking to him? Michael never wanted anything to do with the Chicago mob."

"I don't know. Like I said, it may mean nothing, but we should keep our eyes and ears open to see if it means anything. Dominic is different than Michael. He may be looking for outside help. Just be sure to keep close tabs on him," Bruce took a drink.

"One more thing." Sammy looked at Bruce.

"Oh yes, Sammy wants to send a message in return for the message he was sent by Michael. Do we all agree?" Everyone nodded. "Great. It will be done before Michael is arrested."

"Don't forget that it needs to be personal," Sammy reminded.

Bruce cracked his knuckles. "Don't worry; it will be a very personal message. He will, without a doubt, know who sent it."

* * *

The whole day had been perfect. They went into the city and had no particular set agenda. The only thing they had were dinner reservations at seven. The day and evening otherwise were to be improvised. The weather had been ideal.

They started their day by walking the magnificent mile, shopping and laughing and just enjoying the time being with each other. Whenever they passed a storefront window, Michael would steal a glance at the reflection of Elizabeth and himself in the window. They had stopped for ice cream and shared it with each other as they sat at one of the tables outside. The sun seemed to make Elizabeth glow.

Michael decided not to be his usual self and instead be a little playful. He took the ice cream cone and dabbed the tip of Elizabeth's nose. He dabbed a little harder than he wanted, and it left a big hunk of ice cream hanging. Elizabeth was all wide-eyed, and her jaw dropped. Michael had never been that aggressive. He was always polite.

"I'm sorry," Michael laughed and reached with a napkin to wipe it off.

"Sure you are," Elizabeth took the napkin from his hand. She wiped the ice cream off and threw the napkin back at him. Michael flinched, knocking the table and the two drinks over onto the sidewalk. They both burst out in laughter as the waitress came over.

"I am so sorry," Michael told the waitress. To Elizabeth, he said, "We better go before we get into trouble."

They both loved being in the city, and Michael couldn't believe he allowed himself to be out on a date. He never dated before, which was his choice, and the thought of him being on a date made him feel good. Michael enjoyed watching Elizabeth shop for clothes. They would laugh and joke about some of the outfits, but each time Elizabeth came out in a different one, she looked even more beautiful to Michael. He had put business aside and all the stress of his life and allowed himself to be a schoolboy who got a date with the head cheerleader.

The way Elizabeth could laugh at herself and the craziness of the day made Michael think, *Why do I feel this way about this woman*? They both laughed as they continued their walk downtown. The whole day had been like that. As the evening approached and the sun began its descent, it cast tall shadows across the buildings. As the lights came on, they illuminated the streets, and the windy city came to life with all the beauty and character it was known for.

Michael took Elizabeth by her hand, "Come on. I have something special for you."

They came to the old water tower—the only building that survived the great fire. They walked around to the north side of the tower, and Elizabeth saw horses and carriages lined up on the street. Michael paid for a ride, and they both climbed into the carriage.

Being that it was the windy city and the sun was on its way down, it grew cool with the breeze coming off Lake Michigan. The coachman offered a blanket and draped it across their laps. Elizabeth nestled up against Michael. As the carriage made its way through the streets, the hypnotizing clopping noise of the hooves made the ride very romantic. Elizabeth and Michael just looked at each other, smiled, and did not say a word.

Little did Elizabeth know that Michael had tipped the coachman well and they were being taken straight to their dinner destination. The carriage came to a stop in front of Lawry's restaurant, and the coachman got out and gave Elizabeth a hand down.

"I can't believe the carriage took us right to dinner!" she said.

They walked in, and the host led them to their table.

Lawry's was a beautiful restaurant with chandeliers and ornate decorations. When you first stepped into the dining room, there were tables that at first looked too close together, but with the tall ceilings, the room opened up and was very spacious.

Michael and Elizabeth followed the hostess to a booth, but not the typical type. The seating bench was against the wall and slightly curved. The table was pulled completely out so that Michael and Elizabeth had easy access. Once again, Michael smelled Elizabeth's perfume, and it had the same effect as before. The table was then slid back into place. They sat side-by-side, very comfortably. Dinner was perfect, as the soft lighting and the glow from the candles made Elizabeth even more stunning.

Michael looked around the room, and even though he had closed out the business side, he could not help feeling they were being followed. After dinner, they walked back down Michigan Avenue and stopped on the bridge crossing the Chicago River. The pedestrian traffic along the river walk looked like something that Elizabeth would enjoy, but a clap of thunder broke the calm.

"Maybe we better hurry back toward the train," Michael said.

"What are you afraid of, a little rain? Afraid you might melt?"

And with that, the clouds opened up. As Elizabeth and Michael ran, they laughed together and held hands. The rain came down hard. There was not a dry spot anywhere to be found on their clothes. "You're running too fast!" Elizabeth called out, "slow down!" Michael turned and looked into her deep dark brown eyes. Even soaking wet, she was beautiful.

They stood there for a long moment as everybody rushed by them trying to avoid the drops of rain splashing on the sidewalk. Now, as they stood in the pouring rain, the memories of the day flooded in. They walked to the train station. By the time they reached their train, they were soaked. The train ride home was cold with the scheduled A/C blowing. Elizabeth didn't seem to mind. She sat close to Michael.

The ride home wasn't as tranquil as Michael would have liked. Why did he feel they were being followed? Perhaps he *should* feel that way. Sammy was angry; the message was sent loud and clear. Sammy, more than likely, knew who sent the message.

The sound the wheels made as they glided on the rails were hypnotizing, and it was not long before Elizabeth nodded off to sleep. The train ride home would take about an hour and fifteen minutes, and it was not long before Michael was also asleep. Through most of the ride, the tall, gray-haired man sitting three rows in front of Michael and Elizabeth was watching them closely. He studied their breathing and watched to see if there was any movement. As the train was slowing to a stop at the next station, the gray-haired man got up from his seat and walked toward them.

In the train car, the recorded announcement could be heard that the doors were about to open. The man walked up to where Michael and Elizabeth were sleeping and reached into his coat. He pulled out a .44 magnum. He took the barrel and pointed it right at Elizabeth's chest. The train stopped. The gunman waited for the recorded announcement. "Caution, the doors are about to close." He would have about three seconds to run to the door, and with the right pressure applied, the doors would stay open long enough for him to escape from the train. He moved the gun an inch closer, and when he heard the announcement, he pulled the trigger.

30

THE SOUND OF the gun going off woke Michael. He sat straight up in his bed, drenched in sweat. Another nightmare. This time Elizabeth died. Because of the dream, Michael came to two conclusions. One, Elizabeth could not and would not be a part of his life or his world. Two, he needed to get in touch with Dominic to plan how they would take care of Sammy, Moe, and Willy. Well, Michael knew exactly how he was going to do it; he just wanted to have Dominic on the same page.

He could not go back to sleep. Too much ran through his mind, which kept him tossing and turning—revenge, payback, murder, and necessary death. Susan, Elizabeth, and Reverend Simmons crowded his thoughts, along with Sammy, Moe, Willy, Dad, Dominic, and Nick. Michael could not clear his mind of all these thoughts. As he sat there, he noticed the videotape sitting on the coffee table. Detective Martin had been so insistent in getting Michael to come and pick up the tape. Why?

Maybe since Michael could not go back to sleep, it would be a good time to watch it. He inserted the tape, sat on the couch, and pressed play. The first thing he saw on the TV brought tears to his eyes and a lump in his throat.

Nick.

Nick just sat there, not saying anything. Michael wiped the tears from his eyes. He heard Nick clear his throat and adjust his seat before he began to speak.

"Mikey, I'm sorry. If you are watching this, then that means I'm gone. I miss you, and I'm sorry for leaving you alone. There are some things that have changed, and I will try to explain. First, I need to warn you that if I'm gone than the rest of Titan is going to try and take you out. I have traced Sammy to Bruce Trait. You remember Trait? Well, they are related by some bloodline that goes in too many different directions to try and figure out. Just know you can't trust Sammy. Moe is with him, too. Willy is questionable, and Paul is dead set against it. Keep him close. Otherwise, he could be taken out as well."

Nick stopped for a moment to take a drink of water. "They also have the police captain and that Monroe judge. I was doing some on-line work when I came across something in the shipping files that linked the three of them together. So, with you and Paul, it will be two against six. You are going to have to call in a lot of favors to win this battle. There may be a lot of bloodshed, also. Or, you can do what I did. That's the main reason I made this tape. I wanted to be sure that you got the same message that I got."

Nick stopped again. It seemed to Michael that Nick was trying to hold back tears. "Mikey, I don't know how to say what all needs to be said. I just know that there has been a change in me. I no longer care for the things of this world. All the money and cars, women and booze…I have come to realize that all that didn't make me happy. I was greedy. My life was empty of everything and anything. I love you, and I want you to be happy and safe. If you have this tape, then that means you have also met Ryan Martin. Michael, he's not your enemy. He is a friend who is willing to help. And right now, I'll bet you need a friend. He's the one who told me about God's love that forgives all I've done wrong. I really don't understand it all, but it's real. Trust me!"

Nick leaned closer to the camera, and Michael instinctively leaned closer to his television set. Tears ran down his cheeks as he watched his brother talk to him. "I don't know how to tell you what I really want to tell you, so here it goes. Mikey, the way we live our lives is wrong. Can't make it any simpler than that, but that's it in a nutshell."

That statement struck a nerve with Michael. To hear Nick say that the way they lived was wrong meant that there had been a big change in Nick's life. "We have hurt people, taken things from people, and left their lives in shambles. We were greedy and selfish. Think about how we lived. It was for greed and self. We didn't care who got in the way. I have taken lives I had no right to take. I'm not God. I deserve hell, plain and simple. But, Jesus forgave me. Don't ask me how. Don't ask me why. I can't answer that Mikey. All I can tell you is that there's something different, and I don't want to do anything to hurt anyone else. Something has changed me inside. I'm not the same. I have experienced what Ryan Martin called forgiveness. He called it….um….what else was it? Oh yeah, grace I think he said. Grace from God. I really don't know what that is or what that means. I just know I feel that there is more to life than things. Things are just things. I have a peace that I never had before. I know that when I asked Jesus to forgive me something happened. That's when I started to feel different."

His tears stopped, but Nick continued, "Remember that time when we were in Russell's Pharmacy and got caught stealing bubble gum? We knew it was wrong, but we did it anyway. Or remember the time I had to pay off that kid so that he wouldn't tell mom about the knife I had? There were also the times we would spend hours on a Saturday sledding down the hills behind the hospital and playing army in the neighborhood until it was dark. Remember being on the same little league team and winning first place or the many games of football with the bigger kids? I would always make sure we were on the same team so that I could watch and make sure no one would hurt you. Those were the days when the simple things were the fun things. I miss them. I'm not there to keep you safe anymore."

Nick took another drink and cleared his throat again. "Our little sister was right. She only wanted what was best for us. I think what she wanted was the same thing I want for you, Mikey. Peace and comfort. I want you to feel the same way that I do. Just ask God to forgive you. Tell him you're sorry."

Nick's face crumpled, and he looked down, taking a deep breath. "Mikey, don't seek revenge. Don't pay back my death with more death. Don't hurt anyone else. Seek redemption, not revenge. I don't want you to avenge my death. I love you, Mikey. Just ask God to forgive. I don't know why He does, but He does. I love you little buddy." The tape went dark.

Michael sat there and wept. His big brother was gone and seeing him on the videotape was just too hard. He tried to comprehend everything Nick tried to tell him. Some of the things Nick had shared, Michael was already feeling. Nick was right when he said that they had been greedy, but Michael's wasn't greed, it was vengeance.

Michael wanted revenge, but Nick asked him not to avenge his death with death. How could he do it then? How could he rid himself of the anger that churned inside his heart? Was the fact that Michael wanted revenge ultimately caused by selfishness? Would that be considered greedy? Nick said something about when he asked Jesus to forgive him that his heart changed. He pleaded for Michael to do the same thing. Something about grace. Michael wiped the tears from his cheeks and took a deep breath.

Okay Nick, here goes.

"God, I cannot even begin to believe how You could ever forgive a person like me or how You could even want such a cold hearted and greedy person to pray to You. Is that what I am doing, praying? I have no clue what's going on here. Can You hear me? Who knows, maybe You won't. Maybe my sins are too awful, and You will refuse to forgive. I can understand that. It would be hard for me to forgive me. But, I am not You. So, how do I begin?"

Michael didn't know why, but he got down on his knees and continued. "God, forgive me for all the wrongs I have done. I'm sorry. Should I list them all to You? All Nick said was to ask for forgiveness so that's what I'm doing. I know that my life has been selfish and all about me. I know I am greedy. I also know that my life is empty, and I feel like a lost soul out of place. That's how Nick said he was feeling. He also said something about grace. God, I really don't know what I'm doing. I just know I don't want to feel that way anymore, and I want to have the peace Nick said he felt. Nick told me to not seek revenge but seek redemption. So, if you can, God, please redeem me."

The phone rang, and it startled Michael. He picked it up, "Hello?"

"Michael, its Dominic. What did you need?"

Dominic's voice made Michael forget about the image on the TV screen, and he shut it off. "Dominic! You need to get over here now! It is imperative." That was the end of the conversation. Michael hung up the phone and sat there on the couch.

What just happened? He was not quite sure what was happening in his mind at the moment. He knew he wanted revenge, yet he couldn't shake the image of Nick telling him to seek redemption and not revenge. *Did I do that?* He wondered. *"What did I just do?"* Michael filed those thoughts away, went upstairs to shower, and began working on his plan.

He stood in the hot shower as the water washed over him just like the flood of thoughts. Whenever he thought of things to do, somewhere and somehow, there were alternatives to take. Michael had always been sure on every decision he made. He never second-guessed himself. Could it be because he was planning the death of three of his closet associates? Could it be that he was even thinking of murder at all?

He stood in front of the steamed covered mirror. His hand squeaked on the glass as he wiped a circle to look at his image. For the first time in a long time, Michael was not happy with the person who looked back at him. He felt insecure like he felt when around his father, but his father was dead and so was Nick. When that thought came to mind, the anger came right along with it. He finished getting ready and continued to work on how he would take care of Moe, Willy, and Sammy. It wasn't murder. It was necessary death. It was revenge, and it would be sweet.

31

THE PLAN WAS set. Michael continued hearing Nick's voice telling him not to seek revenge. But, he also remembered Nick saying, "Mikey, haven't you learned yet that when there is a problem, you have to take care of it—right away, all the way?" He was sure now how he was going to handle it.

He remembered the image of Nick on the television, when there was a single knock at the door. Dominic. They embraced; then, Michael stepped back. "We are going to take care of Moe, Sammy, and Willy, and we need to do it now before I change my mind."

"It's about time you've come to your senses. I've been waiting for you to make this decision. How do you want to handle it?"

"First, I want you to know that we are going to do this my way. I want them to feel what it is like to have a gun stuck to the back of their head just before the trigger is pulled. I want them to feel the fear Nick felt. I want them to know fear."

"You got it. They'll feel fear that's for sure. So, what needs to happen?"

"I called Willy's wife and told her I needed to talk to him. She told me that he was at the Blue Willow with the rest of the group. You need to call that big guy you always use. What's his name?"

"Luther?"

"Yes, Luther. You need to call him and have him meet us outside the restaurant. Can you get in touch with him?"

"Not a problem," Dominic said.

"The three of us will wait 'til each person leaves, and then, we will follow them. We will grab them up before they get home. Then, we will meet on the green of the fourth hole at the country club. That is the furthest hole from the clubhouse. Once we are there, I will take care of them."

"What are you going to do?"

"You will just have to wait and see. You need to call Luther. Then, you can tell me if you had anything to do with burning Salluci's building."

Dominic got off the phone and said to Michael, "I can't tell you anything. That would put you in danger of being an accessory. You need to stay out of my way and let me work."

Michael and Dominic drove separately. Michael wanted to be sure they had the means to follow Moe, Sammy, and Willy. It was a short drive to the Blue Willow, and when they arrived, Michael watched as Luther walked up to Dominic's car. They talked briefly, and Luther went back to sit in his car. Dominic got out and walked up to Michael.

"I told Luther to follow Sammy. I'll follow Moe, and you get Willy."

It didn't seem long before Michael noticed Sammy step out into the early morning darkness followed by Bruce Trait. Seeing Trait sent a cold shiver down Michael's spine. It had been over fifteen years since he had last seen or heard from him. Maybe this was a bad idea.

Sammy and Bruce embraced.

No…this was a good idea. A very good idea.

Bruce walked to his car and Sammy to his. When Sammy started up his big Buick LeSabre and pulled away, Michael noticed Luther pull out right behind him. Michael wanted to pull his car right in front of Bruce's, but Willy had stepped out of the restaurant and was walking toward Michael. Michael slid down in his seat so Willy wouldn't see him. When Willy left the parking lot, Michael pulled his bright red 69 Nova behind him and headed south down Wolf Road. It wasn't going to be a long drive for Willy, so Michael would have to act fast.

Willy flashed his right signal to turn onto Route 7. That's when Michael took his Nova, a car he cherished, and floored it so that it struck the back of Willy's car. When Willy turned his BMW, it did a tail spin and came to stop in the parking lot of a strip mall. That late hour meant that there was no traffic and the strip mall was empty. Michael got out of his car and walked slowly over to Willy's.

Willy still gripped the steering wheel, shaking his head as if to clear it. Michael wrenched open his door, and the first thing out of Willy's mouth was, "Don't you know how to drive you stupid, no good, son—" He looked up and when he realized who it was pleaded, "Michael, I can explain. Please let me explain. I was forced to turn against you by Sammy and Moe. I never wanted to hurt you or Nick. I thought—"

"Shut up!" Michael yelled. "I don't want to hear excuses, I don't want explanations, and I don't want to listen to your lies. What I want is to see you beg for mercy and plead with me not to take your life because you're mine now! So is Sammy and so is

Moe. Tonight, there is no forgiveness. There will be no mercy, and you will know just how Nick felt before he died. This, I promise you." Michael raised his fist and smashed it into Willy's face. He then grabbed him and shoved him into the trunk. He pulled from the lot and headed toward the country club.

* * *

As Sammy stood on the green of the fourth hole, he could feel the dampness from the early morning dew on his bare feet. Luther made him take of his shoes to discourage trying to make a run for it. He saw Michael and Willy. Willy's nose was swollen and looked broken. He heard Michael ask, "Any problems?"

"There had to be a little persuasion, but they finally gave in," Luther said with a smile.

"What do you think you're doing?" Sammy yelled.

Sammy hated the fact that Michael ignored him. He saw that Willy's and Moe's hands were tied just like his. Michael went over to stand right in front of Sammy. "I don't think you're in any position to ask questions."

Sammy was taken aback by the fact that Michael was speaking out of character. That was something new and different. Michael sounded cold and deliberate. "In fact, I don't care what you think or what questions you have. Just shut up, and in a matter of minutes, you'll know what I'm going to do. I want the three of you to kneel right here in front of the fourth hole. Go ahead. Kneel!" Michael commanded.

Willy was the first one to drop to his knees, and he whimpered like a child. Moe reluctantly went second. Sammy refused to kneel.

"I said kneel!" Michael yelled.

Luther took a steel pipe and struck Sammy right behind his left knee. He screamed and went down. The pain was intense. He took deep rasping breaths and then looked up. "So, what's next big man? You going to beat us up? Make us say we're sorry? Well, you can forget it! I don't apologize to anyone for anything. For all I care, you can go straight to—" This time, the steel pipe struck Sammy in his left shoulder. Again, he screamed out. Even as the pain seared through his shoulder, his disdain for Michael grew stronger.

"If I want to hear you speak, I'll ask. Until then, just shut up," Michael warned. To Sammy, he sounded so cold and calculated. "How about you, Willy? What do you want?"

"Michael, I already told you how sorry I am. I was forced into this. I don't want to die. This is not my fault."

Michael stooped down to whisper into Willy's ear, "Not your fault? Well, my friend, I see no one here to blame but the three of you. You want mercy? Then beg for it."

"Don't you dare beg for mercy!" Moe spouted off. "You're just as guilty as the rest of us. I'm not asking for it, and I know Sammy won't. Be a man. We screwed up. We got caught. Don't give in and give up. Just keep your mouth shut."

"Oh another bright one," Michael backhanded Moe across his face splitting his upper lip. "Let him speak for himself. We already know what happens when you speak for him."

"I want to live," Willy whispered

"What was that?" Michael said.

"I want to live. I don't want to die. I'm afraid to die. Please don't kill me!"

Dominic smiled and looked at Luther. Willy had soiled himself. Dominic leaned toward Michael. "I have never seen you display such power, so much anger. You are in complete control of what is going on. I love it."

Dominic's words chilled Sammy, but didn't seem to affect Michael. He continued his verbal assault on Sammy and the others. "Are you asking me to spare your life? Did you think about sparing my brother's life? Obviously not, otherwise, he'd still be alive." Michael leaned right into Willy's ear and yelled, "But he's dead!" Willy cringed and started to cry.

"Are you kidding me?" Michael taunted. "You're going to cry? What kind of man are you? You'll order the death of someone else. Yet, when the time comes for you to pay the piper, you're going to cry?"

Sammy watched as Michael stepped away from the three of them and then turned to look at them. He just stood there and stared at them, eyeing them up. Sammy knew Michael was watching to see which one would give the other one up as the mastermind of the whole thing. Dominic snickered.

Michael turned and looked at Dominic. "Do you think this is funny? Do you think this is for kicks? I see nothing funny about taking a human life. What is happening here is very serious. Someone needs to pay for what they did to my brother. That's nothing to laugh at. This is payback for treason, for turning your back on a friend, and for taking the life of a family member. I don't think there is any humor in that. Paul, my close friend, was murdered by the same garbage that took the life of your father because he knew how wrong it was."

He turned back to the three men on the ground. "Why would you do something like that? I wouldn't. What about you, Dominic? Would you turn on someone who gave you a good life?"

Dominic's ears were red.

"What about you, Sammy?" Sammy didn't look at Michael and said nothing, but was exasperated to hear that Dominic was Rhino's son. *That explains everything.*

"Why would you turn on someone who made you rich beyond what you could have done on your own? Family?" Michael finished.

Sammy shot a look at Michael. He just looked at him and winced. He was able to mutter out a question. "How did you find out?"

"You don't think I watch what goes on around me? I trust no one! I constantly keep my guard up and always keep those close to me safe."

"Well, you failed to keep your brother safe," Sammy told Michael in a matter of fact tone of voice.

Michael pulled out a .45 and shoved it in Sammy's mouth knocking out his top two teeth. The pain was intense and shot through Sammy's mouth. He tasted blood. "Don't get smart with me. You're in no position to say anything that won't make me pull this trigger and spray your brains all over this manicured grass."

Michael looked over at Moe. "Please tell me that you had better sense than to follow this fool." Moe said nothing and just looked at the ground in front of him.

"So, this is what it all comes down to? I got one who cries like a baby and can't control himself and another one who can't look me in the eye or admit he made a mistake and followed a fool. Lastly, I have the fool who thinks he can turn against me and convince you guys he could take me out and get away with it. I know it wasn't this bunch I chose to form Titan. I asked men who knew what they wanted, men who stood with me and helped me run a city and make us all wealthy, men who would be honest with me, and men I trusted with my life. I guess that maybe I'm the one who was a fool. But, who is standing right now and has control? I do!"

A maniacal laugh escaped him, "You took something from me that you had no right to take! You killed the only person I loved! What were you thinking? Did you really think you could take me out? Did you? You make alliances with old enemies and expect me just to give in or give up? This is my life; this is all I know and all I care about. I got nothing else to lose. You are nothing but fools with a foolish notion that you could take me out. So, I want you to feel just like Rhino felt before you had him killed. I want you to know what it's like to feel the barrel of a gun pressed against the back of your head and wonder when the bullet's going to leave the chamber and enter your skull, taking your last breath. I'm sure that's what my brother was thinking. So now, so will you."

Michael shoved the gun in his front pocket then reached behind his back and pulled out two more .45 caliber handguns and cocked them both. The sounds echoed in the quiet, still air of the early morning. It was getting lighter out, and Sammy could see the morning dew hanging in the air.

Willy cried even harder.

He saw Michael hand Dominic and Luther the guns. They walked around behind the three men. Sammy could feel the barrel of the gun press against the back of his head. Dominic and Luther did the same to Moe and Willy.

"So, this is how it's going to end?"

Michael still badgered. "I thought I had close friends that I would be able to trust all the way to the grave. Doesn't look like that will happen."

Willy was now in complete tears. Moe continued to stare silently at the ground. Sammy was still his arrogant self, trying to talk Michael down. "You don't have the guts to do it."

"On the count of three, we'll pull the triggers." He heard Michael order.

"One! Two..."

"Please, Michael, I don't want to die!" Willy cried out.

"Three!"

At once, the three of them pulled the triggers.

In the silence of the morning, all Sammy heard was the clicking of empty chambers. Willy fell forward crying. Moe had a look on his face like a deer hypnotized by the headlights of an oncoming car. Sammy looked back at Michael. Michael stared at the gun in his hand. Dominic and Luther looked at each other.

"What's going on?" Dominic asked. Luther just stood there. "Michael, what just happened? Why were there no bullets in the gun?"

"I told you all I wanted was for them to feel what it was like for Nick before they took out his life." As Michael looked at Willy all rolled up in the fetal position crying like a baby and Moe sitting there thankful that his life had not come to an end, he proclaimed, "Seems like I got what I wanted."

Sammy sneered. "Just couldn't pull that trigger, huh? I didn't think so. You are nothing like your brother."

Dominic started toward Sammy. "I'm going to knock the—"

"Stop," Michael said in a voice he'd never used on Dominic before. "Just stop. One of the last requests from your father, from my brother, was not to seek revenge for his death. I want to honor that request to honor him. He told me of a change he made in his life, and I feel that I have made that same change. I no longer want this type of life. After seeing my brother and how he pleaded with me to change, I was drawn to examine the life I lived and the man I had become. The lives that were ruined so that I could gain, I just felt so guilty. Nick asked that I seek redemption instead of revenge. I think I did."

Dominic and Luther gaped at him. Willy still cried on the ground.

"So, what happens next?" Dominic questioned.

"I'm really not sure." Michael started to walk away.

"Wait! Michael! I need to know what we do next. Are we going to kill these guys or let them go?" Dominic sounded scared and frustrated.

Michael stopped and faced him. "You do what you want, but do not take away their lives."

"What? We're not going to kill them? They killed my father! They killed you're brother! Did you forget that?"

Michael shook his head, "No, I have not forgotten that. I just do not want anything to do with murder. I never did. That was a part of the business I never wanted to believe happened. So, I made myself ignorant, immune, separate from that, and tried to think that I was not part of a world that had no respect for life. Obviously, I was wrong. Now, because of my world, my brother is dead. What gain is there in that?"

Sammy shook his head and laughed, "He's babbling like a baby, making no sense at all."

Luther struck Sammy in the face with his gun, breaking his nose. "Shut your mouth. You're still in no position to get smart."

Though in excruciating pain, Sammy watched Michael walk away.

Dominic continued his plea, "Michael, are you just walking away from this? What about Titan? What about me?"

"Dominic, I have loved you since the first day you came into my life. I raised you and taught you just like you were my own. I love you and will never walk away from you; but, this life is a life I want no part of anymore. Titan is yours. I have always had controlling interest in Titan. I alone owned it. Everyone—Paul, Sammy, Willy, and Moe—they all worked for Titan. They never had a share in the ownership. I am sole owner. I now give it to you. But, if you continue to run it in an illegal manner, you'll regret it. Remember, I know about something that can put you in prison for life."

Dominic froze, "Are you blackmailing me? If I don't do what you want, you'll tell on me? How childish is that. You're giving me one of the most powerful companies in this city, maybe in the state, and you want to change how it's run? I don't think you know how to run it yourself. One thing I learned from my dad is that when there is a problem, you have to take care of it. Right away. All the way. You didn't take care of this problem. If you leave your enemies alive, they will come back one day and try to wipe you out. If you walk away with this unfinished, I will have no respect for you."

Michael turned away from Dominic and started toward the clubhouse.

"Michael!"

Michael continued walking.

"Michael!"

32

BRUCE TRAIT SAT at the large conference table at the Wooded Hills Country Club, in the very seat Michael would occupy. Moe, Willy, and Sammy were seated, also. Sammy still nursed the shoulder wound he had received from Luther and walked with a cane. The smile on his face was highlighted by a set of new teeth, compliments of Michael Marello. As they sat at the table, no one noticed the little red light that activated the recorder.

"Do you really think we should be meeting here with Bruce sitting where Michael is supposed to be?" Willy asked sheepishly.

"What! Are you still going to be wimping out on us because of Michael?" Sammy shouted.

"No need to shout Sammy," Bruce encouraged. "Willy my friend, you don't need to fear or worry about Michael. That's being taken care of."

"I'm not worried about Michael, but what about that nephew of his—Dominic?"

Now it was Bruce's time to be angry. "I could care less about that young punk. He's nothing. He's got no backing, and he has no business sense. The best thing Michael could have done was give Titan away to someone who has no idea of the power he holds. We will be able to take care of him. He is no threat. With him out of the way and with Michael out of the way, we will have complete control of Titan, just like we planned from the beginning."

"How will Michael be out of the way?" Moe asked.

"I've taken care of that, not to worry," Bruce stated with confidence.

* * *

Michael sat in his living room in the quietness of the early morning with Susan and Elizabeth. He was still unsure what happened. He told Elizabeth and Sue about the events of the last couple of weeks. He sat there, and Sue sat next to him on the couch. She was still crying from watching the video of Nick. Elizabeth dried her eyes with a tissue.

"I can't believe what I just saw. I can't believe that after all these years my prayers have been answered. Your life is going to be so much better now," Sue finished.

"I have to laugh at you, Sis. I just made my life even more dangerous."

"How do you figure?" Elizabeth asked.

"I left my enemies alive. That means I'm a target. Not only that, but since I didn't take care of it *all the way*, I created new enemies."

"You don't think Dominic is now you're enemy, do you?"

"Dominic was a perfect student of everything I taught him. If he remembers what he was taught, I will be his enemy. He has to protect what is his. At all costs. Period. So, because I gave it all up and have the potential to take him down, then yes, I am now his enemy. Now, I have him to worry about, also. Tomorrow, I will go and talk to that Detective Martin and see what happens next."

The three of them sat in silence. The calm of the late morning was soon filled with the sounds of shattering glass and splintering wood. Michael jumped to his feet as policemen rushed into his house.

"Police, freeze!"

They forced Michael to the ground. Two policemen grabbed his arms as another stepped on his neck. "Don't move."

Michael knew better than to try and fight the police, so as calmly as he could, he waited until they had him handcuffed. They stood him up as other officers started to rummage through his personal stuff. Susan and Elizabeth were also placed in handcuffs.

"I hope you have a warrant, Officer," Michael said, annoyed.

The officer did not respond. Captain Altman stepped from behind him, "Oh yes, Mr. Marello, we have a warrant. Don't you worry." He slapped it across Michael's chest. "We are following the law to the letter, and we are going to make sure you get what you deserve."

"Look, this is my sister and her friend. They have done nothing wrong. Could you please release them?"

The officer looked at Altman for a response. Altman told the officer, "Keep them cuffed."

Altman would have to die. That thought was soon replaced by the word's Nick had said in the video, *"Don't seek revenge seek redemption."* That was not going to be easy. No matter what prayer Michael prayed, it did not make him want to seek redemption. He wanted and would get revenge. He stood there and believed this with all his heart, as Captain Altman began to read him his rights.

"Mr. Marello you have the right to remain silent..."

* * *

Dominic stood from across the desk of the Chicago mob boss, Vincent Garvallenci, and shook his hand, "Thank you Mister Garvallenci for your time. I feel that the arrangement we've agreed upon will be the best for both sides."

Garvallenci took Dominic's hand and reassured him, "Not to worry Dominic. If anyone goes against you, they now go against us, and they won't like that!"

Dominic looked very intensely into Garvallenci eyes, "What about Michael?"

Garvallenci just smiled.

Printed in the United States
By Bookmasters